Making sure I had his full attention, I slowly unzipped the jumpsuit. Down to the tops of my fake breasts. Pause.

His pen stilled.

Zip. Over the girls, past the hips, down to the crotch. I gave one shoulder a shimmy shake sending the silicone girls bouncing as I stripped the jumpsuit off one shoulder. Then the next. I'd watched Logan's strip aerobics DVD a time or two and it was coming in handy now as I worked up to the grand finale.

I gave my bottom a healthy wiggle as I scooched the overalls past my hips and stepped out of them, one elongated leg at a time.

His gaze was glued to my crop top. When I looked down, I realized it was plastered with sweat against my body in much the same way as a wet T-shirt clings. I kicked the coveralls into the corner and stepped directly in front of him, feigning trying to get a glimpse of my chart. In reality, I was just giving him a better look down my blouse.

"Hey, you were a real trooper." His tongue was thick on his words. He was looking down at me. I was looking up at him, standing way too far into his personal space. "Five times isn't bad. Great big, brave policemen don't do any better."

Our gazes locked.

"Thanks."

He cleared his throat. "You probably better send the next CT in."

"You're probably right." I reluctantly stepped back and turned to leave. I paused at the door to call to him. "Bet no one else is as good as me." I winked and raced out, giving him a wave over my back, being careful not to turn and let him see the big, fat grin on my face. Let him figure *me* out.

SPY CANDY

GINA ROBINSON

Nancy —

Wishing you many

happy escapes!

Gina Robinson

ZEBRA BOOKS

Kensington Publishing Corp.

www.kensingtonbooks.com

ZEBRA BOOKS are published by

Kensington Publishing Corp.
850 Third Avenue
New York, NY 10022

Copyright © 2008 by Gina Robinson

All Kensington titles, imprints and distributed lines are available at special quantity discounts for bulk purchases for sales promotion, premiums, fund-raising, educational or institutional use.

Special book excerpts or customized printings can also be created to fit specific needs. For details, write or phone the office of the Kensington Special Sales Manager: Attn. Special Sales Department. Kensington Publishing Corp., 850 Third Avenue, New York, NY 10022. Phone: 1-800-221-2647.

ISBN-13: 978-1-4201-0472-1
ISBN-10: 1-4201-0472-1

First Printing: November 2008
10 9 8 7 6 5 4 3 2 1

Printed in the United States of America

For, Jeff, I love you.
Thanks for always believing.

ACKNOWLEDGMENTS

With a debut novel, there are always so many people to thank. I'm blessed to have a large family and many friends who've supported me in my dream over the years. I'm particularly grateful to my husband and my three Js, my children, for their unwavering support, love, and faith. Thank you to my parents for so many things, beginning with driving three hundred miles to watch the kids so I could go to my first writers' conference, right up to the present, for driving those same three hundred miles to celebrate my sale with me.

I have a fantastic critique group. They've read my work, given me tough literary love, and laughed and cried with me over the years. Thanks so much to Joleen Wieser, Gerri Russell, Heather Hiestand Pruett, and Judith Laik.

Thank you to my fabulous, tenacious agent, Kim Lionetti, for choosing the idea for *Spy Candy* from my pile of story ideas, for her suggestions that improved the book, her guidance, and her belief in my work. And of course, I'm indebted to my excellent editor, Peter Senftleben, for buying the book, making suggestions to improve the story, and guiding me through the publication process.

Chapter One

"Chocolate martini. Shaken, not stirred." I crossed my legs and attempted a sexy Domino-style, vixen-like perch on my bar stool as I awaited my spy camp contact in Martini Junction, an airport lounge at Phoenix Sky Harbor International Airport. In the process of tugging down my skintight miniskirt, I wobbled precariously.

The bartender, obviously adept at handling drunks and travel-weary patrons, reached across the counter and caught my elbow, steadying me. He spoke directly to my silicone-bra-insert-enhanced cleavage. "You want a Hershey's Kiss in that?"

"Make it two." I sighed, wishing I'd been blessed with the sexpot gene and knew how to take advantage of that stare. Frankly, even though I'd just crossed a big milestone birthday, I didn't have much experience with men ogling me.

Turning thirty wouldn't have been so bad, really, if my life had been more Bond girl and less Money-penny. Just because I have a head for finance and am good with numbers doesn't mean I want to spend the rest of my life approving loans and assessing some guy's bottom line from across a desk.

The day my deadbeat dad, Jack, took me to my first Bond flick, *The Living Daylights,* I instantly fell in love with Timothy Dalton. Ever since then, I've dreamed of being a Bond girl. What girl *wouldn't* want to spend her time saving the world on the arm of a daring, handsome spy, with some hot sex thrown in for good measure? The only downside I can see to being Bond's sidekick, besides the danger, is the naming convention. Dr. Warmflash? Honey Ryder? Pussy Galore? Holly Goodhead? Come on.

Fortunately, my name is plain old Jenna Jarvis. Family and friends call me Jen. I live one ordinary day after another. Shut off the alarm at six thirty every morning. Put on the suit. Commute to work. Run the numbers. Just what you'd expect from a banker.

But for one week, I'll be known by my camp-assigned code name, Domino, like James Bond's bodacious brunette love interest in *Thunderball.* I'm supposed to dress and act the part, too. It's all part of the deluxe fantasy adventure vacation that my friend Logan gave me for my birthday. All part of my cover. Which I've been warned *not* to blow.

Fantasy Spy Camp, or FSC, as they like to be called, sent a dossier and a sample costume prop— a hot-pink bikini top. When I tried it on, it looked like a limp string connecting a pair of deflated balloons from a Barbie birthday party. Logan laughed at me when I came out of my bedroom to show her. Either someone at spy camp had a warped sense of humor, or Logan had set me up.

"You look like Joey in drag." Joey is Logan's ten-year-old nephew. "You can't be a boy-figured Domino, Jen. You just can't. It's not right."

I didn't like the wicked gleam in her eye. And with good reason. I've known Logan since junior high. Her mission in life is to make people happy. If that includes making them over, so much the better. I love her despite this flaw.

Now, less than twenty-four hours later I found myself remade into a twenty-first-century version of Domino, courtesy of Logan's lottery winnings. Brows waxed into a perfect arch, acrylic nails professionally applied, hair extensions, and silicone bra inserts for that babe-o-licious bounce factor, as Logan put it. It made me want to hide out in my room. I'm not the kind of girl who's used to strutting around on stiletto heels with her bosoms spilling out for all to see.

Logan won a thirty million–dollar Powerball lottery last year all by her little lonesome—single jackpot winner–take-all. Logan has *always* been lucky. And fiscally careless. For her sake, I founded a lottery winners' support group, the Unexpected Money Institute, UMI, and made her a charter member. If not for me, Logan would have blown through her winnings already and been one of those sad, broke-and-living-in-a-trailer lottery stories you hear about from time to time. Well, maybe not the trailer, but definitely broke and selling her Manolo Blahniks on eBay to raise rent money.

The bartender set my drink in front of me.

"This hasn't been shaken," I said as I glanced at it. Maybe it was stupid to call a hunky, burly guy on his lack of drink-making skills, but I'd never been accused of having a lot of social smarts. "Clear as a bell. No bubbles." I pointed to my glass.

He shrugged.

"You know, shaking is good for business. It enhances the flavor of the drink. Not to mention it ups the antioxidant activity, which reduces the risk of stroke and heart disease. And cataracts. Shake all your martinis and I bet you could market them as health drinks. It's a good angle." Well, it was a good plan if the FDA or whoever was in charge of those things would let him get away with it.

He gave me a straight face, obviously absolutely underwhelmed by my idea. After stealing a final glimpse at my breasts, he walked off to the far end of the bar, shaking his head in a way that indicated it was too bad I was such a crazy broad because I had a nice rack. Obviously, that was the only shaking he was going to do this evening.

Okay, I know a lot of Bond trivia. Maybe more than the average person. Maybe too much. I'm more of a Bond geek than a Bond girl. Like I know Bond's martini contains 130 calories, the approximate amount he burns having sex. In a single encounter. Mine probably had a few more calories and I knew I wasn't going to burn *any* off having sex.

I fished one of the chocolate Kisses from my

drink and sucked on it while I scanned the room for my contact. My instructions said that after deplaning, I was to go directly to Martini Junction, where I'd receive instructions on where to find a blond woman reading a copy of the *Wall Street Journal* with the left-hand corner turned down. I was to approach her surreptitiously, repeat a code phrase, and she'd give me directions to the camp bus.

I had expected someone would "bump" into me and slip me a note. Only so far that hadn't happened. I pulled the FSC dossier from my bag and took a quick look at the photo of the woman I was supposed to be looking for.

I couldn't help smiling at the warning on the FSC cover page: "Because of the nature of this vacation, potential campers should not divulge to others their reservation at FSC. Failure to observe the confidentiality of a reservation may affect eligibility to have fun." The wording was right off the MI6 employment page. Though I suppose most people wouldn't know that, either.

On any account, their secrets were safe with me. I hadn't told a soul. Only Logan knew my top-secret vacation plans.

I scanned the room, catching the eye of a dark-haired, fortyish man seated at a table a few feet away. A bowler hat rested on his briefcase. He stood and I got my hopes up for about half a second that he was my contact. Then he walked right past me, stealing a peek at my cleavage as he went by.

There was something familiar about Bowler Hat Man. Before I could place him, a page sounded over the PA system, interrupting the steady flow of light hits of yesterday and today that played in the background.

"Ms. Jarvis. Ms. Jenna Jarvis. Please pick up a white courtesy phone."

I started and, without thinking, slid off my stool, ready to rush to the phone. I'd seen one in the hall outside Martini Junction. I grabbed my purse and bag. If something was wrong at home, Logan or Uncle Bob would call me on my BlackBerry. My heart skipped a beat. Must be my contact calling!

I stepped outside into the bustle of airport foot traffic, immediately falling into one of those annoying little "let's get around each other" dances with a harried older woman pulling a flowered suitcase stacked with a hatbox and suit bag. After three or four unfortunate blocking moves, she grabbed my arm.

"Stop where you are. Just let me get around you. I have a connection to catch!" She looked me up and down and shook her head disgustedly as she shoved past me, muttering something about brazen young women who should stop dressing like hookers and learn some modesty.

I was taken aback and froze in place. No one had ever accused me of immodesty before. I was a paragon of modesty. I looked down at my outfit. But Domino wasn't. And I was supposed to *be* Domino.

That's when I began to think like Domino and had a lightbulb moment—why would my contact be paging the real me? What if this page was a setup to see if I'd blow my cover? What if this was a test? I mean, if I picked up the phone, anyone watching

and paying attention would see that I was plain old
Jenna Jarvis and *not* Domino. On the other hand,
what if I just had a vivid imagination and by not an-
swering I missed my directions? How long would the
FSC bus wait for me? I stood watching the phone
and debating. My first spy conundrum. What would
James Bond do?

I glanced around, looking to see if anyone was
watching the phone. Like I was some kind of big spy-
detecting expert. Fortunately, unlike Logan, who
could walk right past her own father without recognizing him, I've always been observant. I suddenly
spotted my airport contact, a statuesque model-type
blonde, sitting in a chair just down the hall from
Martini Junction. And just to remove any doubt, she
was holding a copy of the *Wall Street Journal* with the
left-hand corner folded down.

I resisted the urge to punch the air in victory and
made my way toward her, taking a seat next to her.
Remembering my instructions and the code, I said,
"I'm looking for a good stock tip." I nodded toward
her newspaper. "Any hot picks in there?"

My contact sized me up in a not totally warm fashion. "I'm finished with it. Do you want it?" She held
it out to me, along with a single sheet of paper
neatly tucked inside.

I nodded at her again, took the newspaper, and
popped into the ladies' room to read my instructions. I stared at my unfamiliar profile in the mirror
for a moment. The silicone bra inserts made my
slender five-foot-five frame positively curvaceous. No
wonder the boys liked them. If I'd realized back

during my painful acne years the *full* power of a pair of stacked breasts to divert the male eye from my face, I would've stuffed my bra.

I slid into a stall in the ladies' room to read my instructions, positively gleeful and full of praise for my own brilliance. I was one smart spy cookie!

Just for fun, after I'd memorized the info on the sheet, I blacked out all the information with a marker from my purse and then tore the page into shreds, stopping just short of flushing them. That was probably over the top. Instead, I stuffed the paper bits into the metal box on the stall wall that was reserved for disposing of tampons and sanitary pads. No one was going to look in there!

I hurried toward the airport exit, full of anticipation and fear. Could a girl like me who mostly only dreams of adventure really hack it at spy camp?

Chapter Two

July back home in Seattle is pleasantly warm. July in Phoenix is simply torrid. Yeah, it's a dry heat, but so what? So's my oven. I wouldn't want to vacation there, either.

The force of the heat hit me the minute I stepped from the air-conditioned cool of the terminal. The average human body is something like 90 percent water. Only Seattleite's bodies are more like 95 percent liquid on account of living in the rain and "marine air," as the weathermen call it. I felt my water content plummet and my lips crack beneath my moisture-whipped lip gloss.

Because Logan coerced me into it, I wore one of my new Domino outfits—low-cut black Lycra tank top, black shrug, wide black belt, skintight black miniskirt, a magenta headband to spice things up, and spiky-heeled magenta sandals—with bows, no less—to match the headband. Dragging my bag behind me, I wobbled on my killer bow-toed sandals toward a crowd waiting for the FSC bus in the blistering Phoenix sun.

Being more of a looks-like-a-sensible-heel-feels-like-a-sneaker girl, I was the perfect picture of discomfort and discomportment, if there is such a word. My black tank top wicked up heat like a superabsorbent paper towel and stuck to my body in a way that would have made the Brawny Man's eyes pop out. Worse yet, sweat pooled underneath my fake boobs. Who knew silicone retained so much heat? I hoped I wasn't getting an underarm ring. Bond girls don't do underarm rings.

I stopped at the back of the spy crowd, stuffed the shrug in my duffel, and lifted the hair off my neck in a search for cool. Probably summer in Phoenix wasn't the best time to go long. I was going to have to master the updo, and quick.

As I tried to surreptitiously unstick my tank top from my body, I noticed the parking lot was awash in gleaming, highly reflective, white vehicles. Why did I get the feeling that black was color *non grata* down here?

The bus pulled up before I had a chance to meet or assess my campmates. The last camper, a lanky thirtysomething guy with receding brown hair, ran for the bus after the rest of us had boarded, flagging it like he would a taxi. The inside of our chartered bus was mercifully air-conditioned. With my mind off my physical discomforts, I surveyed my fellow campers. There was only one other woman in the group. She sat in the seat in front of me and looked to be in her late forties. Thin, fit, even buff in a stringy, slight way, with short, cropped, bleached blond hair. Definitely an athlete's build of the long-distance runner variety. She introduced herself as Emma Peel, but she wasn't wearing the skintight catsuit characteristic of John Steed's spying cohort of *The Avengers* fame. Maybe they'd sent one to her as a prop, and like me, she'd thought better of wearing it on the plane. I pegged her accent as Australian laced with a dose of American, like she'd spent several years in the States.

"British?" I asked nonchalantly. The Aussies I know are outgoing and gregarious and revel in their individuality. Without exception, they take offense at being mistaken for reserved Brits.

"Aussie."

"Wow, and here I always thought Mrs. Peel was British." I flashed her a smile that told her I'd caught her falling out of character.

She grinned back at me, undaunted. "Yeah? Most people are terrible at placing accents. They assume because I married a Brit and spent some years in England that I am a Brit. But I was born in Australia. Brisbane, to be exact. Once an Aussie, always an Aussie." Her tone and expression dared me to take issue with her loose interpretation of the character, while her eyes danced with humor.

Evidently there was wiggle room with the charade. If she could play it as she saw it, I could, too. I liked her.

"Domino. Pleased to meet you . . . Emma." As I extended my hand, I let my intentional pause tell her it was a nice, but not thoroughly convincing, attempt at recovery. Amateur.

The bus pulled away from the curb and headed out of the airport as we shook hands.

"And you've gone blond now, too." I made a point of staring at her hair. "I like it. Going under-cover?"

"Aren't we all?" She winked and gave her hair, such as it was, a playful shake. "No." She laughed as she fluffed her hair with her hand, "This here's my chemo 'do. I'm quite proud of it. A few months ago, I was a baldie. Now I've got this beautiful blond mane growing in. Shocked the hell out of me that it didn't come back in brown."

She spoke so matter-of-factly and with such good humor that I was completely taken aback. My surprise must've been evident, because she grinned broadly like she'd been expecting my reaction, creasing the wrinkles around her lips and eyes. She looked weath-ered, like a person who'd spent too much time out-doors. I realized too late that she had the look of someone who'd undergone chemotherapy.

"Oh." I didn't know what to say. I'm such a verbal klutz in situations like this. "I'm sorry—"

She held up a hand to stop my stammering apol-ogy. "No need." I still had no idea what to say next, but I had to say something, so I just stumbled on. "You're okay now?"

"Oh, no worries! I had breast cancer. Stage two and a half. Spread to the lymph nodes by the time they caught it. I'm the breastless wonder now, but I'm cancer-free and ready to live. Which is why I'm here.

To have some fun and a few thrills!" Her expression became serious. She put a hand on my arm. "Get your yearly exams. Promise?"

I nodded. "Always."

"Good." She leaned back against the window and stretched her feet out on the seat. "Ahhhh." She sighed happily. "No nausea. The stamina to get through the day without a nap. The things we take for granted when we're healthy."

I reassessed Emma's age, taking into account the effects of illness and chemo. She was probably much younger than I'd originally guessed. I felt suddenly protective. "Are you sure you're up for adventure?"

"Absolutely!" She sat up, indignant at my suggestion. "And I've no time to waste. Breast cancer's notorious for coming back, you know. I'm not letting life pass *me* by. I've booked the whole next year. Gonna do everything I ever wanted to do.

"After spy camp, I'm signed up for comprehensive skydiving lessons, rock climbing, whitewater rafting, flying lessons, dance lessons, voice lessons, bungee jumping, mountain climbing . . ."

Just listening to her itinerary left me exhausted. "Um, most of that sounds very . . . dangerous, doesn't it? Maybe you should take it a little easy?"

Emma gave me a puzzled look. "That *is* easy. If I had my full strength, I'd have packed more in."

"But the danger—"

She shrugged, looking a little disappointed in me. She probably expected more bravado from a spy camp attendee. "You can't spend your life being so cautious you don't live!" Her deep-blue eyes skewered me with a penetrating, challenging look. "Look at me. I led a responsible, safe life and cancer nearly took me out all the same.

"One thing about facing my own mortality, it's made me fearless," Emma continued. "I'd rather die having fun and trying new things than in a sickbed, wouldn't you?"

I nodded slowly, still unsure, because there was a certain beauty to living as long as possible, regardless. And probably dying in a sickbed was more comfortable than lying shattered and broken on a pile of rocks, should, say, one's parachute fail to open, or one slips while rappelling. I suppressed a shudder. I have a horrendous fear of heights. The camp brochure mentioned rappelling down a building as part of the experience. I'd already planned to ditch that session.

"Thanks to the lottery, I've got the money to do anything I want." Emma rearranged herself on the seat.

I wasn't surprised that Emma admitted to being a lottery winner. She probably assumed I was one, too. Logan had told me when she presented me with the trip that she'd booked me into a special ultra-deluxe custom camp experience with a group of lottery winners. In fact, she'd heard about the trip from one of the women in UMI. When that gal had to drop out at the last minute, Logan booked me in her place.

"Since you're hell-bent on living dangerously, I hope you took your winnings in a lump sum," I said, only half-teasingly. You can throw the banker out of the bank on a fantasy vacation, but you can't take the bank out of the banker.

"Of course. It only makes the most fiscal sense, anyway." She adjusted an air vent to throw more cool air her way.

I smiled at her, liking her even more. A sensible lottery winner. What was not to love about that?

Emma winked at me and whispered, "What do you think of the rest of our adventure mates? Looks like some of them are wearing their props. Care to guess their code names?" She nodded a few rows back to the man with the bowler hat I'd seen in Martini Junction. "I'd lay odds his code name is that of my old boss, John Steed."

I did a mental head slap and nodded my agreement. Of course! That's why he'd seemed familiar and yet I couldn't place him. He did look a bit Avenger-like. Emma and I scanned the bus, looking to make more identifications.

"Across the aisle. Third row back. A Maxwell Smart clone. Has to be," I whispered, pleased at my own astuteness in noticing the camper wearing a blue vest, dress shirt, and tie, a signature Max Smart outfit.

Emma leaned forward and whispered to me, "We'll know for sure if he goes for his shoe phone."

"Or his cone of silence."

"Right, chief," Emma said and we broke out giggling.

The others, a motley crew of men of varying ages, mostly past thirty, stumped us.

Emma grimaced as she did a quick scan of the bus. "Let's hope none of them are James himself. I couldn't stand it. Might put me off 007 for good."

"Heretic! Nothing could put me off Bond."

"Not even these guys?" And she laughed.

"Not even these guys." I was loyal to a fault. Ask Logan. She'd tell you that's why I've stuck with my boyfriend, Daniel, for five years through our on-again, off-again, decidedly noncommittal and open relationship.

Logan wasn't exactly right on that one, though. I had other reasons, too. Daniel isn't Bond, doesn't have Bond's daring or sense of adventure in the slightest. But he's attractive in his own short, gray-haired, stout way. By far the most attractive man I've ever dated, which admittedly doesn't put him on par with the 100 Most Beautiful People.

And he's successful, though Logan accuses me of being too impressed by his money and connections. And fun to be with when we aren't fighting. Which, unfortunately, is practically every time we spend more than a day or two together, leading me to the unfortunate suspicion that Daniel is probably right about insisting we not live together.

Even if he is fifteen years older than I am and a little staid and set in his ways, I could do a lot worse, believe me. After all, he puts up with my Bond fetish, even if he never fulfills my ultimate fantasy by acting Bond-like in any way other than wearing nicely tailored suits. I've told him repeatedly that he could humor me and order a suit or two from Brioni's, Bond's tailor of choice. He says hell will freeze over before that happens. He doesn't need me looking at him in a Brioni suit and fantasizing about James Bond. Guess I won't tell him that sometimes I fantasize about Bond when he's out of his clothes.

I did a mental run-through of all the Bond spies I could remember, trying to place characters. I finally nodded toward a middle-aged man wearing a Hawaiian shirt. "Jake Wade, CIA. Calls Bond 'Jimbo.'"

Emma scrutinized him. "Dunno on that one. Could be he's just a notoriously bad dresser. He could be John Strangways, MI6, and that shirt is just his way of expressing his strange ways." She grinned again. "I'll wager a twenty that you're wrong."

Classic lottery winner. Once a gambler, always a gambler. I knew the type.

"Make it a five and you have a deal," I said.

"Ever the cautious one." She shook her head in amusement. "Guess we'll find out at camp. You know, if we girls stick together, we can kick some serious spy-wannabe boy butt."

"Absolutely." I nodded my agreement as the bus pulled away from the city and headed northwest from Phoenix.

The landscape became barren, punctuated by a saguaro here and there. Emma and I fell into companionable silence. Actually, Emma's eyelids drooped as she fell into a nap. I resolved to let her sleep.

As I was easing myself back into my seat, she said, "Don't get any ideas that I'm not feeling up to par. We've got a long ride to camp ahead. I'm just napping to kill the time." Then she was out.

Spy camp sat on five hundred secluded acres on the site of a little-known former CIA training facility, known to insiders as The Grove, outside Surprise on the road to Wickenburg. Just under an hour and a half after embarking, the bus pulled off the main road onto an exit advertising The Grove, FRESH ORANGES AND CITRUS SEASONALLY. Nothing about spies and extreme fantasy vacations. I liked it.

The White Tank Mountains sat to the south, picturesque against the barren, brown landscape. The Hassayampa River meandered along the countryside, but I use the term *river* loosely. If not for my guidebook, I wouldn't have recognized it as such. In Washington state, when we refer to a river, there's usually some actual water flowing in it. Dried riverbed was probably a more apt description, so dry, it looked prehistoric, something carved by the Great Flood, never to have seen water again.

Ocotillo grew along the road, leafless from lack of rain. I was going into green withdrawal when suddenly a dusty citrus grove came into view.

I was caught off guard and hurled against the window as the bus turned abruptly into irrigation heaven, an orchard of deep-green trees filled with tiny, unripe fruit. An oasis in the desert. I felt like I'd taken a step back into nature. Calm, peaceful nature. Back to the earth and a grow-your-own-food life. What could possibly go wrong in a place like this?

No sooner had these thoughts of peace and tranquility crossed my mind when a guard shack and a razor-wire-topped chain-link fence sprung into view. The bus driver pulled to a halt while a guard with a bomb-sniffing dog and a worker with a mirror on a long pole worked the bus over before waving us through. Wow, now I felt like we were in *The Recruit*. Too bad Colin Farrell *wasn't* on our bus!

Bomb search complete, the bus continued through orchards, winding past a parking lot, shacks with corrugated metal roofs, around a private road, past a large, Southwest-style home, the prosperous kind of house you'd expect to find on a successful citrus plantation. We came to a stop at a big open space across from another large building of the same architecture. On closer inspection, I realized it was actually two buildings connected by a breezeway, Frank Lloyd Wright style. Natural architecture.

The bus doors opened. We were hit with a blast of heat.

Emma sat up and rubbed her eyes. "What a stinker of a day!"

"We're here," I said unnecessarily.

The bus driver stepped out and began opening the cargo bays beneath the bus. Several campers, led by John Steed and his bowler hat, followed his lead and debused. I peered out the window, hoping for a better look as I enjoyed the air-conditioning for as long as possible.

"You'd think they'd send a greeter," I said to Emma.

"Maybe we're early," Emma said.

I glanced at my watch and shook my head.

She shrugged and stood.

"Kind of anticlimactic." I grabbed my duffel and purse from the overhead storage rack and shuffled down the aisle, following Emma out, shielding my eyes against the harsh sunlight as I stepped off onto the roadside. "If this is just going to be like a regular vacation where we check in at the lobby, well, that's kind of dull, isn't it? Shouldn't some kind of spy trainer or someone greet us? You know, like M, to give us our assignment?"

Emma turned toward me and opened her mouth to reply.

A sudden brilliant flash of light at the end of the road, followed by an explosive roar that reverberated through the air and shook the bus, cut off her response. Debris rained down on the asphalt at the end of the road, tinkling like bells against the bass of the explosion. My ears rang as complete pandemonium broke out among the campers. People were pointing and running while I stood rooted in the heat-softened asphalt as if stuck there by the melting tar.

An abandoned car at the far end of the road, now missing a door or two, and all its auto glass, was engulfed in full flame. I wrapped one arm over my head for protection from any errant, falling debris, thinking, "Cell phone, cell phone." I had to call out for help! Then I was going to call Logan and verbally kill her for sending me to meet my end in the hot Arizona desert. Like she couldn't send me to Maui instead? Then, irrelevantly, I wondered how long it would take the fire department to arrive from Surprise.

I was digging in my purse for the phone when a volley of what sounded like gunfire erupted. It echoed off the building walls along with a woman's scream. I looked around for Emma, but she'd disappeared, which is when it dawned on me—*I* was the screamer. I was going to die! Someone had sabotaged spy camp and killed all the trainers, just waiting to ambush us supposed lottery winners and rob us as we arrived. Well, who better to mug than a host of lottery winners? Tell me that!

My trembling fingers somehow pulled the phone from the deep recesses of my purse and I was wildly stabbing at the buttons, trying to punch 9-1-1 without success. Something had happened to my small motor skills. Damn it! Why had they failed me now?

Thick smoke now obscured the view of the explosion. The volley of gunfire died away. I dropped the phone back in my purse without hitting send and patted myself down. Okay, I was still here and apparently whole. No holes that I could feel.

I'd squinched my eyes closed in hear-no-evil-see-no-evil fashion once I'd given up on the phone. I'd have to open them to take a peek at assessing the damage. I'm squeamish and I really didn't need the sight of blood and gore to make my day. Only someone might need help.

Oh, God, help me! I went into rapid-fire prayer mode as I pried one eye open, hoping that one eye would see only half the carnage, I guess.

As if from an action-adventure movie trailer, a

big, buff man emerged from the haze of the wreckage and smoke, striding in what could only be called a cocky, "I'm a real badass" walk.

Okay, now both my eyes popped wide open.

He was six foot two if an inch. Black hair worn longish in a snowboarder style. Black tank top that showed off a chest sculpted like he had muscles of stone. Jeans, my gosh, jeans in this heat, jeans that showed off buns of regulation steel! Combat boots. No Uzi. I was practically certain he wasn't packing. Well, not a gun anyway.

The only thing light about him, in manner or otherwise, was the glint off a diamond stud in his left ear. Not even a sheen of sweat. What kind of human being doesn't break a sweat in hundred-degree heat and utter mayhem?

My knees shook and I felt faint at the sight of him. But I wasn't sure if it was relief, fear, heat-stroke, or uncontrollable lust. Truth is, I'm an in-control type person. I've never felt *uncontrollable* lust before. All my loyalty to Daniel flew out into the open desert as I had a vision of urgently doing the dirty deed with Badass Guy.

"Freeze!" he yelled. "No one move." He surveyed the lot of us from behind his tinted Maui Jim sunglasses.

Complete obedience; that was us. No heroes in this crowd. He could have been Dr. No himself, but no one made a move to jump him. I was afraid to even breathe. And darn it all, but I felt a trickle of sweat running down between my breasts and an itch on my nose as I frantically tried to obey his order.

"Welcome to The Grove." Badass Guy stopped a few feet in front of me. "That was a simulated car-bomb attack. As our first exercise, on my command, you're going to take your pulses." He held his left arm in front of him so he could read his big, clunky, black, guy-type watch. Probably had all the gizmos. He held his right hand up in a starter's pose, like "runners to your mark."

"Go!" he yelled.

And I counted. "38 . . . 39 . . . 40—"

"Stop!" He looked around the frightened faces of the group again. "Multiply by four to get your heart rate."

One-sixty for me. And not slowing a whole heck of a lot. Especially not when his penetrating stare fell on me. Well, I assume it was penetrating. On any account, my reflection in his sunglasses scared the hell out of me. How did my hair get so wild? Evidently long hair took a little more brush maintenance than short. And I think my pupils were dilated. And you know, they really should make sunglasses with better reflective optics. My reflection looked round and fat, funhouse style, instead of slimming. If they were going to make reflective sunglass—

"Anything over one-forty-five and bad things start happening to the body. Complex motor skills break down." Badass Guy took another step toward me, looking down at me from behind his glasses. "Yo, cell phone girl."

I gulped. My heart rate spiked back into the danger zone.

"You get your call off to nine-one-one okay?" he asked.

The combination of his nearness, the excitement, and the heat, rendered me speechless. I resorted to a meek headshake.

"Thought not. Never yet have had to call off the emergency services." He took a deep breath and lowered his sunglasses on his nose. "Anything over one seventy-five and cognitive thinking completely breaks down. We become no better than dogs."

Why was he looking at *me* like that?

Okay, I'd done the scared-dog equivalent of dodging out in front of a moving car and freezing with fear, but hadn't everybody? I blushed under his unnerving stare and felt my ankles go wobbly.

He gave me a quick, intimate wink, which could not mean what I thought it meant. Hot guys just did *not* look at me like that. Ohmygosh, I thought I was going to melt. Mercifully, he turned to scan the group before I lost complete composure and the ability to remain standing on my tiny, spiky sandals.

"Blood withdraws to the core muscles, hardening the body like armor and preventing rapid blood loss in the event of injury. At that heart rate, some people literally piss in their pants or void their bowels. If anyone needs a shower, you'll be dismissed to your barracks in a few." He cut his gaze back to me.

Hey, I was fine. Strong bladder and fear of public embarrassment.

"You!" he barked at me and I jumped. "You're dead within seconds, had this been real. You don't call for help until you've secured adequate cover. Got it?"

Touched by his concern, I nodded mutely as he pushed his glasses back up and walked around the group, pointing out dead people. With him out of personal-space range, I regained a low enough pulse rate to bounce out of dog thinking back into the human zone and looked around for Emma. Badass spy trainer found her flat on her stomach on the ground behind a tire on the far side of the bus as the rest of us trailed after him looking for her.

Badass Guy started clapping. "Congratulations, trainees. Exactly one of you lived through that little welcome exercise."

He gave Emma a hand up and a pat on the back. "Good job, CT. The proper technique to survive in the line of gunfire, which we simulated with firecrackers: Get down and stay down. If you're outside, get behind a car and lie behind a tire on the opposite side of the volley. A bus is even better. Stay down until the gunfire ceases." He shook his head as he surveyed the rest of us. "If there are no vehicles present, lie in a gutter. Do anything to make yourself the smallest target possible." His gaze ran the length of me, lingering just a second longer than necessary on my newly acquired curves. The look in his eyes said he definitely wasn't thinking they were small targets.

Emma came to stand next to me.

"Impressive," I whispered to her.

She was looking at the spy trainer. "Him or me?"

"You." But I was thinking *him*, definitely *him*.

"Sheer survival instinct. I have a strong one." She turned to look at me, shaking her head. "I thought you were the cautious one. Ducking for cover only makes sense, doesn't it? You've got to toughen up, Domino. This here's a dangerous world."

True. But who expects a car-bomb-firecracker-gunfire welcome to camp? It wasn't something I'd trained for.

Badass Guy stood front and center of the group in a military at-ease stance. "My name's Torquil Toricelli. You can call me Torq." He grinned. "I'll be one of your trainers. Grab your bags and follow me."

Being the big, spy-loving dork that I am, I wanted a picture of that scorched car for my scrapbook. I mean, it was right out of a Bond movie! Ever counted how many cars bite the dust in a single show? I have—gazillions!

Just wait until I told Logan about it. She'd be thrilled! Not to mention a tiny bit jealous. I pulled my camera from my bag, and using my zoom lens, took a few discreet snaps of the car before Emma gave me a nudge to get going.

Just as we'd begun to move as a mob, Torq stopped short suddenly. "One more thing. This is hot country. Heatstroke's a killer here. Carry a water bottle with you at all times. You'll be issued a camp bottle and carrying strap inside. Move out."

"And you thought camp was going to be boring," Emma whispered to me as she eyed Torq's red-hot steel buns.

Chapter Three

"Torq here's our James Bond, no doubt about it. Bond can be our pet name for him," Emma said, voice filled with awe and lust, gaze glued to Torq's hind end as we followed him into the air-conditioned training facility, pulling our wheeled suitcases behind us. "What do you think?"

"Bond?" Okay, color me confused. "Rambo maybe. What makes you think Bond?"

"You don't see the resemblance?" She looked at me like I was the crazy one.

Because I am basically a pleaser, I squinted, trying to see what she saw. "A younger, darker, Italian James Bond from the wrong side of the tracks. Bond on mega-steroids, maybe." I couldn't hide the skepticism in my voice. I was really stretching the point. He was sexy and handsome and presumably a spy. Those were the only similarities.

"Look at that butt! That's a Bond butt. Don't tell me you haven't noticed? You have to have a great butt to be Bond." She looked incredulous. "And you call yourself a Bond aficionado!"

"James has sensitive eyes," I said. "Think Pierce Brosnan. That's what gets the ladies." And me.

Emma rolled her eyes.

"Okay, okay. I concede. He has the butt to be Bond. We can call him Bond Butt if you like." I grinned and changed the subject, sort of. "Look at him. He's not sweating," I said. "Not a drop. That's a sign of dehydration, right? I think he needs hydrating. He probably needs a big bottle of that water he was talking about."

"Worried? Isn't that sweet!" Emma chuckled. "He's former Special Forces. Special Forces guys are superhuman. They've learned how to live without water and food for days on end. They can control not only their pulses, but their body functions, to the point where they don't sweat if they don't want to. The control thing, that's what makes them great lovers." She winked.

My turn to roll my eyes. "Where do you think he was hiding until the bomb went off? He just appeared out of nowhere like a spook."

"He's also ex-CIA. CIA guys are spooks. And Special Forces guys are expert hiders. Combine the two and you've got a super spook."

"What'd you do, memorize the camp brochure?" I muttered to myself.

Inside the lobby, Torq removed his sunglasses, revealing a very fine pair of deep-chocolate Italian eyes more on the steely side along with his buns than in any way sensitive. Still, I might have drooled if I'd had any spit left in me. Where was that water he'd promised?

Torq introduced us to Agent Rockford, the senior member of the instruction staff whom Emma and I immediately dubbed Chief, an aging hulk of a man with cropped gun-metal-gray hair, impressive, imposing, ramrod posture, and the bark of a drill sergeant. Rockford handed us each an arrival packet that contained our barracks room assignment and key, a water bottle emblazoned with the FSC logo, and a bag to drop all our valuables—wallets, purses, and ID—into for storage in the camp safe. Compliance mandatory. "Because we'll be playing spy games, folks" is how Rockford explained it as he collected our storage bags.

"Dinner's at eighteen hundred hours, followed by orientation in the training center at nineteen hundred hours. Lights out at twenty hundred hours. Days begin at oh six hundred. There are refreshments set up at the end of the lobby. Help yourself. See you back here in"—he glanced at his watch—"seventy-two minutes."

I looked around for Torq, curious to see if he'd allowed himself to sweat yet, but he'd disappeared as stealthily as he'd come.

I pulled my BlackBerry from my purse to check for messages from Daniel. He was on business in London and didn't know about my surprise trip. I'd left him a message on his voice mail, telling him about my fantasy vacation. But he hadn't responded yet. Probably he'd sent me an e-mail. We had a date scheduled for the upcoming Friday night and I wanted to make sure he knew we'd have to reschedule.

I tried imagining his reaction to me at spy camp but came up empty. Amused, surprised, or perturbed, he'd probably keep his opinion to himself. Daniel and I kept our relationship fresh by leading separate lives and rarely interfering in each other's pursuits. Logan calls our relationship apathetic. I call it broad-minded.

"Don't waste your time with that thing." Agent Rockford's voice boomed from behind me. "We don't have cell or wireless coverage out here."

I glanced at the screen, confirming he was right, dropped the BlackBerry back into my purse like a chastened child, and turned to face him, putting on my professional nice voice. "I'm expecting an important call. Do you have a message service?"

Agent Rockford gave me a stony face. "We have a business phone in the office."

"I don't suppose you could check to see if anyone's left a message for me?" I gave him a helpless good-girl smile.

"No." Rockford shot me a look warning me not to be trouble and walked off.

Emma, who'd watched the interaction, came up beside me, shaking her head disgustedly in an imitation of Rockford. "A good spy knows when and how to use her sex appeal to get favors and information. Ever hear of Mata Hari?"

Emma nodded toward my chest. "You've got a good package. Use it. Work those girls to your advantage. Stand up straight and thrust them out.

Lean into the target." She demonstrated. "Put a little sultry into your voice. And crikey, woman, learn to make bedroom eyes."

Emma grabbed her wheeled suitcase and headed for the refreshments. "This phone message business is all about some mate, isn't it?" The disgust in her voice spoke for itself. "Don't waste your time on a mate who doesn't call."

I wheeled my suitcase, trailing behind Emma. "I'm not wasting anything." I was sure I sounded defensive, so I changed the subject. "Look." I pointed to an iced pitcher on the table. "Tea."

"What is *that*?" Emma came to an abrupt stop in front of me so suddenly I almost ran into her.

"Iced tea," I said, slamming on the brakes. "Don't tell me Aussies don't ice their tea?"

"No, I meant her."

I followed Emma's line of sight. "Oh."

A curvaceous brunette decked out in a flowing white knee-length dress strolled in through the lobby doors on a pair of six-inch gold heels like she was born to walk on them. She wore a diamond of at least ten carats on a gold chain around her neck. I was betting it was cubic zirconia. Who'd be dumb enough to bring the real bling to camp?

The newcomer exuded confidence. As every male in the room turned to gawk at her, she smiled like she'd been expecting the attention and wasn't disappointed.

"Hello, boys," she said, completely ignoring Emma and me. Her voice was sultry and low. "Have I missed anything?"

"Oh, God," Emma said, rolling her eyes.

"Exactly." I echoed Emma's disdain. The newcomer was exactly the kind of woman who made me feel small and insecure and ugly—feelings I tried hard to avoid, especially on vacation. At least at the bank, I could hide behind the authority of my position for confidence.

Emma nudged me. "What do you say we skip the refreshments and head right to our rooms?"

"I'm with you. You lead," I said, following her out.

The brochure said that some guests may have to share a connecting bathroom. Wouldn't you know that they gave that honor to Emma and me, two of the only three women at camp.

"These spy trainer boys are sick puppies," I said to Emma when we discovered this dilemma. "Like the men need private bathrooms to brush their teeth and run a comb through their hair."

"It could be worse," Emma said, dumping half the cosmetics section of Walgreens on the bathroom counter. "We could be sharing with *her*. Who do you think she is?"

"White dress. Gold shoes. Diamonds galore. Octopussy. Without doubt." I tried not to sound as unhappy as I felt about the new arrival.

"I'm not even going to wager on that one. I think you're right." Emma shook her head in disgust.

"Which probably means she'll be sleeping with our Bond before long." I shrugged, attempting to sound light and casual as I pushed aside my feelings of jealousy and disdain, wishing for once that I had the confidence of an Octopussy. That someone like her didn't make me feel so insecure merely by showing up.

"Give him more credit for brains than that." Emma gave my arm a little squeeze. "Our Octopussy is an inferior spy. Couldn't find her contact and missed the camp bus so she had to hire a cab to take her here. She's more like Agent 3.14 from *Spy Hard*. A comic farce." Emma shot me her winning grin, which I was certain was meant to boost my confidence.

"Either that or she's cunning and planned that grand entrance. Remember, she is Octopussy." I paused, as a more innocuous thought occurred to me. "Or maybe her flight was simply delayed."

"Killjoy," Emma said to me as she wandered off to her room to unpack. "I like my explanation better."

I closed the door to our connecting bathroom, set my suitcase on the stand provided for it, and surveyed my room.

No phone in sight. A twin bed, small dresser, lamp, clock radio, and desk. A clock hung on the wall next to the ubiquitous and obligatory dreamcatcher in muted Southwest pastels. I fiddled with the clock radio and found a station I liked, hoping a little music would cheer me up and bolster my confidence. Restless, I went to the window.

My view consisted of a couple of orange trees, the White Tank Mountains in the distant south, and the blown-up car being strapped to a tow truck. Oh, and Torq squatting and inspecting the left rear quarter panel of the car.

He did have a fantastic butt, a bottom line a girl

could really appreciate. He ran his fingers over the side of the car, frowned, and inspected a bit more. I was intrigued . . . by more than just his butt. Why was he inspecting the car? It was obviously totaled. Time to turn it over to the junkman and be done. Yet something was bothering him.

Just then he stood, catching sight of me standing at the window, admiring him. Just as quickly I blushed to my hair-extended roots and snapped my curtains shut. An automatic and childish response that only underscored the fact I'd been spying on him. Not to mention drooling a bit in the process.

You'd think I'd leave the window. Just walk away from the fire. But I didn't. Fueled by curiosity, I pulled back a tiny corner of the curtains and peeked through. Torq had returned to examining the car and frowning.

"Emma! Emma, come here and look at this!" When she didn't answer, I went to find her. "I have something I want you to see."

She came with me to the window, but when I pulled back the curtain, Torq was gone and the tow truck was idling, the driver nowhere in sight.

"A tow truck, so what?" she said.

I explained about Torq. "So why would he be checking out the car?"

Emma shrugged, unconcerned and uncurious. "He probably just wanted to see how well his bomb had worked."

"He looked worried about something . . . and puzzled."

Emma shrugged again. "You're imagining things.

Come on. Better finish unpacking. We don't want to be late and have the Chief bark at us."

After Emma left, I checked out the vacation pictures I'd taken since leaving home this morning. The burned-up car pictures were definitely my faves. I studied them carefully, zooming in and blowing them up, wondering how they'd look poster-sized on my office wall. Blistering paint. Holes. Charred seats. All of it totally in focus. Sweet stuff! Simply awesome photos.

Emma banged on my door, startling me out of my reverie. "Ready to go?"

I glanced at the clock. Shoot! I'd lost all track of time. I was going to be late.

"Hold on. Give me a minute!"

I slid the camera into an empty dresser drawer and filled in around it with my brand-new Domino wardrobe of tanks, blouses, shorts, pants, and skirts, and sexy lingerie from Victoria's Secret. I wasn't sure why I was hiding the camera. It just seemed the spy thing to do.

I slammed the drawer shut, reached for my brush and one of those big clippie things that look like an overgrown mouth of teeth, and opened the door to our joint bathroom to fix up.

Emma was waiting for me with an accusing look on her face. "What in the world have you been up to? You haven't even fixed your face or done your hair yet?"

"Thinking and unpacking."

Emma shook her head. "You have to be the slowest unpacker I've ever known." She had the good grace not to call me a slow thinker, too.

I shrugged. "I'm meticulous, what can I say?" Yeah, right. I just hoped she didn't check out the jumble in my drawer.

I hadn't owned so much as a barrette for about twenty-five years. As Emma watched, I studied the pictorial diagrams on the cardboard the clippie came on, trying to follow all the arrows and doing half a dozen contortions with my arms as I tried to emulate the picture. I pulled my hair extensions back, winding them into a rope, and trying to claw them shut before too many strands fell out without much success.

"Oh, give me that before I die of frustration watching you. You act like you've never done it before." She pulled the clippie from my hand and, shaking her head, expertly clipped my hair up and arranged several strands around my face to soften the look. "There."

"Wow."

"Yeah, I'm good with hair." She sounded regretful as she tousled her own short hair with her fingers. "Before the cancer, I used to have hair down to the middle of my back." She spied my look of sympathy. "Go on. Get your lipstick on before we're even later."

A quick swath across my mouth with Domino pink, a blot on a tissue, and I was ready. Almost. I had to use the bathroom. It was a Jarvis thing. We always have to use the bathroom at the very last minute. Doesn't matter if we just went two minutes ago. The habit had been drummed into me by my mother with her unfailing litany, "It's time to go. Have you used the bathroom? Gotten a drink of water?"

I turned to Emma. "I have to use the facilities."

"I'll wait for you in the hall." She rolled her eyes and departed.

Minutes later I joined her outside our rooms. Just as I pulled the locked door closed behind me, I remembered something from one of the pictures. But was I remembering right? Or had I simply imagined it by thinking too hard on it? If Emma hadn't been shoving me along, I'd have gone back to check out my memory right then.

As it was, she played mother hen, shooing me toward dinner. Checking the pictures would have to wait until after dinner. . . .

Chapter Four

Dinner was served mess-hall style at long tables in the cafeteria. Despite putting the rush on, Emma and I arrived late and had to gulp down our food to make it to the orientation on time. We sat in the back next to the Maxwell Smart clone, who preferred to be called Max and had donned a suit jacket for the occasion. Octopussy strolled in even later than we did and took a seat right in front, crossing her legs provocatively, the big suck-up.

Agent Rockford, alias Chief, gave the welcome address. "Welcome to The Grove. A lot of you came here expecting James Bond–type adventure. We're gonna give you that. And while we don't have a license to kill, we do have something Bond doesn't— a license to thrill." He grinned at his own cleverness.

"While you're at FSC we'll refer to you as CTs, Career Trainees, just like the CIA does. We'll treat you like real CTs and that means giving you the standard warning—in the spy world you can't believe anything you see, hear, or experience. You can't believe or trust anyone, except yourself. Truth is a scarce and valuable commodity, and lying's cheap and par for the job. Skepticism and intuition are your two best friends."

The group did a collective squirm.

"If you've read your mission notes, you all know the mission scenario, but I'll repeat it just the same.

"You've been selected by a top-secret paramilitary unit for a covert operation deep in enemy territory. The mission will culminate in terrorists kidnapping one of you. The others will mount a rescue attempt."

Next to me Max whispered, "It's the old kidnap-a-CT trick."

I rolled my eyes.

Rockford leveled his gaze at us. "Let me just say that in all the missions I've overseen, the rescue rate runs about fifty percent. Last mission the hostage ended up dead." He gave us a slow, evil smile. "You'll be facing every kind of simulated danger imaginable."

"And loving it!" Max piped up.

The class laughed.

Rockford looked like he wanted to make Max drop and give him ten but chose to ignore him instead. "To prepare for this mission you'll be trained by my handpicked group of contract mercenaries and some of the world's toughest Special Ops folks.

"During your six days here you'll learn such spy essentials as face reading, pistol marksmanship, unarmed self-defense, CPR, rappelling, close-quarter battle techniques, police and bodyguard training, panic control, hostage negotiation, and evasive driving techniques." Rockford took a sip from a glass of water on the podium. "Now let me introduce the staff. Boys, come on up." Rockford motioned a group of men up front.

"First, your driving staff." Rockford slapped a fifty-ish, balding man of average height on the shoulder. "This is Davie Edwards."

Davie gave us a wave.

"He has twenty-six years of professional auto racing experience. He's trained hundreds of security chauffeurs, law enforcement officials, and bodyguards in evasive driving techniques. He taught driving at the Bondurant School of High Performance Driving for six years. What Davie doesn't know about driving hasn't been invented yet."

Rockford pointed farther down the line of men to two fortyish guys. "Next we have Jim Wexel and Greg Helmer. They've got thirty-five years of on- and off-road racing experience between them and both of them belong to the Hollywood stuntmen's association.

"Now for the combat staff." Rockford grinned at Torq and a tall, handsome blond with snapping blue eyes, a lazy, laconic stance, and a killer grin that was fixed in my direction and made my toes curl in a reflexive lust reaction.

Wow! Two instantaneous crushes in one day. That was some kind of record for me. Maybe it's true that women come into their sexual prime in their thirties. Guess there was an upside to getting older after all. If it hadn't been clear that there were only the three of us women in the room, I would have looked around to see whom he was aiming that grin at.

Just as I was about to return it, Emma leaned into me and whispered, "Dibs on the blond. I got a thing for blonds."

"You can't dibs an instructor," I hissed back.

"I just did. Look, he's smiling at me." She gave him a little finger wave and whispered to me while looking straight ahead at him. "Besides, you've got a mate."

"But you said I should drop him," I whispered back, giving the blond my own little wave.

"Don't believe everything you hear," she said.

Rockford gave Emma and me a hard stare and cleared his throat before giving his own qualifications as combat instructor—sixteen years in the U.S. Army Special Forces. Several tours of duty in Vietnam. A stint with the British SAS and several other counterintelligence agencies. Then he introduced Torq, telling us about his six years with the CIA, four years with Special Forces, and two years of civilian service. "He's an expert in intelligence/counterintelligence and has a black belt in karate."

Torq gave an enigmatic head nod and went back to his seat at the front of the class. So much for Mr. Personality.

"And this"—Rockford slapped the blond on the back with obvious affection—"is the guy who keeps camp lively and fun. He hails from Texas and served twelve years in the U.S. Army Special Forces. He's trained more than a hundred SWAT teams nationwide. He can drink anyone in this room under the table. He's a hell of a driver, and a nice guy, too. Everyone, meet Alex Fry."

Alex nodded to the class. "Y'all can call me Fry. I prefer it to Alex." He flashed that grin again.

Emma and I were trying hard not to swoon. You had to love a Texas accent.

"There's our 006," Emma whispered to me. "His name is Alex and he even looks like a young Sean Bean."

"006 went bad," I said.

"No worries. I like 'em bad." Emma gave me a wink. "The badder the better."

Fry sat down.

Rockford had us introduce ourselves by our aliases. The cast of camp characters read like a who's who of pop culture spies—Emma and me, Max, John Steed, Octopussy, "but please, just call me Pussy" followed by a salacious wink, Bill Tanner, Q, Ethan Hunt, Tom Bishop, and Jack Wade.

I held my hand out, palm up, to Emma when Jack introduced himself. "Guess I'm the winner. Pay up."

"Sorry. I don't have anything on me."

"OK. But just so you know, I'll be charging usury-type interest until I get my money." I gave her a grin.

"Nothing doing. Double or nothing Wade blows his cover first," she said.

I rolled my eyes. "Cheater."

She grinned back.

Rockford passed out the schedule for the week and rattled on about camp policies. I stopped paying attention a few minutes in when I noticed a row of three desktop computers along the far wall. Aha! A way to contact Daniel.

I was startled out of my thoughts by the feel of Rockford's hard stare on me. "And for cripes sake, CTs, dress appropriately for camp. This isn't some goddamn beauty show."

I felt myself blush. So what was "appropriate" attire? His staff had sent me a bikini top. Maybe I should show up in that instead.

"Class dismissed. See you back here at six hundred hours." Rockford turned and left.

Emma stopped to visit with some of the other campers, but I begged off and went back to my room, stopping by the vending machine to grab a soda on the way.

I popped the top and opened my dresser drawer, eager to take another look at my fabulously fun photos. Only . . .

The camera was gone! Poof! Vanished.

I tore through the drawer, tossing clothes on the floor like a madwoman as I went, trying to convince myself I'd just overlooked it. I hate it when things go missing. Drives me nutso until I find them.

When the drawer was finally empty and still no camera, I had to admit defeat . . . and disappointment with the human race. Someone had obviously broken into my room and stolen my camera. What other explanation was there?

The hairs on my arms stood up. It's amazing how creeped you can feel when someone has violated your personal space and pawed through your underwear.

I looked around the room, as nervous as if I expected a SPECTRE agent to jump out from behind the curtains and attack me. The air-conditioning clicked on. The curtains rustled. Scaredy-cat that I am, I jumped and froze, hand on heart, a real easy face-on target for any junior marksman. Definitely *not* a Bond-girl stance.

When no one jumped out firing an automatic weapon at me and my heartbeat slowed back down enough to allow rational thinking, I made a vow. I was going to pay attention in unarmed self-defense class 'cause acting like a chicken was no way to face a real threat.

I went to the window and pulled back the curtains. The window was definitely closed and latched. I couldn't see any sign that the window had been forced in any way. Not that I was an expert, but I didn't see any pry-bar marks or broken glass. To the best of my recollection, with the exception of the things I'd tossed on the floor, everything in the room looked just as it had when I'd left it. Which meant it either had to be an inside job or I'd been hit by a real pro.

I took inventory of the rest of my things. All my brand-new sexy panties were accounted for. We weren't dealing with a pervert. Nothing else was missing. Time to face facts—someone, probably one of my fellow campers, had stolen my camera. How low could you go—a big lottery winner stealing from poor little me?

I evaluated my options. I could report the theft, but making accusations wasn't going to win me any friends. And what could really be done about it now anyway? Instead, I decided to keep an eye out for it. If it didn't return itself by camp's end, I'd report it and collect the insurance.

It was getting late and, given the traveling I'd done, I should have been dead tired. But I couldn't settle down, too wound up to even get ready for bed.

I did a little pacing. Maybe it was time to check out the computers in the orientation room. Doing something would take my mind off the current mystery, and a little distance of time would probably put the creepiness factor at bay. If I could get on those computers, I could contact Daniel.

I glanced at the clock. Oh, darn. It was after curfew. What would 007 do? I grinned. As if I needed to ask!

I pulled on my pink sneakers and headed out.

Well, actually, old 007 would probably be curled up in bed with Octopussy burning off his 130 calories per boink. But eventually he'd get to the computers.

The door to the orientation room stood cracked open. These spy camp guys were trusting souls. You'd think they'd have more security. Maybe this was all another test. Maybe they had hidden security cameras and bugs everywhere. In a minute a SWAT team would be all over me.

I peeked in. The lights were on. The room was empty. I cautiously slid my hand along the door frame, prepared to run. Nothing. I slipped inside and closed the door.

Inside the room, I did another quick scan for people. All clear, so I popped over and sat down in front of the nearest computer. When I touched the mouse, the screen came to life.

I took another look around the room to make sure I was still alone before returning my attention to the screen. I tried logging on to my Web mail account, typing in my username and password.

A message popped up. "Invalid password. Please check your password and try again."

What? Invalid password, my hind leg. I tried again. Same response.

Idiocy is repeating the same behavior and expecting a different response. I typed really carefully the third time.

"Access denied. To apply for a new password please provide your birth date and the last four digits of your social security number . . . a new password will be sent to you. Or call customer service . . ."

"Shit!" I banged the desk with my fists, then froze and looked around, fearing I'd given myself away. It was then I realized I'd been typing in the password for my online banking account. And I couldn't even blame my mistake on jet lag. During the summer, Phoenix is on the same time as Seattle.

Well, that's what I get for following instructions on how to protect your online presence and making up different passwords for different accounts, using a combination of letters and numbers that form nothing but gibberish. Who the hell can remember gibberish, let alone keeping all those gibberish pass-words straight?

I was stuck. I couldn't call. Grrr . . . Daniel would just have to wait. I should have felt more let down about that. Instead, I felt a surprising sense of relief at being incommunicado. I didn't have to feign any loyalty or lovey-dovey stuff while battling that pesky niggling bit of guilt about the reactions I was having to Torq the Bond Butt.

I heard a door slam down the hall. I swiveled in my chair, heart racing, fully expecting to get caught. Male voices approached. I held my breath.

Following a perfect Doppler-effect pattern, the male voices grew louder, then receded into the dis-tance. I let out the breath I'd been holding. I'd just settled back into my chair when the hairs on the back of my neck stood up and I froze, sensing the presence of someone behind me, watching me. I paled. What would super spy girl do in this situation?

I jumped and spun around in my chair to find Fry staring down at me, or rather, appreciatively down my fake cleavage. Fortunately for me, while my real breasts liked the attention enough to bud right up, my silicone inserts remained undaunted and anatomically correct, but at ease. I was the Ice Princess. Totally cool and unflappable, just like a real Bond girl. I put my hand to my heart to slow it down from the start and from Fry's nearness. "You scared me!"

"Sorry." He was grinning as he pulled up a chair next to mine. "Didn't mean to give you a fright."

"How'd you sneak up on me like that? I didn't hear a thing."

"If I told you that, I'd have to kill you. It's a trade secret." Fry flashed me a flirty grin and nodded toward the computer screen. "So what are y'all doing out and about after curfew?"

I'm neither a good actress nor an accomplished liar. But I'm pretty good at partial truths. I explained about my BlackBerry not working. "I'm expecting an important message," I said, conveniently leaving out the "from my boyfriend" part. Spies never tell the whole truth anyway. "No one said anything about these computers being off-limits to guests."

"CTs," he corrected. "Not by me, they aren't. Rockford might shit bullets, though." He winked. "Don't worry. I won't tell. But it's getting late. First full day of camp's a real butt burner. You'll need your rest. Why don't I just see you safely back to your room?"

And see me safely back, he did. Without putting any smooth 006 moves on me, more's the pity. You know, Six was one of Bond's best friends. They were in MI6 training together and had covered each other's backsides on more than one mission. That's what made his betrayal of Bond and country all the more heinous. So I expect Six had a lot of Bond's talents with the ladies, too. Just like I imagine Fry does. After all, isn't everything bigger in Texas? I grinned to myself at the thought.

Chapter Five

I woke on Monday morning after a night of fitful sleep. Fuming about my stolen camera and being a tiny bit fearful that the perp might come back for more of my goodies made for light sleeping. I did my best to push aside uneasy thoughts of someone breaking into my room.

By morning's light I'd halfway decided the theft was just a camp test to see how I'd react or how secure I kept my things . . . or something. It made sense. As far as I could remember, everyone had been at orientation, giving all the CTs alibis. Which didn't mean I wasn't keeping my eyes peeled for the camera's return or that I wouldn't be on the lookout for a guilty party. Or that I'd think it was funny when the Chief handed it back to me when camp was over.

Excited and nervous about the day's upcoming activities, I dressed in my tan Lycra sport bra top, matching bikini panties, spanking-new desert fatigue pants, and combat boots. Getting into the paramilitary aspect of camp, I was going for the Domino as GI Jane look. Yes, I was still wearing the signature Domino headband . . . in camouflage to match the outfit. That Domino is a regular style maven. Plus, I'd seen Bond wear his fair share of military attire.

I met up with Emma in the bathroom, where we fought over the sink and mirror space as we raced to get ready. Eager for confirmation, I was dying to share my camera-stealing-camp-test theory with someone and desperately trying to think up a way to see if Emma knew anything about my missing camera. After all, she couldn't have stolen it; she was with me the whole time and I beat her back to the room. But she might have seen something that would be helpful in getting it back.

"Emma, what would you do if you had a secret? Would you tell?" I looked into the mirror and massaged makeup primer onto my face the way the beauty consultant at Nordstrom had showed me, watching Emma's face closely while trying to keep mine impassive.

Emma stopped applying her mascara midstroke to stare at me suspiciously. "Depends on what it is. And how much someone tortured me to pry it out of me. Why?" She stretched the question out in a singsong voice.

"I'm having a hard time keeping something to myself and I'd like to tell you. I want your opinion," I said as nonchalantly as possible.

She turned to face me. "I'm good. Out with it."

"Only if you promise not to tell anyone."

"Cross my heart." She made the appropriate gesture.

I bit my lip, trying to phrase my accusation carefully. Finally, I gave up and just spit it out. "My camera disappeared while we were at orientation last night."

She looked genuinely surprised by my claim. She frowned slowly. "No way. Are you sure? You didn't misplace it, did you?"

"Positive. Someone took it from my drawer. I'll show you."

She followed me into my room, where I showed her the crime scene.

"You took everything out? You've looked everywhere?" Emma asked, scanning the room.

I nodded.

"Was it expensive?" Emma plopped onto my bed.

"A couple hundred dollars. Chump change." To all of them, anyway. "Not worth stealing."

"Unless we have a klepto in our midst." Emma paused, obviously mulling over the possibilities. "I can't see why any of the campers would take it, unless maybe someone took it as a prank."

"But we were all at the orientation," I objected.

She nodded slowly. "Could be a maid."

I'd thought of that myself. "But the room was already clean. Why would a maid be in my room?"

Emma didn't offer an explanation. "So what are you thinking, then?"

I told her my theory.

"Could be," she said when I finished. "What are you going to do about it?"

"I have no idea." I looked at her hopefully, but she seemed as clueless as I did.

"Have you reported it?"

I shook my head no. "I thought I'd give it some time to see what develops. I'll mention it if it doesn't turn up by the time we leave. In the meantime, why don't we keep our valuables locked up and our eyes open?"

"Oh, I'm all up for spying on people." She grinned. "Count me in."

You have to win the trust of your allies, or you'll end up dead meat. That goes for banking, spying, or life. I figured now that I'd confided in Emma and warned her to be careful, we'd be more likely to bond and she'd be more likely to share any information she discovered with me. She didn't have to know that I wasn't planning on sharing *everything I found out at camp with her.* Dear old Mom taught me there are a few things you should never share— your man and whatever gives you an edge.

Eight o'clock in the hot, hot morning found my fellow spies and me in the war room, the main training-center conference room. Rockford started in on a lecture on the realities of spying, counterintelligence, and special ops. I listened with half an ear, the other half being busy with some surreptitious surveillance spy stuff, Jenna-style.

Fry and Torq sat at the front of the class as Rockford lectured. Torq focused his attention on me. Why? God only knew, when he could've been look-

ing up Pussy's skirt as she did a Sharon Stone a few
rows over from me. He didn't look away even when I
met his stare and did the visual caught-you-looking
thing. Instead, he flashed an enigmatic half smile.

"People come to camp thinking this is all James
Bond stuff," Rockford said. "Fast cars, fast women . . ."

At the mention of fast women, Torq looked at me
again. Okay, this had to be genuine interest on his
part. With Emma's admonishment to use some
Mata Hari type spy seduction ringing in my mind, I
flashed him my best shot at a sexy little smile. When
he grinned back, there was definite lecher in his
eyes. I smiled to myself and looked away.

". . . and lots of gadgets. But the real world of
spying and special ops is no Bond fantasyland.
You'll have no special gizmos, no rocket-launching
bagpipes, piano-wire garrote watches, laser-firing
cameras, or machine-gun-firing BMWs to get you
out of scrapes. But neither will the bad guys. You'll
have nothing but this." He tapped his head. "And
this." He indicated his body. "Our goal is to teach
you competency with these two most powerful
weapons."

I tuned in and out of Rockford's little speech, pondering everything from how cold the air-conditioning
was set to my chances of getting my camera back.

"The number-one Murphy's Law of combat is 'Anything you do can get you killed, including doing
nothing,'" the Chief continued. "We'll teach you
how to act instinctively under stress so you up the
odds of making the right choice." His fierce gaze
bounced around us. "Having people trying to kill

you makes you a fast learner. Soldiers who learn by experience end up dead."

I swallowed a lump in my throat. No learning by experience? And here that was my main learning style. What happened to "Experience is the best teacher"?

Rockford paced in front of us; the guy had too much energy to stand still. "Situational awareness is your key to survival. Fighter pilots are masters of this; they may be upside down pulling Gs, but they know where up and down are, where the enemy is, and where their friends are."

I didn't even know *who* my friends were here. Hadn't he just told us to trust no one? And now he wants us to have friends? The man was a pacing conundrum.

"To survive this special ops mission you're going to have to go into combat mind-set—anything to survive. Use discipline. Fight like you train. And use your weapon"—the Chief pointed to his head again—"with precision. You'll have to learn the art of invisibility—the job of the spy is to find the enemy, or information about the enemy, and return without being caught.

"Now, we're going to divide the group into two squads for the morning. Torq will lead Squad A. Fry, Squad B. Squad B will learn the fine art of breaking and entering and planting a bug . . . in the other five CTs' rooms. One of the goals of this mission is to discover a clue to the other CTs' real identities." Rockford grinned evilly. "Hope you picked your panties up, boys . . . and girls." He laughed.

"Squad A will run through face recognition and Grace-Under-Pressure training." Rockford found something about Grace-Under-Pressure training especially amusing. His smile spread in an imitation of Dr. Evil's. I was beginning to think Rockford had one warped sense of humor. I instantly knew I was not going to like Grace Under Pressure.

Rockford began calling out assignments. Emma, who'd been sitting next to me during the intro, gave a hoot and pounded the air with a victory punch when she was called into Fry's group. She leaned into me and whispered, "Told you I had dibs on him."

I got her back by laughing when Rockford assigned Pussy to her group.

I was assigned to the stoic, scary Torq's squad, along with Max, John, Ethan, and Tom Bishop. It would have been a perfect group if Ethan and Tom had looked, and behaved, more like their Tom Cruise and Brad Pitt movie counterparts and less like adolescent morons.

Those of us in Squad A got the pleasure of remaining in the freezing conference room while Torq set up to show a video. I got the idea that while my panties weren't lying around for all to see, I'd like to secure my valuables, such as I had left. My BlackBerry was still up for grabs. I got up and tried to slip out.

Rockford had none of it. He stopped me at the door. "No one leaves the room."

I raised a brow. "You want us dancing in here?"

Rockford called my bluff. "We got paper cups in

here. You can take a whiz in one of those or I can escort you to the ladies'. Your choice."

I sat down, grumbling as I went.

I noticed Torq watching our exchange as he worked, ever the spy. He called the CTs over when he was finished. We gathered in the middle of the room before the fifty-inch plasma TV screen and Rockford left his post as guardian gargoyle.

"That Rockford's a regular card," Torq said in a monotone, his face impassive. "If I've told him once I've told him a thousand times to introduce this session as what it is—mind reading." He looked to the group of us for our reaction. "Intrigued?"

Next to me, Max snorted. "It's the old mind-reading trick. Seen it a million times."

I sat up straighter, mostly because my poor posture made my fake boobs droop, and tried to look like I was paying attention.

"Next I suppose you'll be teaching us defense against the dark arts." I perched on the edge of my chair and smiled straight at Torq, wanting to see if I could crack his serious-guy veneer.

To my surprise, Torq laughed. "I like a girl with a sense of humor. And the answer would be yes. At some point. Almost everything we do is cloak-and-dagger stuff. But we don't teach Quidditch. Our own version of Q hasn't perfected the flying broom yet."

Was it just me, or were we connecting just the tiniest bit?

Personally, I didn't believe in mumbo jumbo. You watch enough *Secrets of Magic Revealed* and you realize everything's a trick. Uncle Bob has the complete series on DVD. We've watched it together at least a dozen times. If Torq tried the old levitating-on-one-foot trick, I was out of here. Even I could do that one.

"Okay, let's begin." Torq looked directly at me, grinning as though he liked my edge-of-my-seat attentiveness. Some mind reader! I'd fooled him with my fake enthusiasm. Or my fake boobs.

"You have a nice AU combination of skepticism on your face, Domino," he said to me.

My mouth popped open like I was intent on catching a few flies—that's what Mom would say. As I snapped it shut again, he winked at me, letting me know he had my number. That was completely scary. Guys aren't supposed to know what we're thinking.

"AU stands for action unit," he said, getting back to business. "AUs are the building blocks of the Facial Action Coding System, FACS.

"The most common judgments we make of other people are what they're thinking or feeling, how we feel about them, whether they're telling the truth or not, in other words, mind reading. Most of us do it without thinking. We're probably right, on average, eighty or ninety percent of the time. But ninety percent isn't good enough in the spy business. We're shooting for one hundred percent accuracy." He walked over and stood directly in front of me, made direct eye contact, gave a small smile, then looked down and averted his gaze.

My heart did a little flip and I felt my nipples contract. I broke into a flush. He was definitely hot and definitely flirting with me now. Right in front of the class!

Next thing I knew, he dropped into a squat so he was eye-to-eye with me. "What was I just doing, Domino? Read my mind. Come on," he coaxed in a smooth, deep voice. "You can do it."

I felt my flush deepen, my mouth pop open, and my tongue go dry.

Torq shook his head and winked conspiratorially at Max next to me before rolling forward on the balls of his feet, leaning in, and focusing intently on my face. "Okay, I'll go first and read yours." He looked deep into my eyes. "I see surprise, embarrassment, hesitation—you know the answer, but you're afraid telling the truth will make you look foolish and vain. I see some fear and . . . yes, a little anger and annoyance for being put on the spot. Your turn."

"You were flirting!" Okay, so I spoke a little louder than I intended. I hadn't quite mastered the cool-cucumber spy mode yet. But the day was young.

"But was I really flirting, or was I faking?" He rose out of the squat and back to his feet away from me in one quick, smooth move.

Good thing, too, because I was sputtering in his face, or would have been if he'd stayed put.

"Hey, that's a very good AU 4-5-7-24 combination, Domino." He grinned at the boys. "Anger." He walked back to the front of the class. "If Domino here was good at reading what we call micro expressions, she'd know the answer to my question. She'd be an expert mind reader. Madam Domino, the all-knowing." He had the nerve to wink at me. "Micro expressions are quick, instantaneous, completely involuntary expressions that cross our faces.

"Our faces don't merely echo our feelings and thoughts, they *are* our feelings and thoughts. Try as hard as we can to mask our feelings, we can't succeed. A micro expression will give us away. See the connection between mind reading, special ops, and spying?"

Torq paused and took a sip of water. "For the spy, it means detecting the liar and recognizing a friend, if there is such a thing.

"Some emotions can be expressed with a single AU; most are much more complex. AU one." Torq's eyebrows shot up. He looked suddenly anguished. "Distress. How about this, AU twenty-four, thinning of the lips." He looked suddenly pissed. "Anger."

Torq went through half a dozen more combinations of AUs, each time transforming his expression. He was so convincing, he should've been an actor.

"As I've said, some of these facial expressions are voluntary," Torq continued. "Some are not. That's why smiles forced for the camera are so obviously fake. You can control the muscles around the mouth, but not those around the eyes that mark a true smile. Learn what a genuine smile looks like and you can unmask the false friend."

I felt a sudden chill. Here was a man who could imitate with precision practically any emotion he wanted at will. How could you trust him? Not like I had good reason to trust him in the first place, but I made a mental note to be *very* cautious around him.

"There's good news and bad news about mind reading," Torq continued. "The bad news first—extreme situations can disrupt our ability to correctly process what we normally instinctively recognize.

"The good news is mind reading abilities can improve with practice. They can be taught." He grabbed the remote. "Let's try a little test of your mind-reading abilities. I'm going to show you a short clip of a dozen or so people claiming to do something they had or hadn't done. I want all of you to write down who's lying."

He clicked the remote and we watched the video.

"Shit," Ethan said when the clip stopped. "That was brutal, man."

Torq collected our tests and took a quick look at our answers, shaking his head.

"AU whatever—disapproval," I called out.

The class snickered. Torq laughed. I think it was actually genuine, though I couldn't be sure.

"Good mind reading, Domino," Torq said. "Too bad all of your mind-reading results came out at about the average for chance guessing." He set the papers down and picked up the remote again.

"I'm going to show you a thirty-five-minute training video that teaches people to read AUs. We use this DVD when we train bodyguards." He dimmed the lights and clicked the remote again. Thirty-five minutes later we were all sputtering in awe of our newfound capabilities as our success rate of reading another test video correctly skyrocketed.

"This is fantastic," John Steed said. "I'm going to use this on my kids. Next time I tell them they're giving me crap, I'm going to know it for sure. No more lying about anything."

"On your kids? This should work on the chicks!" Bishop said.

I was thinking more along the line of interviewing loan applicants. I could be the banker girl with the lowest loan default rate in the history of banking, meaning big profits for Uncle Bob and me. All I had to do was get expert on recognizing the AU for deceit and insincerity.

Torq shook his head. "Just remember the involuntary micro expressions and don't get cocky." He stepped away from the podium. "Take five. Then the fun begins—Grace Under Pressure."

Chapter Six

When Torq said "take five," he meant five and not a second more. Class reconvened before I'd even had time to fully recover from his flirt exercise. As all of us CTs faithfully gathered around him, a faint aura of anxious anticipation hung over the group. Or maybe that was just the odor of nervous perspiration. Probably partly my own. During the break Torq had singled me out to put on an orange jumpsuit, which didn't bode well—in all likelihood I was going to be made a fool of first.

"Time for Grace Under Pressure. You're up, Domino," Torq said.

Why was I not surprised?

"Put this on." Torq handed me a mask of sorts. Kind of a pair of goggles with a flexible face mask that covered not only the eyes, but also the nose, mouth, and chin.

Holding it in my hand, I hesitated, stalled by equal parts fear and annoyance. I was in no mood to be maimed, not so soon after being gorgeoused up. Nor did I feel like ruining a good hair-extension day. I cocked my hip and put my hand on it, trying to look calm and Bond girl–like. Not easy in the baggy orange jumpsuit Torq had made me wear. "Where's my matching bulletproof vest?"

"A vest would be overkill," Torq said.

I didn't really like the way he emphasized "kill."

"The mask's just for insurance purposes, to keep our rates low." Torq gave a grin that reached his eyes as he helped me put the mask on and adjusted the straps so tightly it rubbed uncomfortably against my hidden cornrows.

"The game's completely harmless." He gave my chin a playful chuck. "Comfy?"

Hell, no. But I wasn't going to tell him that. I did a mind-read of *his* face. If there was a micro expression of lying or lust, I didn't see it. I probably needed a bit more mind-reading practice and vowed silently to get the "experience" he'd mentioned earlier.

"You look like Freddy Krueger as a beekeeper," Max said, admiring my getup.

"Thanks. You really know how to flatter a girl," I said.

"And she's the good guy in this scenario." Torq winked at me. "Mask must fit. Sounds like you can speak just fine." Torq took my arm and strapped a heart-rate monitor on it before I could protest. Then he handed me a strap that contained the transmitter and told me to put it around my chest under the jumpsuit.

To say I was getting leery about this exercise

wouldn't be exaggerating. But as I was in spy-girl mode, it was show-no-fear time.

"Here's the scenario," Torq said. "You're each going to take a turn playing my bodyguard. I'm going to call for help, and you're going to come to my rescue—"

"But we haven't had any bodyguard training," I objected.

"Think of this as a pretest, Domino." He turned and walked back to the podium. "I'm going to evaluate your instinctive reactions and how you handle pressure in an unknown situation. Since you haven't had any time on the firing range yet, you can just use your fingers as a gun." He made a gun out of his hand and gave it a friendly wave.

"Remember, bodyguards never fire their weapons unless they have to, so use restraint. If you get the drop on the bad guy, I'll let you know." He snagged a pair of sunglasses from the podium in front of him. "I'm going to take you outside one at a time. Domino, come with me. The rest of you stay here and relax." He slid his sunglasses on as I dutifully followed him outside and down the road to a small corrugated-metal shack that looked like a packing building for the oranges.

"I'm going to go inside that building. When I call for help, you charge in and save me."

I gave him a skeptical look, but I don't think he could read it because of my mask. "Okay, but what's all this for?" I gestured toward my jumpsuit and mask.

I don't know what AUs it took to do it, but he

gave me an "I know, but I'm not telling" look and walked off, calling over his back, "Remember, on my signal, you come in and save me."

I did a little huff. It was just barely ten in the morning, but the day already felt over one hundred and the air smelled arid and dusty. The stupid orange jumpsuit I wore had long sleeves and long legs, completely negating the cooling properties of my crop top. As I waited for Torq to call me, I moved into a shady spot beneath an orange tree. But the shade wasn't discernibly cooler. A trickle of sweat formed on my brow under the plastic of my mask and dripped into my eyes. Good thing I'd used that makeup primer. At least my foundation was staying put.

"Are you ready yet? You're taking your sweet time and I'm melting in this heat." I squirmed uncomfortably and shooed a sticky fly away. "I'm from Seattle, where a 'dry heat' means fifty-five and rainy. Much longer out here and I'm going to dry up and blow away and there'll be no one to save you. You'll be on your own, buddy."

"Stop exaggerating. You're not blowing anywhere. There's no breeze," Torq yelled back, sounding kind of maniacally pleased about the no-breeze deal. "Now wait for my signal." He paused. "And drink your water," he added as an afterthought.

"I haven't got it." The only appendage I was used to carrying around was an umbrella. Very thoughtful of him to remind me now so I could dwell on my thirst, maybe even become delusional and start seeing mirages.

"I think I hear a noise," he finally yelled.

"That's it? You hear a noise?" I started for the shed, my playing-cops-and-robbers hand at the ready. "Kind of wimpy for a big guy like you. Why don't you just check it out your own self and call me when you have a real problem, like a hangnail."

I was all false bravado. I really didn't want to go into that building. There had to be a reason the insurance company wanted me to wear this stupid mask.

"Just come check it out." I didn't need to see his face to detect an uptick in his irritation level.

My heart was doing a bit of a pitter-patter, but nothing major; probably it was just in the cautious range. I followed his voice into the shed and guardedly stepped over packing crates as I made my way through the small front room, scanning for intruders and noises as I went.

Something skittered out from under a box in the shadows of the corner and scampered across the room. I let out a squeak of horror, jumped back, startled, and put a hand to my heart, completely forgetting to shoot my pretend gun at it.

I thought I heard Torq give a heavy sigh from what looked like a storage room just off the room I was in. There were no lights on, just natural light filtering in through a dingy window, so it was hard to tell. As I calmed down, I muttered to myself, "Why doesn't someone call an exterminator around here?"

I peered around the corner into a hall no longer than eight feet long, my loaded finger at the ready.

A refrigerated room sat to one side, a storage room on the other. No one in sight so I slipped around real stealthily and flattened myself against the wall just like they do in all the spy movies. The thump of a motor turning on gave me another start and I jumped. Damn it! Where was my calm? It was nothing more than the hum of a refrigerator cycling on. I took a deep, calming breath and relaxed with my back against the wall.

I heard another click and spun around just in time to hear a gun fire and take a bullet square in my left silicone breast. Just like in the movies, the impact sent me staggering as I grabbed my chest. I had the irrelevant thought that the physics of it was wrong. I'd seen *MythBusters*. Bullets slicing through you don't send you flying. All this passed through my mind in a nanosecond, but it was like time had slowed. I let out a yelp, more of surprise than pain.

Before I could wonder why my life wasn't flashing before my eyes, I was shot dead-on in my chest. It all happened so quickly I didn't have time to process where the attacker was hiding. I felt something oozing down my jumpsuit, something sticky to the touch, like blood. Did I mention I'm *really* squeamish?

Another shot rang out. I covered my head with my hands and started screaming, trying to call for help, but only gibberish rolled off my tongue.

On the verge of pure hysteria, I ducked my head down and raced back toward the entrance as fast as my wobbly legs would carry me, nearly colliding with Torq as he came around the corner into full view, carrying a lethal-looking rifle thing and shaking his head.

"Anyone ever tell you it's not smart to run into the line of fire?" He shook his head. "No survival instinct. You are so dead."

Seeing him, I nearly collapsed with relief, followed immediately by embarrassment and anger as I realized the truth of the situation. "You! You were the one who shot me."

"Who'd you expect, the Easter Bunny?"

I looked down at my jumpsuit, expecting to see blood and saw—

"It's paint," Torq said, "from this. It's a paintball gun." He shook his head again and gave me a "duh" look. "You'd think the paintball mask would have given you a clue."

Instinctively, I reached up to touch the mask. I yanked it off and shook it at him. "Paintball mask! How was I supposed to know this was a paintball mask? I've never played paintball. Decent people don't play paintball." Now I was glaring.

I dropped the mask and rubbed my chest, mostly to make sure my falsies hadn't slipped. Nope, they felt fine. That's when I realized Torq was watching me and enjoying the view of me fondling myself.

"Oh, stop it!" I yelled at him and brushed a lock of hair out of my face. "Decent people don't shoot innocent people coming to their aid. Besides, that hurt!" Or it would have if that had been real me in my crop top and not falsies.

"It stings." He shrugged, looking mostly stoic. But I saw a micro expression of amusement cross his face, I swear. "The bad guys are going to use more firepower than washable paint. You gotta be prepared. This drill's for your own good."

"Yeah, well, I could use more firepower, too. How come you get a paintball gun and all I get is a finger?"

"'Cause I'm the instructor." Of all the insolence, he grabbed my arm. If he thought he could just lead me around by the arm—

But before I could tear it away, he read the heart-rate monitor strapped to me. "Peaked at one seventy-five. Dog-thinking mode."

His smile was the slightest upturn of the corners of his mouth. On him, I found it incredibly sexy. He should have dropped my arm. Instead, his warm thumb was doing a neat little rubbing trick on the tender inside of my wrist, which had unexpectedly pleasant consequences all the way down to my G-spot.

He glanced at the monitor again. "Looks like your heart rate is spiking."

I yanked my arm away and gave him a glare.

He smiled to himself, gave his head another shake, then walked to a small cooler that I hadn't noticed before. "Let's try it again."

"No way," I said, rubbing my wrist, trying to rub out the sensations he'd caused and cover my embarrassment.

He pulled out a chilled bottle of water and handed it to me. "Chicken?"

Oh, damn him. No one called a Bond girl "chicken" and got away with it!

"Fine. Only this time I'll be ready. And don't take

so damn long setting up. It's hot out there." I jerked the cap off the bottle and took a big drink as I stormed outside.

A few minutes later, he called out again. "I hear a noise."

"He hears a noise. I'm going to make him hear a noise, all right," I muttered to myself as I ran to the shed, heart racing, opened the door, and—

Bang! He shot me in the chest again.

"Yeaouch!" I gave him a glare as he came around the corner, smiling.

"You sadistic bastard, you're enjoying this," I said as soon as my heart rate slowed down enough for me to form words. "And stop shooting me in my girls!"

"You want me to shoot you in the head instead?"

I kept glaring. "How about in the arm or leg? Did that ever occur to you?"

"Bad guys aren't going to be aiming for your arm, Domino. They shoot to kill." He grabbed my wrist. "One seventy-five. Let's go again."

I yanked my arm away before he could try the thumb trick again.

And so it went. He called. I approached with my racing heart. He shot me and took my pulse. Until finally, I wasn't afraid anymore.

He called. I approached, hand-as-a-gun at ready and much smarter about how to check out a building and keep behind cover.

I didn't exactly get the drop on him. But just as he shot me, I managed to keep my finger aimed at him and say, "Bang, bang!"

He took my pulse. "Ninety." He grinned. "Congratulations, you're now inoculated against stress."

But not against him.

"Yeah? I look like a Jackson Pollock painting!" I did a little victory dance. I was covered in paint and drenched in sweat, but I'd never felt so exhilarated.

"You can drop the mask and the coveralls in the corner and head back to the barracks for a shower." He looked down to record my heart rate on some kind of chart, but not before I caught his smile. "Don't let the other CTs see you or talk to them. The element of surprise is key in this exercise."

Surprise? I grinned evilly to myself as I had a Domino moment. I paused. He looked up from his charting.

Making sure I had his full attention, I slowly unzipped the jumpsuit. Down to the tops of my fake breasts. Pause.

His pen stilled.

Zip. Over the girls, past the hips, down to the crotch. I gave one shoulder a shimmy shake sending the silicone girls bouncing as I stripped the jumpsuit off one shoulder. Then the next. I'd watched Logan's strip aerobics DVD a time or two and it was coming in handy now as I worked up to the grand finale.

I gave my bottom a healthy wiggle as I scooched the overalls past my hips and stepped out of them, one elongated leg at a time.

His gaze was glued to my crop top. When I looked down, I realized it was plastered with sweat against my body in much the same way a wet T-shirt clings. I kicked the coveralls into the corner and stepped directly in front of him, feigning trying to get a glimpse of my chart. In reality, I was just giving him a better look down my blouse.

"Hey, you were a real trouper." His tongue was thick on his words. He was looking down at me. I was looking up at him, standing way too far into his personal space. "Five times isn't bad. Great big, brave policemen don't do any better."

Our gazes locked.

"Thanks."

He cleared his throat. "You probably better send the next CT in."

"You're probably right." I reluctantly stepped back and turned to leave. I paused at the door to call to him. "Bet no one else is as good as me." I winked and raced out, giving him a wave over my back, being careful not to turn and let him see the big, fat grin on my face. Let him figure *me* out.

My exhilaration hadn't faded by the time I reached my room. Maybe I did have the thrill-seeking gene after all, just like James. When I'd read on my favorite Bond fan site about scientists isolating the thrill-seeker gene, I'd been depressed because I didn't need a DNA test to tell me I'm mostly a thrill-dreamer. Or thought I was. Until now.

I pulled out my magnetic key card and unlocked my door, pausing with my hand on the knob. Wasn't someone supposed to be bugging the room while I was gone?

I cupped an ear and listened at the door for spurious bug-planter noise. Not hearing any wild rummaging going on in there, I stepped inside and pulled the door closed behind me, freezing just inside the room to survey it, wondering if my room had been hit yet.

After fourteen years of being the first person to arrive at the bank after Uncle Bob opened it in the morning, I had a lot of practice taking stock of a room before entering.

Ever security-minded, Uncle Bob, who was always the first person at work, let himself into the bank, checked it for intruders, and then returned to the lobby, where he changed the date on the front desk to the current date. If I arrived and the date hadn't been changed, I was to assume something was wrong, leave the area, and call the police immediately. Yes, we had a security system, but you could never be too careful at a bank. The thought of free money, lots of it, had a way of inspiring a certain type of person with amazing ingenuity.

For my part, I always scanned the lobby for more than just the changed date, looking for other signs that something was amiss. Fortunately, I'd never had occasion to call the cops yet.

I used those same observation skills as I surveyed my room. The window was closed. The door hadn't been obviously jimmied. Neither had the bathroom door. If someone from the other squad had been here, it looked like Fry had simply let them in with a key.

My gaze bounced around the room as I did a comprehensive visual. I paused at the lamp shade. No one who'd watched even one Bond movie would bug a lamp shade. Too obvious. I'd check it later anyway just in case someone was going for the too-obvious-to-be trick. Then I spotted the wall clock and grinned. It was an impostor. How did I know? It had a second hand. The clock that had been there when I left didn't. And this one was five minutes fast. I'm kind of compulsive about synchronizing my timepieces. I shook my head. Sloppy, sloppy spy work. A real dead giveaway that I'd been bugged. Wonder how much they could hear? One thing was for sure, I wasn't giving them a show.

I turned on the radio to cover any noise I made removing the clock. Wham! Static and white noise blasted into the room. I jumped, startled. It took me a sec to adjust the station and set the volume to a comfortable level that covered the sounds of me moving about the room. The idiot had obviously bumped the control dial when they switched out my clock. I shook my head. Amateur!

I surveyed the rest of the room, trying to decide how much dirt I'd left out that could give my identity away. With a sigh of relief, I pretty much decided I was in the clear as far as blowing my Domino cover.

After my shower, I checked the lamp shade just because I'm a thorough person and I'd said I would. As suspected—nothing. I debated for a second what to do with the clock.

I'd watched enough spy shows and cruised enough spy equipment Web sites to know that it was possible the clock contained a transmitter, an electronic bug. But since I didn't have a receiver, it was worthless to me. It might also simply house a voice-activated recorder, which I could use *if* I had an instruction manual and knew how to remove the device from the clock without damaging it. I decided to take the clock to Rockford and ask for my original back. I really didn't have any other option.

Mission accomplished, I caught up with Emma and the others in the lunch room. She sat with Max and John at one end of a long table. All three of them were munching down subs and fries. I slid in with my tray at the end of the bench. From the far end of the table, Ethan leered at my fake breasts and elbowed his buddy Bishop.

Ignoring them, I turned to Emma next to me. "Was it you or one of your cronies who bugged my room?"

"Like I'm going to tell you. Mum's the word." She popped a fry in her mouth and grinned at me.

I shrugged. "No matter. I'm bug-free now." I'd made a very surprised Rockford give me back my original clock, even making him run his bug-detecting wand over the original before I'd take it back. Remembering his surprise made me smile with pleasure.

"How do you know?" Emma asked.

"I found it, of course. Didn't I tell you I'm a spying genius?"

She had surprise written all over her face. "Okay, genius, how?"

"Two can play the secret-keeping game." I opened a little pack of mayo and spread it on my sub.

Emma had no choice but to change the subject. "How was face recognition?"

"You mean mind reading?" I put my napkin on my lap and reached for my sub. Being pelted with paint had given me an appetite. "Terrific."

Max, who'd been listening with rapt attention, broke into our conversation. "Emma here was saying that some of the gang are heading into Surprise tonight to barhop. Want to come?"

I turned to Emma, who nodded her affirmation. My first inclination was to decline. "How are you getting to town?" If they were taking the camp helicopter, I might consider going.

"The camp bus," John said.

"They're letting us out of this joint after only a day?" I took another bite of sub and tossed back a cola chaser.

"Fry's driving," Emma said.

I started to shake my head no.

"Oh, come on," Max said. "It'll be fun."

"Are you bringing your shoe phone?" I asked him.

"I can, if it makes a difference whether you'll come or not." Max cocked his head. "Do you hear that? I think I hear it ringing now." He reached down and tugged off his right shoe, putting it to his ear. "Right, Chief. Would you believe she's sitting right here?" He offered me his shoe. "The Chief wants to talk to you."

I waved a hand in front of my nose and pushed his shoe away. "Ask the Chief what he wants."

"I think that's obvious," Max said. "He says your mission is to go out drinking with us tonight . . . and love it!" He thrust the shoe back at me again.

"All right," I said, laughing as I pushed the stinky shoe away again. "Tell him I'll come."

What the heck? My BlackBerry would probably work in Surprise. I could call Logan and check for messages from Daniel, too.

Just then Pussy strolled up with her tray and paused before Ethan, leaning over to give him an eyeful of her considerable cleavage. "I hope all you boys are going out to the bar tonight." She slid her gaze along all the men at the table, ignoring Emma and me. "I must have a dance with each of you."

Emma and I exchanged disgusted looks as Ethan stumbled over his tongue to assure her he'd be there.

As Pussy walked off, Ethan came out of her spell and spoke loudly for Emma's and my benefit, I'm certain. "That woman is one sexy acrobat. Imagine the acrobatics she could do in bed." He let out a low whistle.

I turned to Max. "Bring the cone of silence, too."

After lunch, Emma and I stopped by our rooms to freshen up before heading out to the afternoon activities, complaining about Pussy as we went.

"Men can be so shallow," she said as I unlocked my door and she followed me into my bug-free room.

"I wouldn't lump all men in," I said, ever hopeful that there was at least one great, nonshallow guy out there waiting for me. A guy who, unlike Daniel, would commit. I pulled the door shut and changed the subject. "Okay, spill it—who bugged my room?"

Emma laughed. "What took you so long to get around to asking?"

"Seriously," I said.

"I don't know," Emma replied slowly. "It wasn't me. They took us back to the barracks area one at a time so we couldn't figure out who'd bugged who."

"Darn!"

"My sentiments exactly." Emma took a seat on my bed.

Suddenly I had the feeling we were playing one huge, live game of Clue.

"Whose room *did* you bug? You tell me and I'll tell you whose room I do and what I find." I leaned against my dresser and waited for her answer. Neither of us made any false protests or feigned any indignation about not stooping to snooping. Spies snooped. Everybody knew that.

"Wade's."

"What did you find?"

"A mess. A closet filled with Hawaiian shirts. Dirty socks on the floor. Half a dozen scratch game tickets on the nightstand, none of them winners." She grinned again. "I checked."

"He's still playing?"

"Evidently."

"His real identity?"

"No clue. Everything the mate had was pretty much Jake Wade."

"Anything suspicious?"

Emma frowned. "Like what?"

"I don't know. Anything, just anything odd."

She sighed. "Nope. Not that I saw. But I didn't have much time."

I tried grilling her about how the bugging game worked, but my interrogation skills, finely honed from years of interviewing loan applicants, failed me. Tough nut that she was, Emma didn't give up a thing.

"You'll see for yourself soon enough. What about Grace Under Pressure? I noticed you took a shower after that little exercise," Emma said.

Nice try, kid. But two could play her spy game. I did tough and inscrutable with the best of them. I masked my expressions, doing my best to keep involuntary micro expressions at bay. "Very observant, Sherlock. I guess you'll be finding out soon enough yourself."

"Well, if you won't play, I call first dibs on the bathroom," Emma said.

I made a note to remember that Emma was big on dibbing and beat her to it next time. While Emma was in the loo, as she liked to call it, I slipped into my drawer, kind of hoping to find that my camera had mysteriously reappeared. Wouldn't it be great to take a few photos when it was my turn to snoop? No such luck.

I jetted through my turn in the bathroom. Emma was waiting for me in my room when I'd finished. We had a few minutes to kill before afternoon class.

"I was thinking," Emma said, drawing out her

words. She had a devilish look in her eye that I didn't particularly like. "Simply going drinking doesn't seem exciting or spylike enough to me. We're on this here vacation for excitement, aren't we?"

"You have something in mind?" I said, speaking slowly myself, wondering what exactly she was up to.

"We need a mission!" She watched closely for my reaction, which made me even more cautious.

"What kind of mission?" Trying to act nonchalant, I glanced in the mirror on the pretense of adjusting my headband.

"You love *The Recruit*, right?"

I turned away from the mirror and faced her. "Yeah, duh." What spy freak doesn't?

"Remember that scene where they take the CTs to the bar?"

"Uh-huh."

"And their mission is to seduce a fellow CT?" Emma spoke in a tone designed to lead me to a specific conclusion.

"You want us to make it our own mission to seduce one of our fellow CTs?" I said, thinking that our fellow CTs weren't exactly tempting hunks of burning love and looking at her like she'd gone stark raving crazy. No way was I letting any of them feel up my fake silicone breasts, let alone getting completely naked with any of them. "I think Pussy's already dibbed them all."

Emma laughed. "Oh, let her have them."

"Who . . ." I had a sinking feeling I knew who, but my morbidly curious side wanted verification.

"Exactly," she said, beaming.

"Not the instructors!" I shook my head no. "Uh-uh. No way." Never, never, I wanted to add, but at the risk of sounding childish, I restrained myself.

"Why not? Because of he-who-doesn't-call?"

She gave me the most penetrating, challenging look I personally had ever witnessed. I felt a nasty twinge of guilt, because Daniel hadn't been in my thoughts at all. I was actually more afraid of being rejected by Fry or Torq than betraying Daniel. My logic, warped as it may have been, mirrored my feelings about money in the bank. While the money's safely squirreled away, there are endless possibilities regarding how to spend it. Once spent, it's gone, with it all of the fantasies of how it could be spent.

I'd never been a head-turning babe. Wallpaper. Background noise. Those are pretty good descriptors. Generally, even regular guys don't notice me. Handsome, dangerous, exciting men—forget about it. Thanks to the makeover Logan had given me, I looked better than I ever had and was actually getting noticed by a wide variety of men. I was building fantasy capital. I wasn't sure I was ready to spend that capital and face the humiliation of probable rejection just yet. I was on a fantasy vacation. It was no time to have all of my fantasies dashed.

I blushed and Emma took it wrong.

"Forget about him! Spies have to be able to set aside their personal feelings and seduce friend, foe, or informant on the spot. Bond girls do it all the time." Still wearing the scary challenging look, she was unblinking and formidable.

"Yes," I said slowly, agreeing with her as I thought

up a good excuse to decline, or at least change the mission. "But they only do it to get information."

"We could get information," she said, nonplussed.

"About what?" I asked.

"Wouldn't it rock to be the first campers in camp history to prevent the kidnapping? I bet nobody else has even thought of *trying*. I bet the instructors know who the victim will be."

"Well . . ." I wasn't exactly jumping up and down with enthusiasm. "I suppose we could seduce *information* out of them." I was trying to appease her and broaden the definition of "seduce" at the same time.

"Seduce." Emma grinned again. "I like it. As long as I get to seduce, I'm happy."

"Seduce *information*," I reminded her.

"Whatever." Emma nodded her approval. "Fry already likes me. I'll work on him. You can have Torq."

"How am I supposed to get him to spill top-secret camp info to me? I'm not sure he even likes me." More accurately, I was confused whether he actually liked me or was merely faking it to pull my chain.

"Pillow talk."

I rolled my eyes. "I'm seducing nothing but information."

"Suit yourself. Just don't question my methods." She stuck out her hand. "Deal?"

We shook.

"All right. But be careful. I don't want us to be the first women in the history of spy camp to get kicked out for sleeping with an instructor."

"I'm always careful. And discreet." Emma grinned

broadly. "You watch yourself. Torq's hot. Hard to keep your hands off a guy like that, especially if there's some drinking and dirty dancing thrown in."

"No worries," I said, mimicking her accent. "A good spy has self-control. Take Kissy Suzuki. She resisted Bond's considerable charm."

"Only until the mission was over," Emma said and grinned like there was hope for me yet.

Chapter Seven

I spent Fry's lecture on electronic surveillance enjoying the view while getting a little daydreaming practice in on the side. Not that electronic surveillance isn't a riveting topic. It's just that I preferred my daydream of a bare-chested Fry perched above me saying, "Brace yourself, Domino," in that sweet Texas drawl of his to becoming the paranoid wretch any sane person was apt to become when they realized that Big Brother, or the evil dude next door, could be listening to you through his Ping-Pong paddle receiver, while simultaneously recording your computer keystrokes and stealing your identity. Listen too closely and suddenly Bond's laser beam, rappelling line, and buzz saw–loaded watch and Max Smart's martini-and-olive radio didn't sound so far-fetched. Living in paranoia isn't good for the soul.

I was startled out of my daydreams and pleasant postlunch sleepiness by Fry announcing the bugging mission specifics.

"It's simple, y'all."

He held up a navy blue pen with the camp logo embossed on it in silver. "I'm going to issue each of you a camp pen just like this one." He picked up another camp pen, a black one. "Y'all will observe it's slightly different in color from a real camp pen. Hard to tell the difference unless you look real close. Kinda like a pair of mismatched men's dress socks—you don't notice you're wearing one black and one navy until you get out into the light." He pulled up his pant legs and made a show of checking his socks. "Whew! Good for me I'm wearing white athletic socks today."

The class laughed.

"Your mission is to talk your way into your target's room. In the barracks hall, you'll find a maid with a cleaning cart. She has a master key. You need to convince her to open the door to your target's room and let you in. . . ."

I gave myself a mental pat on the back for being smart enough to realize that entry hadn't been forced.

"Once inside the room," Fry continued, leaning back against the podium, "you swap the real pen— every room was equipped with a real pen before you checked in—for our 'bugged' pen and get back out and return to class without being noticed." He paused. "Of course, y'all know the 'bugged' pen's a dummy, right? FSC respects the privacy of its CTs." He winked because the statement was so obviously ludicrous.

Probably the truth was FSC didn't want to spend the money on real bugged pens. I knew from my experience checking out spy gear online that a real voice-activated recorder pen could set you back several hundred, while a bulk pen with the FSC logo on it would run under a dollar.

The class let out a collective groan of disappointment that made Fry grin wider. I congratulated myself that I hadn't wasted time dissecting my clock.

"All right, who wants to go first?" Fry looked around the class with his gaze ending up on me. "Domino, how about you?"

I suspected Fry picked me first thanks to his Southern manners—ladies first, please. And while I appreciate the ladies-first mentality when it means I get to take the first chocolate from a box of candy, in this case, I hadn't yet had time to construct my plan to get into my target's room. Not to mention that my fellow CTs looked like they were getting tired of me having first stab at things.

"Uh . . ."

"Great! Thanks for volunteering," Fry said as he handed me a folded slip of paper. "Everything's set up and ready. You can read who your mark is on your way to the barracks. As for the rest of you, I'll be going over the basics of both tailing a mark and losing a tail."

Personally, if Fry wanted my tail, I'd let him have it. But I didn't have a choice as he nodded toward the door. "Go on. Have at it."

I'd just grabbed the doorknob when Fry called after me. "Oh, I almost forgot." His tone said he was lying. He remembered clearly enough. He was already holding a timer. "You've got ten minutes to complete the mission, Dom, and be back in the classroom. Longer than that and we get to storm after you." He glanced at the timer and held his arm up like he was calling a race. "Time starts . . . now."

I nodded and zipped out of the room as fast as I could without breaking into a run, trying to look calm while my pulse roared in my ears and my stomach did backflips. Just outside the classroom door, I unfolded my assignment. *Octopussy, Room 110.* At least one thing had gone right—she was my first choice of mark. Feeling the clock ticking, I sprinted to the barracks.

As Fry promised, the maid, who wore a name tag proclaiming her Maria, was in the hall with her cleaning cart. Trying to get the ticking clock out of my head, I took a deep breath and screwed up my courage, ready to do what every actress and good spy dreams of—give the performance of my life. As I walked past Maria, I smiled and pulled my own key card from my pocket. I marched directly to Pussy's room, stuck the key in her lock, and waited for a green light I knew wasn't coming.

I put on a perplexed look, removed the key, and tried, tried again. I repeated this charade one more time, finally feigning frustration by pounding on the door.

"Shoot!" I said loud enough for Maria, who was ostensibly getting cleaning supplies from her cart, to hear. "My key doesn't work. It must have gotten demagnetized or something."

I looked around, searching for an answer, and

made eye contact with Maria. "Do you have a key? Would you mind . . . ?"

Maria gave me a wary look and shook her head no. "This is not your room." She pointed down the hall to my real room. "I know you stay there. I clean it for you. I see your clothes."

Damn! I'm not good at thinking up lies on the fly. So I tried the truth, sort of.

"Look," I said, "my digital camera disappeared from my room yesterday. I think the lady from this room may have 'borrowed' it." I made quote marks with my fingers as I said "borrowed." I also watched Maria closely for any telltale micro expressions that she was our camera-stealing klepto.

"I'd like to get it back without making a scene. Can you help me?" I gave her my best pleading look, which was totally lost on the surprisingly steely and not the least bit guilty-looking Maria.

"Not my problem. I let you in, I lose my job."

I sighed. The clock was ticking. I hated to resort to bribery. It made me feel supremely slimy, but it was the best shot I had. No way was I going back defeated. Fortunately for me, I always kept a little cash on me. I pulled out a twenty and held it out to her. "Would this help?"

She grabbed the twenty and pocketed it. Without saying another word, she let me in.

"You're a lifesaver," I said dryly as I stepped inside Pussy's room.

Maria shrugged. "I know nothing of this." Then she went back to her work.

I closed the door, gave the air a quick victory punch,

and looked at my watch. Exactly two minutes had passed.

Even though I had plenty of time, I was feeling rushed and shaking as I located the pen on Pussy's desk. I had to take a deep breath and make myself concentrate on the condition of the room and the exact placement of the pen before acting. I angled my pen above the original so that the two exactly lined up and then swiftly swapped it out for my dummy pen.

After that I headed for her dresser and became snoop extraordinaire. I carefully opened her drawers.

Sheesh, I expected Pussy would have more glamorous lingerie. Some guy was going to be disappointed when he got her down to her skivvies because the drawer was full of Spanx and other serviceable garments designed to cover figure flaws.

Another glance at my watch. Five minutes to go. Still plenty of time, I told myself as I breathed deeply and tried to stay calm and not *rush*. When I rushed, I made mistakes.

I opened the closet—scads of spandex and plunging necklines. I put on an evil grin, considering causing a little mischief with the wardrobe, like hiding one of the pushup bras or Spanx panties that made wearing these getups possible. Hey, I'd seen the *What Not to Wear* duo on *Oprah*. A good pair of tummy-control panties goes a long way toward slimming and smoothing out unsightly bulges.

I went back to the drawer and grabbed a nice full-bodied Spanx panty, size M. My gaze bounced between the bed and the dresser. How hard would it be to imagine that she'd dropped this while unpacking and it "accidentally" got kicked under the bed? Feasible, I decided as I got down on my hands and knees, ready to toss the lingerie under. Did I feel guilty? Nope. Pussy was the enemy. Well, all right, definitely the competition, anyway. And we all know that all's fair in love and war . . . and spying.

Old Pussy had a family of dust bunnies living under her bed. Maria evidently didn't consider sweeping under beds part of her job description.

I tossed the panties under. *Take that! Just you try wearing that skintight stuff now, Miss Pussy.*

As I started to stand up, the bedspread caught on my head. Lovely. Still kneeling, I shook it off and, in doing so, noticed a bulge between the mattress and box springs. Curious, I reached in between them and pulled out . . .

A handgun!

I dropped it onto the floor with a clatter, shaking so hard I was in a complete panic. I stifled a scream, finally gaining enough control to bend over to look at it, thanking my good fortune that the gun hadn't gone off.

I knew only two things about guns—this was one and Bond's favored handgun is the Walther PPK or the P99 (more recent, more firepower), depending on the movie. He sleeps with it under his pillow. *Shudder.* The gun under the pillow was quite possibly the only downside to sleeping with Bond. Evidently even Pussy was more cautious, preferring to keep it under the mattress. Not as accessible, but I wasn't arguing with her choice. I had no idea if the gun on the floor in front of me was a Walther anything. Guns scare me spitless—a definite detriment to becoming a real card-carrying spy.

The sight of the gun fueled my vivid imagination. What in the world was Pussy doing with a gun here? How did she sneak it in? Was it for protection? Was she afraid of someone? Lots of lottery winners developed phobias, thinking that someone was out to get them for their money. That could be her problem.

Hopefully her problem wasn't that she was planning on going postal. But Pussy hadn't displayed any violent tendencies that I could see. Her only predatory actions appeared to be sexual.

I wondered briefly whether I should tell Rockford. Then I thought better of it. Surely Pussy wasn't smart enough to sneak a gun in without the staff's knowledge? And I wasn't a squealer. Instead, I made a note to keep my eye on Pussy. If she acted suspicious at all, then I'd talk.

I was running out of time. Finally, holding the gun by two fingers as if it were a dead rodent, I carefully put it back where I'd found it, all the while praying I didn't accidentally shoot myself in the process.

I rearranged the bedspread, convincing myself no one could tell I'd messed with it, and skedaddled out of there, nodding to Maria as I ran back to class. "I'm late," I explained.

By the time I'd reached the classroom, I was breathing hard and I'd convinced myself that Pussy probably had a concealed-weapon permit and a

perfect right to carry the gun. Why she had it
stuffed under her mattress was her business.

Evasive driving followed Fry's class. He led us directly to the course, where we met up with the other
squad.

Waiting for the other four CTs in my group to do
their bugging had given me plenty of time to think.
There was only one smart course of action—keep
an eye on Pussy and gain her confidence. Maybe
she'd let some clue slip as to why she felt the need
to take a gun to camp. Girl like her could have a
stalker, I supposed. Or some deranged ex. As dis-
tasteful as the thought was, gaining her confidence
meant hanging with her and getting to know her.
Such was the spy game.

At the track, Davie Edwards, the senior member
of the driving staff, greeted us. I finagled a place between Max and Pussy, having to elbow Bishop out of
the way to get next to the ever-popular vamp. From
across the group, Emma shot me a surprised and
perplexed "what's up?" look. Hoping she'd learned
something in mind reading, I returned her look
with one that I hoped communicated "trust me."

The guy CTs flocked around Davie like groupies at
a rock concert. Sickening, really. So he could drive?
So could almost everyone over the age of sixteen.
Didn't impress me much.

Next to me, girly girl Pussy sighed and looked
bored, evidently not happy with a driving instructor
stealing the center of attention from her. Thinking

to break the frosty atmosphere between us, I turned to her and whispered, "I don't see what's so great about NASCAR. All they do is drive around in circles. Go fast. Turn left. So what?"

"Care to repeat that for the entire class, Domino?" Davie asked, voice booming.

Looking around the group I realized I'd lost some major brownie points with the boys. They were gawking at me like I'd committed heresy.

I blushed. "Ummmm . . . no, really I wouldn't."

Emma grinned at me, clearly on my side.

"Those cars drive around the 'circle'"—he punctuated with his fingers—"at two hundred miles per hour, feet, ladies, *feet*, off each other's bumpers. Heard the phrase 'burn rubber'? NASCAR guys burn several sets of rubber just driving the course."

Get Davie worked up and he loves to lecture, that's what I learned. He just kept going on, talking about reaction times and the skill involved in high-speed driving.

"Still don't think NASCAR takes skill?" He shook his head disgustedly. "Get over here and get in the vehicle." He opened the driver's door and motioned me in.

"Every goddamn person in America thinks they can drive. Most of them are asleep behind the wheel, accidents waiting to happen." He focused back on me.

I'd already buckled my seat belt and adjusted my seat and mirrors. He didn't scare me. I'm a fantastic driver with a completely clean slate—not even a parking ticket since I got my license at sixteen.

"Let's see what we've got here." Davie leaned over to inspect my handiwork and shook his head. "You drive with your seat too close. Like most women. Stop suddenly and you'll break your wrists . . . or worse."

Q, Bishop, Tanner, Ethan, and even Max and John were all smirking smugly like they were God's gift to driving, mouths lathering in anticipation of getting their turn to show how it's *really* done. You can take the boy to the city and civilize him, even metrosexualize him, but put him near a sports car and his machismo comes raging back in all its glory.

I rolled my eyes and stuck my chin out, determined to win one for the girls. Hey, we could drive, too.

"If the airbag deploys, you're gonna risk some serious injury. Stretch your arms out." Davie reached for the seat adjustment lever and slid my seat into the proper position. Taken by surprise, I let out a startled gasp.

Around the car, the guys elbowed each other and chuckled.

I was still shooting them a glare when Davie attacked my mirror positioning—"How the hell are you going to see your blind spots with all your mirrors aimed to see directly behind the car?"—and my 10 and 2 hand positions on the wheel—"Nine and three gives you more control." Then he broke into a lecture about oversteering and understeering and loose and tight and heaven only knows what else.

Finally he made driving assignments. There were three instructors and three courses. "Ladies first," Davie said, assigning me to his vehicle and Emma and

Pussy to the other two cars while the guys jockeyed for position to get to drive in the next round.

Davie hopped into the car with me and handed me a helmet. What was it with this camp and helmets? They were hell-bent on destroying my perfect Bond girl 'do.

"Okay, let's see what you've got." He handed me the key and I fired up the engine. "Remember—the secret to high-performance driving is smoothness and precision."

An incredibly short half an hour later, Davie had me pull over and he drove the final lap, cruising the straightaway at over two hundred mph! Then my turn was over. I got out of the car on a complete speed high. My thrill-seeker gene was at full throttle.

Emma and Pussy pulled up about the same time and got out of their cars. The guys all crowded around us like a flock of reporters shooting questions. "How was it?"

I caught Emma and Pussy's attention. "Better than sex, boys. Wouldn't you two girls agree?"

"Definitely." Pussy spoke up before Emma and winked at me. Wow, her first acknowledgment of me, and other female life-forms, since camp started.

"Dinner was excruciating," Emma complained as soon as we'd tucked ourselves in our rooms to get ready for the evening ahead.

Emma watched as I made a quick check of the pens in my room to make sure none of them were the "bugged" ones, just in case. I assumed all the other group had swapped was my clock, but a spy needed to be extra cautious. The pens all came up clean. I turned my attention to preparing for the evening.

Emma grumbled about Pussy sitting with us and her annoying habit of competing for the attention of anything male within a hundred-mile radius. "Why did you ask Pussy at dinner if she was going with us tonight?"

"Surveillance," I said, distracted by looking through my new wardrobe for just the right outfit for an information-seducing mission. What did one wear? "Besides, she knew about our outing and was planning on coming anyway."

"Surveillance?"

I turned from my task to find Emma glaring at me with her hands on her hips.

"The way I figure it, Pussy is the enemy. Well, at least the competition. We need to keep an eye on her."

Emma's unhappy expression didn't waver. "Why?"

She had me for a second. I couldn't very well tell her about the gun. "Because if we don't, she'll monopolize all the guys. And then . . . and then . . . Well, I don't know." I paused. "I just don't trust her." Then I grinned. "I bugged her room and did a little snooping. Her great curves are compliments of Spanx." I launched into my tale of peeking into her drawers. "Wish I would have had my camera."

My description of Pussy's underwear absolutely delighted Emma. "Not-so-perfect miss, is she?"

"No," I said, feeling suddenly a little ashamed and

guilty for sharing Pussy's pushed-up and sucked-in undergarment secrets. "She's trying awfully hard to play this role. I have to wonder why."

Emma shrugged. "I don't know, but I don't trust her, either." Emma grimaced. "She'll steal the show at the bar tonight."

"She'll distract all the guys, including bar regulars, while we go after our information," I said, correcting her.

"Maybe," Emma said, looking unconvinced as she headed back to her own room to change.

I finally decided on a tight, short, low-cut pink dress, spray-on hose, and killer pink stiletto heels. The monochromatic look was supposed to be thinning. I wore my hair extensions loose and flowing for that male-enticing, run-your-fingers-through-it look and squirted my pulse points with my brand-new "fuck me" perfume, as Logan called it.

"The sex it inspires is wild," she'd warned, wearing a smirk that dared me to ask for details, which I'd pointedly ignored. I've never liked picturing my friends naked and romping. "If you're going to wear it, go sparingly. And you'd better be using some strong protection."

Ignoring Logan's warning, I rubbed another squirt on my wrists. What was the point of a mission if it wasn't dangerous?

Just as I leaned into the mirror to apply my Lip Venom, a spicy, tingly gloss guaranteed to plump the lips into full pout mode, Emma strolled back in. We sized each other up like two beauty contestants vying for the crown.

Damn, she looked good. Without reason, I felt defensive. Why should I let her have all the fun while I ended up as Miss Congeniality? There was a flaw in that reasoning somewhere, but at the moment I didn't see it.

She applied her own lip gloss and gave a pucker to check the coverage. "Get your purse and let's go, yeah?"

Since Rockford had collected our valuables upon arrival, he'd arranged for the bar to put our drinks on our camp tab, which relegated our purses to cosmetic bags. Mine was stuffed.

I grabbed my BlackBerry, turned it on, dropped it in my pink evening bag, and followed Emma out. I was halfway down the hall when I remembered I'd left my Lip Venom on the bathroom counter and begged off to go back and get it. "I'll meet you at the bus. Don't let them leave without me!"

Venom retrieved, I was just leaving my room when I heard a door open down the hall toward Pussy's room. I ducked back into my doorway and peeked out. Sure enough, Pussy's door was open. To my surprise, horror, and ultimate disappointment, Torq stuck his head out, surveyed the hall, and sneaked out of her room. I carefully slid my door closed and waited for him to clear the hall before heading for the bus myself.

Damn that Pussy! Had she already had a secret tryst with Torq? The little slut! If not trysting, what was Torq doing in her room?

When I arrived at the bus, only somewhat calmed but trying hard to be calmer, Fry sat in the driver's seat, looking majorly hot in a cream linen blazer, sage T-shirt that highlighted his eyes, and jeans. His blond hair was tousled, giving him an endearing, boyish appeal. I suppressed an appreciative sigh and had a momentary fantasy of doing some tousling around with him myself.

"Hey, don't you look gorgeous!" He gave a little head shake to emphasize the compliment. "Heard that y'all were the star student in the Grace Under Pressure exercise. Saw the overalls for myself." His gaze cut to my boobs, which nubbed right up for him. "FYI, Torq's an expert marksman. He can hit whatever the hell he wants. If it was hit, he was aiming for it." He winked.

Emma, who had been waiting for me outside the bus, was right behind me. Before I could respond, she gave me a shove forward. I stumbled and caught myself before I fell off my heels, catching an amused glance from Torq, who must've beat a quick path to the bus. He sat well in the back.

Emma hissed into my ear. "Your mark is in the back. Get going. We just have this one night to find out what we need to know." Then she turned and smiled seductively at Fry.

Sure enough, Torq sat in the back of the bus with his back against the window and one foot up on the adjoining seat. Emma slid into the seat behind the driver's seat and cooed to Fry. From the reflection in the bus window, I saw her give Fry an intimate touch on the shoulder.

Grumbling to myself, and irritated at Torq for using my breasts for target practice, then having a secret assignation with Pussy, I made my way back.

I hate the back of the bus. Exhaust fumes. Spitballs. Pot smoke. Foul language. Those were the associations I'd had with the back of the bus since junior high. With his longish dark hair, earring, black T-shirt, and lean, muscled physique, Torq looked dangerous and right at home there.

I had the option of either taking the seat behind him or the one in front of him. I chose the seat in front because it put me in the position of power. It'd be damned hard for him to turn around and ignore me if I was the one doing the turning.

I paused before my seat, striking a pose and counting one thousand one, one thousand two to give my potential mark plenty of time to check me out.

"Go ahead and sit. No one's going to bite you." Torq nodded toward the seat. I swore he wore a sardonic expression.

I meant to lean over to give him a good look at my cleavage before leading with my hip as I slid in. Only I caught my heel on the metal rung of the bus seat and more like toppled into the seat. *Very graceful.* I felt myself blush as I composed myself, straightened out my skirt, tugged it down, and brushed a lock of hair out of my face.

Torq was trying hard not to smile, probably amused by my utter lack of sophistication in the flirtation department.

The bus seats were the tall, split kind with headrests.

I sat in the aisle seat and tipped it back so I had a clear view of Torq in the seat behind me.

"How's your trigger finger feeling?" If I couldn't do flirtatious, I could at least do incensed pretty darn well. No way was I leaving him amused at my shortcomings. He'd see that I was pretty steely myself.

He gave me a puzzled look. Got him.

"Sorry. My mistake. I just assumed. I mean, since your aim was off today." I gave him a look that said I had his number.

His eyes lit up with amusement, and even admiration, which left me completely puzzled. He was supposed to be embarrassed. I would have been.

"Where'd you hear that?" he asked.

"Fry."

"Don't believe everything Fry tells you."

I shrugged and sat up straight in an attempt to preserve my dignity and look as huffy as possible. "Well, they do say the shot follows the gaze. Maybe your finger wasn't at fault."

Torq laughed and wisely changed the subject. "How'd your high-performance driving lesson go today? Did it scare the shit out of you?" His eyes lit up like he enjoyed that thought.

I shook my head no. "Why? Should it have?"

"Your camp application says you've got a clean driving record. No speeding tickets. No accidents. I just assumed you're the cautious kind."

"Maybe I'm just good."

"Time will tell." He used that low, sexy voice of his and a tone that said he wasn't talking about driving anymore. Plus he shot me a grin so full of flirt that it made my toes curl.

Either Pussy hadn't been enough woman for him—insert evil grin as I thought about the tummy-control panties—or their meeting had been of another nature. Food for thought. Or . . . maybe he was like Bond, who perpetually had the libido and stamina of a twenty-year-old.

"I still haven't come down off the high from the ride," I said.

"That good?"

I was suddenly nervous. This conversation wasn't going the way I'd hoped. I wasn't good at this flirtation stuff, so I just told the truth. "Davie drives smooth. Turns out I *love* smooth. Smooth moves. Speed. I have a whole new appreciation for NASCAR."

"So that explains why so many women love NASCAR," Torq said, his voice indicating feigned enlightenment, his eyes dancing with amusement. "I'm pretty good on the track myself. Fast. Smooth. And I drive hard."

I felt my vagina contract and the rest of me flush at the innuendo in his voice. Fortunately, I was saved from making a reply. Max, Ethan, and Bishop boarded the bus, jostling and joking among themselves. They spotted Torq and me and headed our way, taking the seats surrounding us, leaving me to sort out my confused feelings of attraction for Torq. Other than the Italian thing, he really wasn't my type. But somehow I had to figure out a way to win his trust and get him talking about camp so he'd divulge something about the upcoming kidnapping.

"So what's this bar we're going to?" Bishop asked Torq.

"Hal's," Torq said. "He's a friend of Rockford's. He's big into Bond, too."

"Excellent," Max said.

Pussy boarded at the last minute and cozied up in a seat next to the nerdy Q, who reminded me of a computer geek. To each her own. I couldn't see how she could go from Torq to Q, but whatever. Neither Pussy nor Torq acknowledged the other. Interesting. Whatever they had going, they wanted it under wraps.

With Pussy finally on board, Fry closed the doors and fired up the bus. "All aboard who's coming aboard."

Chapter Eight

A young, trendy crowd spilled into Hal's lot. The place was hopping. A sign over the door said, HAL'S. EVERYONE WELCOME. WE DON'T CARE WHO THE HAL YOU REALLY ARE. Ironically, a bouncer stood directly beneath the sign . . . boldly turning people away.

Fry pulled to a stop and opened the bus doors. "Here we are, folks. Enjoy. The bus rolls out at the stroke of midnight. Be here or plan on finding your own ride back."

I grabbed my purse and stepped into the aisle behind Wade and Q, who had his hands possessively on Pussy's shoulder.

"Popular place." I guess I'd been expecting a quiet dive. Some old geezers and beer. Not teeming nightlife.

"Hal brags he makes every martini on the planet, including several dozen he invented himself," Torq said from close behind me.

"And how many have you tried?" I asked in a teasing voice.

"How many haven't I tried? I'm a member of his frequent drinkers club." He grinned and glanced out the window at the crowd. "Must have been a game tonight. There's a ballpark here in Surprise."

Then he leaned in and whispered in my ear, "Stick with me, Domino. I'll get us in. Hal likes spies."

Torq led the group to the front of the crowd and spoke to the bouncer, a square-jawed giant with a mouthful of metal. "Hey ya, Jaws. Looks like business is booming tonight."

"Torq." Jaws nodded. "This your gang?" He indicated us. "All of them spies?"

"But of course." Torq made a brief round of introductions, skimming past Pussy as if she were no more than another camper, and finally finishing up with me. "And this is Domino."

Jaw's grin widened. "Welcome, Domino. Any friend of 007's is a friend of Hal's. No cover and half-priced drinks for the ladies." He had the deep Jaws voice down so well it was scary.

Almost involuntarily, I stepped closer to Torq, who put his hand at the small of my back and led me inside. "Don't worry. Jaws won't bite." He put a taste of tease in his tone. "Nibble maybe, but never bite."

"Really?" I let Torq guide me, enjoying the heat of his hand on my back. "And here I thought biting was his forte."

"Only in the movies. Hal's tamed him."

Just inside the door, the gang dispersed. Pussy walked past Torq on Q's arm toward the bar without even bothering to put a wiggle in her walk. So what was up with that? No sly look. No jealousy. No sign of familiarity—on either's part. I made a mental note to grill Q tomorrow and resolved to enjoy the evening and Torq's company while I had him to myself.

Music thumped and reverberated, shaking the walls. A disco ball cast multicolored light from the domed ceiling over the pulsating crowd on the dance floor. I recognized the dome as a replica of Elektra's Maiden's Tower. Bond paraphernalia decorated the walls. Movie posters. Aston Martin ads. Guns behind glass frames.

I was overwhelmed. I loved this Hal guy's taste. Maybe *Hal* was the man I'd been waiting for all my life.

"Like it?" Torq asked.

"Like it?" I let out a long sigh. "I could live here. Think Hal'd hire me as a cocktail waitress?"

Torq smiled and I added, "Hal isn't single, is he? I think he and I could make beautiful spy music together."

"Married over thirty years," Torq said.

"Why are the good ones always taken?"

Torq arched a brow. "Always?"

I grinned back at him. "Most always."

Hal's was a fantasyland, like Disneyland for grown-ups. The atmosphere put me in the mood to strut my stuff, thrust out my chest, wiggle my walk, seduce a few secrets out of someone, and maybe even put on a Russian accent before tumbling into bed with a sexy spy guy. The atmosphere was that powerful and right out of my fantasies.

"Hal indulges his Bond fantasies—"

"And what fantasies," I couldn't resist adding.

"And caters to his clientele," Torq continued, smiling at my enthusiasm and unperturbed by my interruption. "Everyone who comes to camp imagines they're Bond."

"Or a Bond girl," I added, still gawking at the wonders around me.

"Yeah, that too." His smile said he preferred Bond girls over Bond wannabes. "Let me show you something." He guided me toward the back of the room with his hand still hot at the small of my back, coming to a stop before a breathtaking nineteenth-century Ottoman mahogany inlaid wood chair complete with arm and neck cuffs. "Recognize this?"

"Oh. My. Gosh! It's Elektra's torture chair." I stared at it in awe and wonderment, hoping that if I blinked it wouldn't disappear, because I sure felt like I was dreaming. "From the movie?"

"An exact replica." He gestured toward the chair. "Have a seat."

"Shut up. I can't sit there."

He gave me a nudge. "Hal won't mind."

"Sure?" I ran my fingers over the smooth lacquered surface, feeling a trill of excitement just at the thought of sitting in Elektra's chair. It didn't even matter that it wasn't the actual chair where Pierce Brosnan had sat.

"Positive." Torq took my arm and steadied me as

I sat. Though, in truth, his touch had a decidedly pleasant, unsteadying effect on my equilibrium.

The wood was cool and slick beneath my legs. I sighed—this was heaven—and put my neck in the open collar, leaning my head against the detailed, inlaid diamond-shaped headrest. "Bond is all about fantasy. That's what I love about his world.

"Take this chair. An instrument of torture and death, yet beautiful, artistic." I paused, searching for words. "In Bond's world, everything is gorgeous, even the women who want to kill him. And they're not just going to kill him. They're going to do it poetically, sensually, almost autoerotically, all the while wearing an eye-catching, formfitting evening gown made of see-through lace so Bond's last view of the world is beauty. What could be more fantastic than that?" I closed my eyes and savored the moment.

"Dying another day," Torq said, deadpan.

I opened my eyes and gazed up at him staring down at me with eyes full of humor and appreciation for my form. He leaned on the point of the headrest, gazing down the arch of my neck at my cleavage, his hands resting on the star-shaped wheel that propelled a bolt into the maiden chair's victim, all the better for strangling them.

"He's not going to let them succeed! That's the other part of the fantasy—being able to escape death no matter how dire the circumstances." I nodded to the wheel. "You're not planning on strangling me, I hope. I don't have Bond's escape skills."

"I wouldn't be so sure." Torq's gaze lingered on my enhanced, thrust-out bosoms. "But it gives a whole new meaning to a good screw, doesn't it?" He did a perfect Bond imitation.

My mouth went dry. Before I could reply, Fry called to us from a nearby corner booth, where Emma had all but surgically attached herself to his side. "Hey. Come join us."

A quick look of irritation flashed across Torq's face before he managed an affable smile. "Shall we?"

I slid in across from Fry and Emma as a cocktail waitress dressed in a tight black leather dress appeared and handed us cocktail menus. I caught the flirty look of appreciation she gave Torq and felt myself growing irrationally territorial.

"I'll have an Aston Martini," Torq said without looking at the menu.

Fry sighed. "An O'Doul's for me. I'm driving." He shook his head like he was making a major sacrifice for campers and country.

"An O'Doul's? You sure?" Torq goaded him, grinning. "They have club soda and Shirley Temples, too."

"Shut up," Fry said, "you're driving next time."

Torq laughed.

Across from me, Emma curled into Fry, stroking his cheek in a "poor baby" motion, obviously thinking pillow talk would be the most fun way to get the info she wanted. Good luck to her. She was working on a stone-cold-sober mark.

As for me, I really needed a drink to up my courage quotient. Not that I believed one drink would turn me into a stunning conversationalist and consummate femme fatale, but it couldn't hurt.

Astute mind reader that he was, Torq saw my

quandary as I stared at the overwhelming number of martinis listed, feeling pressured to make a quick decision because the waitress was hovering and making definite eyes at my mark. Or maybe it was the lip biting and my poor, balled napkin that gave me away.

He gave me a sympathetic look. "Like chocolate?"

I nodded.

"Try the Flirtini. You'll love it." He gave me the flirt look again, just like in class. Damn, he was good at it. It sent my poor little heart pitter-pattering out of control, while the rest of me prayed it was the real deal.

Determined not to let him get the upper hand or see my stupid girlish hope that the look was real, I turned to the waitress. "I'll have a Flirtini. Sh—"

"Emma, what about you?" Torq rested his hand on my thigh and gave it a squeeze, which I think he meant as a warning signal to shut up. It rendered me speechless, all right. Not to mention left me feeling shaken and stirred myself, and achy-breaking for more intimate hand-to-thigh, mouth-to-mouth, hip-to-hip contact.

As the waitress turned her attention to Emma, Torq leaned into me and whispered, "All Hal's drinks are shaken. You don't want to insult him by asking." He removed his hand from my leg, leaving a scorching-hot handprint and a wave of major disappointment in its wake.

I pushed aside the feeling of being a bona fide social klutz. The atmosphere in Hal's didn't tolerate insecurity.

We made small talk until our drinks arrived.

I finally screwed up my courage to ask Torq about his inspection of the blown-up car. Curiosity must be stilled. "What were you looking for in that car you guys blew up at the welcome?"

"Spying on me?"

He knew exactly what I was talking, and curious, about.

I blushed. But in the dark, who cared? No one could tell. The cover of a dimly lit room gave me courage. "That's the name of the game here. That thing was obviously totaled. You were looking for something. What and why?"

Torq and Fry exchanged a quick look and shrugged in unison.

"We've had some trespassers," Torq said. "People who ignore our posted NO TRESPASSING; NO SHOOT-ING signs. We're out in the open. People like to sneak in and get some target practice in. Take out a few rabbits or snakes. I was concerned they'd been taking aim at our car."

"Before or after our arrival?" I asked.

Both he and Fry laughed. Neither answered the question.

Emma ignored our conversation, eyeing the dance floor the entire time, feet tapping away, shoulders swaying, head bopping, all but doing the tango on the tabletop, obviously itching to dance. Finally, Fry couldn't ignore her hints any longer.

"Let's dance," he said, taking her arm to help her up. Fry flashed us a Texas-sized grin and they were off, leaving me to entertain Torq.

"Do you dance?" Torq nodded toward the dance floor.

The dreaded question. I realized I'd been twirling the pick in my drink and folding and unfolding the corner of my cocktail napkin as if I'd suddenly developed an origami fascination. I forced myself to drop the pick and look Torq in the eye. "Not well. I prefer . . . watching."

I wanted to dance. I wanted to dance with *him*. Badly. I was just afraid I'd be a total moron on the dance floor and turn him off completely with my stiff, self-conscious, jerky dance style.

We sat in silence, staring at the dancers and then each other. Not for the first time, I rued my lack of scintillating conversation skills. The view was good, but we couldn't go all evening without talking. Besides, I had information to gather. We spoke over the music at once.

"How do you like—"

"So," I said, "the kidnapping is—"

We laughed together.

"Go ahead," he said, leaning close, his mouth to my ear, so that I could hear him. "You were saying?"

I blushed. "Oh, nothing. Just wondering about the big camp finale. I'm looking forward to it . . . I think." I laughed nervously, hoping it wasn't obvious that I was fishing for information. The nerves were real enough, anyway. Maybe that was enough to foil an expert mind reader like him.

"Nothing to be afraid of. Just some good, clean fun." He gave a friendly, reassuring smile.

I gave him a shaky smile in return and leaned in

to speak in his ear. "I read an article in the paper once, about what to do if you're kidnapped. . . ."

"Yeah?" he said. "Are you hinting that you'll be a hard target?"

"Maybe." I paused, trying to lead naturally into questioning him about the intended victim and the plan. "I suppose you're all busy planning for it, selecting a victim, discussing the kidnapping. . . ."

Torq laughed. "Hardly. Rockford selects the victim and makes the plan. He fills us in at the last minute."

"Oh." I hoped I didn't sound as disappointed as I felt.

"I'll put a bug in his ear that you won't go down easily," he spoke lightly.

"Thanks." I felt the tension ease out of my shoulders and leaned back against the bench. I really didn't want to be the victim.

"Don't thank me yet. Not unless you have your heart set on being the victim. We like a challenge." He winked.

"In that case, 'gee, thanks.'" I took a deep taste of my drink, hoping it kicked in fast. "Delicious." I swirled the glass and took another drink, licking my lips, a bad nervous habit of mine. "Kind of like a chocolate martini without the Kiss."

Torq raised an eyebrow, his gaze focused on my lips. I'm not sure whether it was the Lip Venom still working its puffing action or Torq's stare, but my lips tingled.

"Hershey's Kiss," I clarified.

Torq put a hand on my arm. "Go easy on that.

Hal's drinks have a tendency to help the floor hit you in the face when you stand up."

Was it just my imagination, or was he finding any excuse to touch me? A girl could hope! I wasn't much of a drinker, but I waved off his concern. I could handle a few martinis.

He dropped his hand and took a sip of his drink. "Don't say I didn't warn you."

"Noted," I said, finishing the drink in an attempt to fend off the fluttery feelings Torq stirred up.

Torq flagged our cocktail waitress. I ordered a Dirty Martini, and Torq ordered another of the same.

"So tell me about yourself," Torq said as the waitress disappeared, watching me like I was Miss Fascinating herself. I don't know how he managed to look like he was all ears and total interest. But it was so flattering, a totally hot look on a man.

I felt myself flush. "And blow my cover?" I teased. "Nothing doing. I'd rather hear about you." I asked him about his CIA experience and his work.

"You want to hear about me?" Man, he looked cute when he played self-deprecating and humble.

"Please. You know I love spy stuff."

He shrugged. We locked gazes and he started talking. I listened with rapt attention to that silky voice of his as he told funny stories of the spook life. Really, I would have listened to him read an assembly manual just to hear him speak. The spy tales were an added bonus. When our drinks arrived, we barely noticed. We sipped them as we talked as comfortably as old friends, *close* old friends, with heads bowed intimately toward each other. We were connecting and it was exhilarating. I was heady with the new-crush feeling of wanting to know everything about him. Well, almost everything.

I was still wondering about him and his spy past. Life has taught me that sometimes the best way to find out is simply to ask.

"Staging mock kidnappings must be something of a letdown after being a real spy." My curiosity was genuine. I really couldn't understand how someone who was a born thrill-seeker could leave the life voluntarily. Can you imagine Bond retiring? No one can. That's why they keep recasting him when the Bond actor of the moment gets too old. "Why *did* you leave the CIA?"

Torq set his drink down and studied me. He'd just opened his mouth to answer when Emma, with her total sense of bad timing, bounced up to the table. "Come with me to the ladies', Dom."

As Fry slid into the booth, Torq nodded for me to go.

Reluctantly, I downed the rest of my Dirty Martini, grabbed my purse and got up to follow her. I needed to call Logan anyway and here was my opportunity. Still. Just when I was on the cusp of discovery. As we walked away, I threw Torq a smile over my shoulder.

Emma took me by the arm. "You've been talking a long time. What have you learned?" she asked as we muscled our way through the crowd.

I fought hard to keep my irritation with the interruption from showing. "Rockford's the only one who knows the plan. The other instructors aren't told anything—

not the victim, not the plan—until right before the kidnapping."

"Excellent. You're good!" Emma exclaimed.

"You?" I asked her.

"Fry's a fantastic dancer. And his body is as hard as it looks." She gave a happy sigh.

"Great. You're some help."

"Give me time," she said.

We swung through the door into the ladies' room and joined the line. The ladies' room was long and narrow, with sinks and mirrors on either side, followed by a row of stalls against each wall. Fortunately, there were only a few women in front of us. A stall opened up and Emma took it.

I dodged back to a spot near the door where I hoped Emma couldn't hear me but I could still keep an eye on her, and flipped open my phone. No signal! Damn, damn, damn! Frustrated, I dropped the BlackBerry back in my purse and zipped into the next open stall to quell my mother's voice in my head asking me if I'd used the bathroom.

I'd just washed my hands and dug my Lip Venom out of my purse, intent on doing a reapplication, when Emma came out.

"Ready for round two?" she asked as she washed her hands.

Emma immediately dragged Fry back out on the dance floor.

"Your glass is empty," Torq said when I sat down. "This one's on me." He gave me a seductive, knowing grin as he flagged the cocktail waitress. He ordered himself a Tequini and turned to me. "May I?"

I shrugged, giving him the go-ahead.

"The lady will have the Orgasm Martini." He looked at me with darkened eyes. Bedroom eyes. "That's the natural progression, isn't it? Flirt. Get dirty. Orgasm."

The drinks and the atmosphere of Hal's made me bold.

"Are you flirting with me?" I asked as the waitress disappeared. "Or is this another one of your tests, like in the classroom?" I put enough flirt in my own voice to cover the puppy-dog optimism I felt. I liked this spy boy . . . a lot. "FYI, in case this is a test, it's way too dark in here to get an accurate AU reading."

He grinned and covered my hand with his, giving it a squeeze. "I like you, Dom."

I had absolutely no retort for that except a trembling smile and a happily racing heart.

The waitress brought our drinks in a flash and Torq handed her a hefty tip.

"The Tequini and the Orgasm are the two strongest drinks Hal makes." He raised his glass. "This puts us on even footing."

"Not exactly," I objected. "One drink tips someone of my height and weight into the DUI zone. You're probably eighty pounds heavier than I am. I'm guessing it takes a few more than one to turn a Breathalyzer against you."

"I had one while you were gone." He lifted his glass. "Cheers."

Okay, maybe he was trying to seduce me. Why? I

don't know. I wasn't the most beautiful girl in the world. But he liked me. And I liked him. Sitting in Hal's with my Bond-girl fantasies dancing in my head like sugarplums, no way was I questioning his taste in women or my good luck. I took a sip of my Orgasm and felt my tongue go numb.

"Like it?" he asked.

I was trying hard not to sputter. I took another sip and felt a pleasant glow settle in. "It's got a surprisingly good afterglow."

"To afterglow." He raised his glass and downed his Tequini with a flick of his wrist.

I savored my Orgasm a moment longer while working up the nerve to get back to my questioning, only partly driven by my game with Emma. Mostly I just really wanted to know him. "So. When Emma interrupted, you were about to tell me why you left the CIA."

"I think it's time to dance." He acted like he hadn't heard my question as he slid from the booth and held out his hand for me. "Come on. Just one."

I hesitated. I sucked at dancing, a consequence of being a lifelong, card-carrying wallflower. Yeah, I could tap, plié, and tendu. I'd had lessons for that. But spontaneous dancing? No.

"Dancing with someone new requires a big leap of faith for me," I said, trying not to sound as nervous as I felt. I made a gun with my finger. "Laugh at me and you're a dead man. Bang! No sexy maiden's chair necessary."

"No laughing. Promise." Then he laughed anyway, grabbed my gun hand, and pulled me from the booth. Graceful me, I immediately stumbled, very maturely covering my embarrassment with a giggle. Torq grabbed my arm to steady me and led us to the dance floor.

I was glowing all over. High on all kinds of hormones and pheromones and alcohol. Torq elbowed us some space on the crowded floor. The music was slow. My heart was beating fast. And the feeling of Torq's arms around me put the pleasant tingles of the Orgasm to shame.

Torq leaned down and spoke intimately into my ear. "You asked why I left the spook business. I left the CIA because I was tired of being someone else. I wanted to be me. Just me." Torq's hands heated my skin through my dress at the small of my back as he held me against him.

His answer surprised me. And yeah, brought dopey sentimental tears to my eyes. Such a sincere, sensitive sentiment. Profound, really. "You're lucky. Most of us wish we were someone else," I said without thinking. I must have sounded wistful. Hadn't I spent most of my life wishing to be more like Logan?

"Why would a beautiful girl like you want to be anyone else?" he whispered in my ear as he tucked a stray wisp of hair behind it. Damned if he didn't sound sincere, too.

"Why?" I repeated his question, utterly flustered. His thighs brushed mine and I could barely think.

"Because my life is pretty dull," I said into his ear.

"I'm single. I live alone. I go to work. I'm pretty much Moneypenny."

His pelvis pressed against mine. And yes, I could feel his package and it was obviously mission-ready and no longer covert.

"Don't knock Moneypenny," Torq whispered as he nibbled my ear. "She's as hot as any Bond girl. And loyal. And true. She loves Bond, knowing who and what he is. I've always thought Bond's a fool to ignore her."

"Maybe James is just afraid to hurt a good woman," I said, coming to Bond's defense. But my eyes were misty with emotion and joy. I had to bite my lower lip to keep from murmuring, "Oh, James."

Torq nuzzled into my neck as his hands strayed south to cup my butt. My breath caught. I was riding a wave of romantic emotion and practically orgasmic at the same time . . . and we were just dancing!

My knees went weak. I leaned into him for support.

"Ummmm," he murmured into my neck, like my perfume was giving him ideas beyond dancing. Torq pulled back and eyed my moist, tingly, Lip Venom–covered lips and his breathing slowed. He lowered his face to mine, hovering just above a kiss.

"There isn't a rule against instructors and CTs . . . um . . . dancing, is there?" I whispered, staring into his eyes with about as much longing as a girl can possess.

"About a hundred," he said, slowly closing the gap between our lips. "But I only pay them lip service."

"A man who can quote Bond—"

His lips landed softly on mine, silencing me, but not my singing heart. No tongue. Just a sweet caress that left me wanting more . . . and more. I sighed and leaned into his kiss. He kissed me deeper . . . and deeper.

His kisses grew hotter. The music moved faster, pulsating around us. We ignored it, dancing our slow dance and necking. Stroking. The music stopped.

I pulled away awkwardly. "I think I need another Orgasm."

"I think we need some fresh air," he said, leading me from the dance floor.

Outside, the night air was warm and balmy. Stars winked overhead and I swayed against Torq as we walked across the parking lot toward the bus. A good deal of my Lip Venom glistened in the moonlight on his lips and neck. I was ridiculously happy. Almost delirious with it.

"Dom?"

"Yes?"

"I had a really good time tonight." He meant it, I could tell. But at the same time, he sounded almost regretful, like he had something to say and didn't want to say it. Like he was calling the night off.

"Me, too." I cuddled into him, not wanting to hear more, not wanting the evening to end.

We reached the bus door.

He paused and tucked my hair behind my ears before brushing my lips with a light kiss. "Much as

I hate to say this, you've had too much to drink. This is where the fun has to stop tonight." Regret weighted his voice.

"An agent and a gentleman," I said, trying not to sound as disappointed as I felt.

He grinned and kissed the top of my head.

From out of nowhere came the squeal of tires. Torq suddenly stiffened and looked over his shoulder. I stared in horror as an inebriated Max staggered out into the aisle from between two parked cars directly into the path of a sedan that barreled toward him, and us, from the far end of the row.

"Shit!" Torq shoved the bus doors open and pushed me up the steps as my purse went flying. "In the bus. Quick!"

Over my shoulder, I caught a brief glimpse of Max silhouetted in headlights. He swayed on his feet in the middle of the aisle, totally unaware of a maniac behind him who apparently had no intention of braking.

Torq yelled at Max to get out of the way, which had the opposite of a saving effect on Max. He froze.

The sickening thud of Max becoming a hood ornament drowned out Torq's shouting and curses. The car accelerated toward us with Max plastered on his hood.

"Maaax!" I screamed.

Torq gave me another push up the steps and followed me into the stairwell just as the car plowed by, missing us, and the bus, by inches. As soon as the car passed us, Torq yelled at me to stay down and stay put, and ran out after it.

My Flirtini-fogged brain knew it should do something. Like get a license number. But it was dark and my eyes didn't seem to want to focus properly. There was also the added disincentive—I really did not want to see a dead, pavement-pizza Max. I focused on the white blur of car. A white sedan—now that narrowed the field. It only described 90 percent of the vehicles in Arizona.

As the sedan sped up the aisle, Max rolled off the hood into the road. I winced and felt my stomach lurch. The car sped off around the corner toward the road and out of sight.

Torq took off at a sprint toward Max. I slid down the steps and fished my purse off the pavement before crawling back up into the stairs. I pawed through my purse, frantically searching, and cursing that no matter what you wanted, it always fell to the bottom of the bag. Where was my stupid phone? I peeked out and saw Torq with his cell phone already to his ear. Thank goodness! Then, miracle of miracles, Max sat up.

I let out a pent-up breath I hadn't even been aware of holding. If Max could sit, he wasn't dead. That was good. I tried to stand, intent on going to Max and Torq, only the world swam and I decided against it. Waiting in the bus as instructed seemed the more prudent option.

Within a few minutes, an aid unit and a squad car rolled into the parking lot. The paramedics examined Max.

This waiting on the bus was the pits. The Orgasm was definitely catching up with me and impeding my thought process.

After what seemed like forever but was probably only minutes, Torq returned with Fry, several CTs, and a cop. I heard them cursing crazy drunks. I was still sprawled on the bus steps, too dizzy, and scared, to move.

Torq opened the bus doors. I hadn't even realized I'd shut them.

"Max is going to be fine," he said before I could speak. "They're taking him to the hospital overnight for observation."

"Being pickled saved his butt," the cop said. "Loose as a goose. A real boneless chicken. A sober person would have tensed and broken every bone in their body."

"But Max bounced." I giggled. There was nothing funny in the situation, but I couldn't help myself. "Someone tried to run him over. Someone tried to kill Max!" I broke out into full-out laughter. "Go find him," I said to the cop as I tried to appear more sober. "He was in a white car."

Torq and the cop exchanged a look. The other CTs and Fry looked sheepish.

"She's no help," the cop said and walked off.

"Oh, baby," Torq said when he turned back to me. And it didn't sound like a compliment. He took my hand and pulled me to my feet.

"Whoa! Too fast." My head swam. "I don't feel so good."

He hauled me gently from the bus. "You need

fresh air. Breathe deeply. I thought you said you could hold your liquor."

"Wine's fine, but liquor's quicker," I said out of nowhere and laughed, feeling silly and unable to stop. "I lied. Didn't Rockford say, 'Don't believe anything you hear'?" I swallowed hard against a gag welling in my throat. Was it just me or were my words slurring?

"Uh-oh." And I didn't mean about the bad guys, or whoever, getting away. "I think the Orgasm did me in."

He looked at me like "if only."

I put a hand to my mouth as a wave of nausea welled up.

"Damn," he said, "I recognize that look." He grabbed my hair and held it back while I wretched Flirtini and Orgasm all over an unfortunate cactus in the median.

Chapter Nine

I woke up in my own twin bed alone, dressed in my new-for-camp nightie. I dimly remembered the bus ride home and Torq carrying me Rhett Butler style, minus the ravish, to my room as Emma fussed over me. I *think* Torq and Emma left before the getting-into-the-nightie part. Even through my embarrassment, I smiled giddily at the thought of Torq. He liked me! Heavy sigh of happiness.

I was glad I remembered the bus ride only as in a haze. Because what I did remember was pretty humiliating and I was hoping it would quickly fade into the dark depths of forgotten memories . . . for all of us. Throwing up in front of your mother is embarrassing enough. But in front of a hot guy you really liked . . .

Plus I'm pretty sure the only orgasm either of us had was the one I drank.

After my stint painting the cactus, Torq was gentleness and concern itself as he forced heinous quantities of water and a large bottle of Gatorade down me.

"Dom, you need to rehydrate and replace your potassium and salt levels. Trust me." He sounded sexy even when dispensing medical advice. And patient, not at all condemning or irritated with me.

Not that he needed to be. I was irate enough for both of us.

I think he threw in some acetaminophen and a vitamin C from the camp medicine cupboard for good measure, too. All part of the cure.

I opened my eyes, bracing for the big headache and . . . nothing but mild, manageable pain. Hallelujah! The nausea was gone. The light didn't even hurt my eyes . . . much. The man was a medical genius. I grinned, sat up, and slid my feet over the side of the bed, way too happy for the day after a drinking binge. I threw on my robe and met Emma in the bathroom.

"Great! You're up! You missed breakfast, but you're up." She nodded her approval, but the sunshine in her voice sounded forced and put on, which put me on red alert. "Good thing I snagged you a muffin and a piece of fruit. Have them in my room. I'll just get them, shall I?" She turned to leave.

Food didn't really sound that bad, but Emma's fake perkiness worried me. I put a hand on her shoulder. "What's wrong? Has something happened to Max?"

"Max, that lucky idiot, is fine." She sounded put

out. "He's already back at camp. He has a few bruises, but he doesn't look much worse than you."

"That's a relief." And I meant it. "Someone tried to kill him."

"Someone was driving drunk," Emma said. She still didn't sound happy.

"If not Max, then what's wrong?"

She sighed and dropped her head, turning back to give me a sidelong look. "Nothing."

"Come on," I prompted. "Out with it."

Ignoring my demand, she looked me up and down. "You don't look much worse for the wear for someone who was nearly run over by a drunk. Evidently, Torq knows what he's talking about when treating hangovers." The false brightness was back in her voice. "He wouldn't let me give you a cup of coffee for the world. How do you feel?"

"Not too bad, really." Which was the surprising truth. "Now stop hedging."

"You'd better take this anyway. Torq asked me to bring it to you." She handed me an acetaminophen and another tablet.

"What is it?" I asked, momentarily letting her off the hook as I inspected the new drug.

"KGB," Emma said. "Key 2 Getting Better. It's an old KGB cure for headaches. Torq asked me to tell you he was sorry he couldn't find the KGB last night. He explained that it has some kind of acid that breaks down the acetal-something-hyde that produces the gruesome effects of a hangover."

I stared at it in my hand. "What a really sweet

thing for him to do." My voice went as soft and gooey as a sticky bun.

"Yeah." Unfortunately, Emma's voice sounded more like stale, dry toast.

"Out with it." I gave her my piercing look.

"It was a game," Emma whispered, looking dejected and miserable.

"What was a game?"

Emma heaved a heavy sigh. "The trip to the bar! The flirting with us!" She bit her lip. "Look, I didn't want to tell you . . ."

And I didn't want to hear. Nooooo! No, no, no! What Torq and I had was real. It *was* real. We'd connected. I knew we had. He may be a master faker, but his smile had reached all the way to his eyes. It *had*. Even he couldn't fake those involuntary micro expressions.

Emma saw my stunned face and put a consoling hand on my arm. "I'm sorry. I . . . thought you should know. I overheard them talking at breakfast. That's why it was so easy for us to win Fry and Torq over. It was all part of the camp. To see how free we are with information. How easy it would be for someone to play up to us and get us to blab our real identities."

I was still holding the KGB and feeling about as happy as if the real KGB had just cuffed me and thrown me in the gulag.

"Don't just stare at it. Drink it up." She handed me a glass of water. "There you go."

Operating on automatic, I popped the pill. "The old '*The Recruit* double cross at the bar' trick. That's the oldest trick in the book." I mimicked Max, trying to sound light but failing miserably, and feeling miserable, too. And stupid. And gullible. Had he really been faking it? My emotional side screamed no, but my logical side thought what Emma said made sense. I wasn't the kind of girl a guy like him fell for.

Emma pried the glass from my hand and set it on the counter. "In retrospect, we should have seen it coming."

"It's always easier to Monday-morning quarterback." I tried to sound consoling. He'd been playing head games with me? Had he? The doubt, and the fear he had been, was enough to make me mental.

I left the CIA to be myself.

Sure thing!

And here I'd been willing to go all the way to "Oh, James" with him. Guess I should've been glad he'd called the game off when he did. Unfortunately, that little bit of data corroborated Emma's story. My head pounded, but not from the hangover.

"How do you feel about Fry?" I asked, using a fair amount of caution.

Emma squared her shoulders. "I wasn't looking for a lifetime commitment. One night of flirting and fun is as good as another."

She tried to cover it, but she still sounded stung to me. We had our pride. I dropped the Fry line of questioning.

I rubbed my forehead, wishing I could rub away last night.

Emma glanced at her watch.

"Go on ahead," I said. "I'll meet you at the dojo."

I wanted a few minutes by myself to get my emotions under control before facing the others. "Trust no one. Believe nothing," I muttered to myself, thinking it was, indeed, a sad way to live.

As she turned to leave, I reached out and gave Emma's arm a squeeze. "Thanks for telling me. Really."

I managed to get dressed and make my way to the dojo for our morning class in unarmed self-defense, arriving just before class began. Anger had begun to replace my humiliation. Ready to take on all comers and beat some serious crap out of bad guys, or anyone dumb enough to cross me, I wore an azure-blue tank top, black Lycra exercise capris, and tennis shoes. For good measure, I also wore my white-framed sunglasses. I wasn't real trusting of light just yet and I had a bit of a puffy eye thing going on.

I wasn't the only one feeling the aftereffects of the night before. Ethan wore his sunglasses, too. And Pussy was conspicuously absent. Too much fun last night with Q? Not a situation I cared to dwell on.

Outside, the thermometer in the breezeway indicated the temperature had already climbed to a brutal 92 degrees, but the dojo was air-conditioned and cool. Of course, we'd already worked up a sweat just walking to class. "Natural architecture" was a fancy way of saying you had to go outside to get from class to class.

I leaned cross-armed against the wall next to Emma, feeling grumpy and upset enough to crave solitude. I looked around for Torq, feeling an unsettling mixture of relief and letdown that he was evidently in full spook mode, as Emma called it—i.e., nowhere to be seen.

"Hey, Domino." Ethan inched his way next to me. "Why don't you let *me* buy you a Flirtini tonight, eh?" He did a grab-ass motion in the air with his hands. From off to my far left, I heard Bishop snicker.

Using one finger, I lowered my sunglasses on my nose just enough to give him a view of my eyes and my freeze-his-*cajones*-off stare, the one I used at the bank to get my "loan denied" message across.

True-blue Emma stepped between us, ready to defend me. "Leave her alone before I have to give you an Aussie lesson in manners."

Before anyone had a chance to say more, Agent Rockford strode to the front of the class.

"Morning, gang. Domino, Ethan, no sunglasses in the dojo during my class. Remove them. Now." He paused, watching us as I pushed my glasses up on my head and Ethan tucked his into a pocket.

"Domino, I believe this is yours." Rockford held my BlackBerry out to me.

I gasped. So that's where it had gone! No wonder I couldn't find it in my purse. I'd lost my beloved BlackBerry and not even realized it! I stepped forward to take it. "How . . ."

"One of Hal's staff found it in the parking lot near the bus." Rockford got right back to business. "I understand some of you had too much to drink last night at Hal's." Rockford used a disciplinary voice and looked directly at me. "Exercise cures a hangover. Anyone who slacks will give me ten push-ups."

"That's the problem with spy school," I muttered to Emma as I gently cradled my phone. "Everyone knows what you've been up to."

"Fry and Torq also reported back that many of you CTs ran off at the mouth last night, revealing secrets about your real identities. Yes," he nodded, "the bar trip was a camp test. You've all heard the saying 'loose lips sink ships.' Last night some of you sank a fleet."

I stiffened. I hadn't blabbed a thing. Not while I'd been sober, anyway. Hadn't I made a point of staying closed-lipped? If Torq claimed I'd bantered secrets about, he was lying. He was lying to cover the fact he'd been hitting on me and not doing his duty. That's what the hope-springs-eternal half of me wanted to believe, anyway.

But my logical side was screaming that Rockford had pretty much just verified that Emma hadn't misheard. The flirting was nothing more than a camp exercise. Either way, I felt about as happy and buoyant as dirt.

"Lesson learned. A spy is always on guard." Rockford launched into his pre-workout lecture, pacing back and forth in front of us as he spoke. "Welcome to Unarmed Self-defense 101. Because we only have three days to toughen you up and teach you the basics, this will be a compressed course tightly focused on the essentials—sharpening your combat mindset. That attacker means to hurt, maim, or kill you. Show him no mercy . . ."

As he used a rubber knife to demonstrate how to disarm an attacker and slit his throat, I waged war with myself, arguing both sides of the "he faked the flirt, he faked it not" thing. By the time the Chief demonstrated how to snap a pistol out of a bad guy's hand I'd come to no firm conclusion and was ready to shoot myself.

"What if you manage to disarm the enemy but then have to engage in hand-to-hand combat?" Rockford said, and my ears perked up. Right now a little get-even foot-to-groin sounded pretty good. "Listen closely, ladies. I'm going to give you some special tips." He looked at Emma and me.

"Use your natural body weapons—heels, elbows, fists, knees." He pointed to each as he spoke, giving a mini demonstration on their use. "Learn proper striking positions and vital-target selection—eyes, groin, top of the foot, pinkies, and thumbs. Learn how to take a punch or kick and defend and escape from holds, grabs, arm bars, and bear hugs."

He stopped pacing dead center in front of us. "First—how to take a punch or kick to the body. Tighten your stomach." He lifted his shirt to demonstrate, showing us a firm, fit set of abs in full flex. "Turn slightly to the side, trying to absorb the impact with your obliques." He demonstrated. "A blow to this area may crack a rib but likely won't damage internal organs. Everyone line up and spread out and let's give it a try together." He paused while we obeyed orders. "Good." He nodded. "When I throw a punch, you all tighten, flex, and turn. Here we go."

He threw a helluva punch into the air, but so did I. Funny what energy being scorned generates.

A few more practices and Rockford gave us a lecture on punches to the head and how to defend against them—straight punch, roundhouse, uppercut. Then Rockford was off on how to escape if an attacker grabbed you from either the front or behind.

"You can go for the groin." He demonstrated a quick knee thrust. "But most attackers know the drill. They're going to be expecting you to go for the jewels and will protect them. If you don't disable him and get him to let go, you're going to make him mad as hell. I'm going to show you some more effective strikes."

By the time we'd gone through how to use our heels to stomp an attacker's foot, breaking at least some of the twenty-six tiny bones there, how to stick our fingers up an attacker's nostrils and draw blood, how to bend back and break his pinky or thumb, and how to gouge his eyes out, I was not only tired, but pretty darn grossed-out, too, and ready for a break.

"Okay, gang," Rockford said. "I can see you're tiring. Take five."

I slumped in relief, dreaming of a nice, big glass of ice water. "Thank good—"

Before I could finish my sentence, a fully padded, masked attacker emerged from the entrance of the dojo. I caught the barest glimpse of him from the corner of my eye in the instant before he rushed me.

Chapter Ten

The attacker grabbed me from behind and locked me against him, my back to his chest, wrenching my breath loose with his vicelike grip just below my ribs. I gasped for air, flailing wildly, tugging at his arms as I fought for freedom.

"Rule number one—never let your guard down," Rockford said as calmly as if he were discussing the latest gun show.

I caught a flash of Rockford's amused grin as Attack Man restrained me with as little apparent effort as it took to hold down a cashed check. I felt my anger rise. It didn't take rocket science to figure out I was being manhandled by either Torq or Fry. And both of them deserved a swift kick between the legs.

Emma must've been thinking the same thing. She lunged forward to help me, bloodlust in her eyes.

Rockford caught her arm and held her back. "Stand back, CTs. This is *self*-defense class. Let's see what CT Domino is made of."

Attack Man spun around with me in a freaky sort

of dance until I was dizzy and disoriented and ruing never mastering that "spot, snap, spin, and don't get dizzy" move in ballet class as a kid. My ponytail tumbled over my face and I had to keep spitting it out of my mouth as I struggled.

Obediently staying out of the action, Emma jumped up and down on the sideline, shouting instructions. "Go for his pinkies. Bend the suckers back." In her excitement, her voice had skipped several octaves higher into shrill territory.

Heart stampeding out of control and pulse roaring toward dangerous dog-thinking mode again, I grabbed at his gloved, padded, interlocked fingers, trying to pry loose his pinkie without success. "They're locked down tight. What do I do now?" I shot Rockford a look begging for help.

He tapped his head. "Use your best asset."

Did he mean the one that was dizzy and disoriented?

"Oh, come on," Emma screamed and jumped some more. "Don't be a wimp! Grab 'em. Bend 'em. Break 'em!" She may as well have added, "Go, fight, win!" and waved some pom-poms.

I pulled and tugged. No dice.

"Eyes! Go for his eyes now! Gouge 'em out!" Emma jumped and bounced some more, adding in a little one-two punching motion.

"From behind?" I screamed back, trying to crane around. "You're crazy. He's masked." I struggled, breathing hard, and addressed my attacker. "Yo, Padded Guy, don't get cocky. Take that mask off and face me like a man. I'd like to give your nose a taste of these." I waved my acrylic nails at him menacingly.

Just to show me who was boss, he twirled me around again. I screamed. So maybe antagonizing my attacker wasn't the smartest move.

Ethan was giving his own words of encouragement . . . to my attacker. "Yeah, get her! Manhandle her. Play rough! Take her down!"

"You!" I was breathless and barely able to speak, but I managed to point at Ethan. "Shut up!"

"You're wasting energy, CT Domino," Agent Rockford warned and glanced at his watch. "In a real attack, he'd have you in the bushes and had his way with you by now."

"Hear that, Padded One," I said, hoping he'd give himself away. "You and I could be having a little fun in the bushes. But you'd have to lose the suit." I struggled, trying to channel my anger into wiggling, prying, or scratching my way free.

"Stop antagonizing him," Rockford shouted.

"I'm just trying to level the playing field," I yelled back. "Do you see me wearing a padded suit?"

Rockford ignored my snide remark. "You're fighting like a girl, CT." He sounded stern. "Use your natural weapons."

"I *am* a girl!"

I managed to get in a brutal backward kick to Attack Man's shin. He dropped me.

"Hah!" I said as my feet touched the ground and I lurched forward to run.

Attack Man grabbed me by my hair and dragged me back against him. I let out a screech.

"Not cool, caveman. This is no way to get cooperation in the bushes." I struggled, but it only hurt more. "Let go! Ouch, ouch, ouch!"

"Ponytails are a built-in handle, ladies," Rockford drawled calmly.

"Thanks for the tip," I shouted as Attack Man released my hair and pinned my arms to my side.

"Stomp his foot!" Emma made her own stomping motion. "Flex your ankle. Raise your knee. Like this." She demonstrated.

Before I could make a move, Attack Man lifted me off the ground, leaving my feet flailing wildly into open air.

"Thanks for warning him!" I said.

"Sorry. Just trying to help." Emma shrugged.

Rockford looked at his watch again. "If he'd gone for your neck with his bare hands, you'd be strangled by now. Get yourself loose, CT."

I flailed my feet. I wiggled. I screamed, hoping to break his eardrums. My attacker didn't let out even a grunt.

Emma yelled something from the sidelines. I could hear her screaming, but I'd stopped paying attention to her words. Padded Guy paused. Seizing my opportunity, I threw my head back into his jaw.

"Ouch! Damn it!" he muttered, loosening his grip enough that my feet touched the floor and I got a toehold.

Torq! I'd hurt Torq. Right now I wasn't sure if that was a good or a bad thing.

I pushed backward, catching him off balance. We toppled to the floor. He landed on his back with me on top of him. As I slid off, I managed a wicked groin shot with my elbow. He let out an "oomph," followed by a groan, followed by a scary bellow. He pulled me back against him, grabbed me, and in a reversal of fortune, rolled over, pinning me beneath him, face to the floor, with his full weight. There's a name for asphyxiation by body weight. I'd seen it on a TV crime-scene show. I just couldn't remember it right now with my life passing before my eyes.

Ethan's lewd suggestions from the sideline grew faint and distant as I struggled for breath beneath all that man and padding and fought the narrowing of my vision that meant I was on the verge of passing out.

"Uncle," I managed to wheeze out. "Uncle."

Rockford strolled over. "Game over, CT. You lose. He could've killed you half a dozen times by now." Rockford glanced at that damned watch of his a third time, probably so he could see if enough time had passed for Torq to have buried me alive in a shallow grave.

"Class dismissed. See you at the firing range in fifteen." Rockford strode off.

"I said 'uncle.' You can get off me now, Torq," I whispered.

"Yeah," he said and gingerly rolled off me.

I took a deep breath and sat up.

He rolled to a sit and peeled his mask and head covering off. His hair was plastered against his head, sweat dripped down his forehead, and blood trickled down his newly fatted lip. He wiped at his mouth with the back of his hand and winced.

My anger evaporated. "Ohmygosh! I'm so sorry."

I kneeled beside him and leaned over to inspect his lip. "So, so sorry!" I couldn't stop myself from apologizing in rapid-fire repeat mode. I felt like a major heel for hurting him. "You need ice." I stood and extended my hand. "Here. Let me help you up—"

He shook his head no. "I'd rather sit. You got me in the lower stomach, too." His voice came out sounding like Mickey Mouse on helium.

Lower stomach must've been guy-speak for groin. I winced and blushed as he clutched his abdomen and took a deep breath.

Several members of the class had crowded around us, dead silent, gazes bouncing between Torq and me. Ignoring them, I bent to kneel beside Torq again. "I'm sorry! I thought that suit was supposed to protect you. Otherwise, I never would have—"

Ethan caught my elbow and pulled me away. "Jeez! Leave the guy alone, would you? Didn't you hear him? You got him in the lower stomach!"

We spent the following hour at the firing range. Wearing those big plastic earmuffs that block out sound and the world gave me way too much access to my own tortured thoughts. From the heights of flirtatious joy to the sandpits of despair and self-recrimination and doubt.

Just what was I thinking, elbowing Torq in "the lower stomach"? Even if he *had* fake-flirted with me, he didn't deserve that. And if he hadn't . . . probably I'd just doomed any hope for a second date, let alone a relationship. Maybe he was the kind of guy who could see straight through to my inner beauty, but could he see past me nearly making a eunuch out of him?

At lunch, Max looked bruised and scraped but otherwise perfectly fine, more like he'd taken a spill off a bicycle than had a run-in with a motor vehicle traveling at high speed. He didn't want to talk about the incident, except to say he hadn't gotten a good look at the driver. He believed the driver had been a man but beyond that couldn't describe him. The police had no suspect. With no license or description, they weren't likely to ever have one, either. Unable to pry more out of Max, we turned to other topics.

Speculation ran high among my group—John, Max, Emma, and me—about where Pussy had disappeared to.

"I heard she went to town," Emma said.

None of us could fathom why.

"With any luck, she won't be back," Emma added before changing the course of the conversation. "What did you think of our girl in self-defense class today? Wasn't she brilliant?" She turned to me. "I guess you showed Torq! Got him where it counted." Emma held up her hand, ready for a high five.

I couldn't make myself return it. Bloodying Torq's lip and giving him a Mickey Mouse voice wasn't nice and I wasn't proud of it.

Seemingly unembarrassed by my refusal to celebrate my "victory," she used her raised hand to give me a squeeze on the shoulder.

Max and John looked uncomfortable.

"I wouldn't call what I did brilliant," I said to Emma.

"Why not?" Emma said, sounding genuinely perplexed. "He was attacking you. You were fighting for your life. Use any means possible to down the bad guy. Right, guys?"

"Well," Max's voice cracked and he crossed his legs, "the elbow-to-the-groin trick was . . . below the belt." He suddenly found something fascinating on his plate. John was looking off into the distance.

"That was an accident," I said, defending myself. "No, really. I feel like scum." Which was an understatement. In actuality, I felt more like slimy, lowly pond scum on a toxic-waste dump.

"I'd rather not be around you next time you have an accident," John said mildly.

Max didn't reply.

Just then Torq walked into the lunchroom, upright and whole. All conversation stopped as everyone's gaze bounced between him and me. I blushed and made a point of staring at my food.

Talk about your relief and assuaged guilt. Evidently his "lower stomach" felt better. In the glimpse I'd gotten of him, I'd noticed that his lip had stopped bleeding and now looked merely puffy, like he'd overdosed on Lip Venom. Now, if he'd gotten his bass voice back, we were in business.

Rockford, who sat at the head of our long lunch table, took the heat off me and saved us from the uncomfortable silence by launching into a series of war stories—being sprayed with enemy machine-gun fire while hiding out in rice paddies, napalm, explosions, and cigar-smoking, drinking binges. Encountering head-hunting cannibals during a brief stint in the Philippines. Oh, and don't forget the Vietnamese whores. Whooey!

Yes, he gave us *all* the gory details. No one else managed to wedge a word in. Finally, unable to take any more of his exploits in the red-light district, and being strangely reminded of a scene in *Catch-22*, I said, "And I suppose these Vietnamese whores all beat you over the head with their high-heeled shoes?"

Rockford looked at me like I was a crazy woman.

"Like Nately?" I added for clarity.

He didn't understand and it was too much to explain. But at the far end of the table, Torq grinned. That was a good sign, right?

Lunch over, we headed to the driving range and divided into three groups. The two NASCAR guys took the other two groups, and I was with Max and John.

I looked around for Davie. Instead, Torq strolled over dressed in a driving suit, a helmet tucked under his arm. After everything that had happened and possibly happened between us in the past twenty-four hours, I couldn't look him in those hot-chocolate eyes of his. I fixed my gaze on Max and John instead.

"Where's Davie?" John asked.

"Called away. Family emergency. I'll be instructing you today." Thankfully, Torq's voice had come down off its elbow-induced helium pitch.

I felt his gaze on me, but I refused to play that game and peered into the sand, concentrating as if *War and Peace* were written beneath my feet.

"I'm also a graduate of the Bondurant Driving School."

Of course. What hadn't he done?

When I didn't look at him, Torq cleared his throat. "Today we'll be tackling the bootlegger hairpin and the moonshine hairpin, which is the bootlegger in reverse. Toward the end of the lesson we'll team up with the NASCAR guys for a little car-ramming exercise." He explained how to perform the bootlegger.

"Slow to between twenty-five and thirty-five mph. Take your foot off the gas. With your left hand, spin the wheel to the three to four o'clock position while yanking the hand emergency brake. *Hard.* When the car's spun ninety to one hundred degrees, release the emergency brake, straighten the wheel and gun it." He looked around the group. "Got it?"

We nodded in unison. But I still didn't meet his eyes.

"Good. John, you're up first." Torq seemed happy enough to be off and out of the tension zone between us.

John suited up and donned a helmet. Max and I stood on the sidelines beneath the meager shade of a paloverde tree and watched as John pulled out and headed up the straightaway. Halfway down the straightaway John pulled the car off the track into the desert sand.

I turned to Max. "What's he doing?"

"Practicing the bootlegger eats up tires, especially on asphalt," Max said. "It's easier on sand and gravel."

"Oh."

Max nodded. "So what's up with you and Torq?"

"Up?" I played dumb.

"Yeah. Up. You seem uncomfortable around him."

I shrugged.

"You're not still worried because you got him in the jewels, are you?"

I shrugged again as Max scrutinized me.

"We all know you didn't mean to maim him." Max spoke with a tease in his voice, trying to cheer me up. When I didn't perk right up, he turned serious. "It's not that, is it?"

I liked Max. He was a sweet guy. But I didn't answer.

"It's about last night and what Rockford said, isn't it?"

I looked at Max in surprise. Who knew he could be so astute?

"Don't let it get you down. From my knothole, I'd say Torq was putting a real move on you. He'd be a fool not to."

I couldn't help it. I grinned at Max and shook my head to hide my embarrassment. "Thanks."

"Don't mention it. And if you ever get tired of waiting around for Torq, I'm here." He had enough tease in his voice that I couldn't be altogether certain he was serious. But it was nice of him to say.

"I'll definitely keep that in mind." I gave him a hug.

We fell into companionable silence and turned our attention back to the track. Through the flying sand, we watched John make several decent attempts at the bootlegger before finally nailing one. He pulled up in front of us, grinning like he'd just sealed a billion-dollar deal.

Torq jumped out of the car and inspected the front tires. Satisfied, he turned to us. "Max, you're up."

Max walked to the car. He paused at the door, shook his head, and waved me over. "Ladies first."

He came back beside me and leaned in to whisper to me, "I can't stand to see you stew. Talk to him."

I shrugged and suited up, nervous, but ready for action. Though not necessarily of the talking variety. My heart pumped with excitement and, okay, some fear. Hot car. Hot guy. Tension. Confined quarters. Forced intimacy.

As I slid into the seat, I turned to Torq and tried to break the ice. "This isn't another one of those exercises where I end up dead, is it?" I was only half-joking.

"Buckle up." He shook his head, but he was grinning.

"Aye, aye." I saluted, buckled into my four-point harness, adjusted my seat and mirrors just like Davie'd taught me, and turned to Torq. "Ready to pull out?"

"I'm never ready to pull out." The grin again.

I tightened my grip on the wheel, and my Kegels, too. I warned myself not to read too much into his statement. I really couldn't handle another fake flirt.

"But let's go anyway," he continued. "Do you remember the instructions?"

"Slow, spin and pull, release, accelerate." I tried hard to concentrate on my driving and *not* on my driving instructor, who despite his treachery was still hot.

"Go for it." He adjusted his sunglasses.

I took us out on the track, accelerating to 50. I had the air conditioning running full bore, but I felt flushed and warm despite that. The car responded to the slightest tap on the brakes and turn of the wheel. I tried to remember what Davie had said about oversteering and understeering.

"Let's slow things down," Torq said. "And head for the sand."

"Oh, come on," I pleaded with more bravado than I felt. "Let me take it hard and fast once around the track." A real spy would *want* to drive fast, and besides, it put off the bootlegger while I found my nerve.

He gave me a look that said he thought I was flirting with him.

"What? I like it fast."

"Could've fooled me." He grinned again. "Once."

I cruised around the track at 70, feeling the exhilaration of speed pulse through me.

"Slow her down to twenty-five to thirty-five and pull off," Torq instructed.

I pulled into the sand in a spray of dust.

"When you're ready, give it a go," Torq said, sounding calm and in control.

Palms sweating, heart pulsing in my ears, I took my foot off the gas, turned the wheel, and pulled the brake. We wobbled but didn't skid.

"Damn it!" I said. I had to be good at something spy. I *was* going to succeed at this.

"Too slow," Torq said. "Get back on the track. Go around, get it up, and try it again."

I took a deep breath and found myself calming as I took us around again. I pulled into the sand, got it up to just over 35 mph, let off the gas, turned, pulled the brake. No skid.

"Now what?" I turned to Torq. "I was definitely in the target speed range."

"You didn't jerk it hard enough. You have to be *committed* to it. Really *want* it."

Was he goading me with a flirt again? It sure seemed like it.

"Pull over and I'll demonstrate."

I wasn't so sure I could handle a demonstration, but I pulled over anyway.

"You take the brake handle like this. Grasp it tightly. Feel it in your hand." He looked me in the eye, his eyes twinkling with challenge. "Grab it. Jerk it. And it'll whip right around." He offered me the brake. "You try."

I grabbed the brake and our fingers brushed. I tried to pull back, but Torq covered my hand with his.

"Give it a good feel," he said and released my hand. "Grip it. Pull."

I struggled with the brake and my scattered emotions. "It's hard."

He looked me in the eye. "That's the way you want it. With a soft brake, you'd brake too fast, too soon. A hard brake will take you where you want to go."

"Right. No premature braking for us." I was thinking of our baby relationship hitting the skids. His smile told me he'd taken my statement in a different way. I blushed.

"Exactly." He nodded toward the track. "Let's give it another try."

I had the feeling, but I'd been wrong before, that he was talking more about us than the bootlegger.

"Okay," I said, feeling uncertain and wary, but also the tiniest bit exhilarated.

I took us around the track, into the sand, and up to just over 35 mph. I let off the gas, jerked the brake, and whipped the wheel around. Sand sprayed everywhere. We came around, but only about 90 degrees.

"What now?"

"Frustrated?" Torq asked.

"Oh, yeah." In more ways than one.

Torq pointed to the wheel. "You didn't whip it around hard enough. Let's try it again. Once more."

"Can I try it on the track? The sand messed me up. I couldn't see as I came around." Okay, I was full of excuses. But I couldn't give the real reason, which was that I was distracted by him and as nervous about this maneuver and our conversation as the day I made my first loan.

He hesitated. I imagined he was thinking of the tires. I gave him my sweet, pleading look.

"All right. Take us home."

I got back on the track. Coming down the far straightaway I saw Max walk to the edge of the track and give the air a little "you can do it" punch. I flashed him a thumbs-up and concentrated.

I came around the corner and hit the straightaway in front of Max, slowed to just over 35 mph, speaking Torq's instructions aloud. "Ease up on the speed. Grab and stroke the brake like so." I grabbed the brake with my right hand.

"Jerk the brake." I pulled the emergency brake. "Whip the wheel." I spun the wheel with my left hand.

The car began its spin. My heart raced into overdrive as I realized we were coming around in a perfect bootlegger.

"Whoohoo! I'm doing it!" It was a pure rush for me.

A loud pop, like the crack of a gunshot, interrupted my euphoria and our perfect skid.

"What the—" Torq said just as the front left side of the car dropped and a strip of rubber slammed the windshield.

The screech of metal grinding on pavement filled the air. Instead of completing the spin, the car tilted, flipped, and became airborne, flying directly at a startled Max.

I screamed. Torq grabbed the wheel. I saw his

mouth moving like he was shouting directions, but I couldn't make any sense of them.

As the car continued to roll, a jumble of images flashed by too quickly for me to process—Torq struggling for control of the car, the sky, Max's horrified face, the sky again, flying sand, random scenes from my life . . .

Chapter Eleven

We landed upside down on our roll bar in a spray of sand and dust, hanging from our four-point harnesses like crash dummies as the blood rushed to our heads. Beside me in the haze and murk, Torq muttered some colorful expletives I'd never heard before.

"Domino. Dom! Can you hear me?" Torq had his helmet off and was unsnapping his seat belt. I heard the click. "Talk to me. Are you all right? Are you hurt anywhere?"

"I'm just peachy, thanks." I coughed. "That was a hell of a bootlegger, wasn't it? I bet none of your other students have ever added a double fakey with a half-flip. I get difficulty points for that, right?" I sounded braver than I felt. Inside, I was quaking. I coughed again and choked on the dust in the air. The car reeked of burnt rubber and overheated engine, a scent guaranteed never to grace a perfume bottle. I removed my own helmet and stretched my neck.

Thanks to the miracle of four-point harnesses, I seemed to have escaped any major whiplash.

"You're the first student to attempt it, Dom. I'd give you more points if you'd nailed the landing."

"Next time."

Torq slid out of his harness and did a *Matrix* kind of acrobatic flip to kneel on the car's ceiling next to me. "Domino, we have to get out of the car." He fumbled at my hips, trying to unlatch my seat belt.

"A little lower." I directed him to the buckle. "That's it."

"Don't distract me." He grinned at me, but his eyes were serious. "We have to get out. Now."

My seat belt unlatched. Torq grabbed me by the shoulders and eased me down onto the ceiling.

"Why?" I brushed a lock of hair out of my face.

He ignored me as he rammed the door with his shoulder. When that didn't work, he gave it a swift kick and it swung open. He slid outside and jumped past the roll bar onto the ground, then reached back in to pull me out and to my feet. I must have been wobbly because he slid an arm around my waist.

From across the course, a crowd of CTs and the two other driving instructors rushed toward us. Fearing the worst, that Max'd become a pancake-thin piece of roadkill beneath our car, I looked around for him.

"Max! We have to find Max!" I turned back to the car.

If Max was there, squashed like a bug beneath the car, Torq didn't want me to see him. He grabbed me

by the arms and forced me to look into his eyes.
"Do you feel up to running?"

"Sure, but—"

"Great, and the trick here would be to run fast,
stay low, and keep your head down until we reach
cover." He took off with me in tow, motioning with
his free hand for the others to get back. They
stopped obediently in their tracks as we ran toward
them.

I slipped and slid in the sand as Torq dragged me
along faster than my own legs normally carried me.
Sand running wasn't really my thing, though it was
supposed to be good for the calves.

"Pick it up, Domino, before I pick you up."

"The sand's slowing me down."

"Where have I heard that before?" he said, pick-
ing up the pace as I panted behind him.

We were maybe a hundred feet from the car
when I felt a blast of heat behind me, followed by
an explosive roar. I watched as my fellow campers
ducked for cover in slow motion just like a scene
from an action-adventure movie.

Torq shoved me to the ground. I fell forward,
scraping my palms and forearms as I tried to catch
myself. I was already sucking wind and my lungs
burned. Hitting the ground took the last puff of air
from me as I landed with an unladylike "oomph."

Torq threw himself on top of me, covering me
with his body. I just had time to cover my ears with
my hands before another explosion cracked
through the air. Little bits of metal, fabric, and
rubber rained down around us. Behind us, I heard

the car break out into a steady crackle of roaring fire, completely engulfed in flames.

"I'm definitely getting used to you on top," I said. "So don't take this wrong, but you're squashing me! Do I have to cry 'uncle' again to get a little air?"

I felt him smile as he rolled off me.

I could breathe again and inhaled deeply. Torq started to speak, but I cut him off. "If you call me a dead woman, I'm going to have to kill you, you liar."

"No way I'd call you a dead woman. Not when I just saved your pretty little ass." He coughed and grinned. "And I'd like to see you try." He stuck his chin out toward me, puffy lip and all. "You want a piece of me, come get it."

In truth, I felt like kissing his boo-boos. It was a real Bond moment—heightened sexual tension in the midst of danger. I couldn't help it, I eyed his crotch like I might take another shot at it. "You're wearing a cup, right?"

He broke out laughing. I started to titter and then lost it.

Finally, I rolled to a sit, still fighting hiccups of hysterical laughter and wiped my eyes. "It must be the stress. This definitely isn't funny." I examined the damage to my hands and arms. Surface scratches and cuts. Nothing some antiseptic and a few bandages wouldn't cure. "Where are the others?"

About twenty feet away, Max stood up from where he'd been lying flattened against the pavement of his own accord. I gave a huge sigh of relief and pointed toward him. "Whoohoo! Max is alive."

"I knew that." Torq took my face in his hand and

turned my head to look into his eyes. "How about you? Are *you* all right?"

I flashed him a huge smile. "Terrific! Fabulous! Never better."

I hate to admit this, but safe and high on adrenaline, I felt ecstatic. When I looked into Torq's eyes, I saw a mirroring rush in his. We simply stared at each other, two adrenaline junkies grinning like we'd just conquered the world.

Finally, Torq stood and gave me a hand up, looking sexy in a hot, sweaty, dusty hero sort of way that sent my meager flirting skills packing and left me practically speechless.

"Anyone ever tell you this camp is hell on automobiles?" I said. Cars, I could talk about. "I suppose this is part of the deluxe, custom spy camp package we paid extra for?"

He didn't answer, just sort of cleared his throat. That's when we simultaneously noticed we were still holding hands and each let go self-consciously.

"Hey," I said to cover the uncomfortable silence, "fifteen years of a clean driving record literally blown to smithereens. This better not affect my car insurance rates or I'll never forgive you guys. That blown-tire thing was not my fault. That was probably a defective tire. And the explosion, no way did I do *that*."

"I'm sure the camp will cover it—" Torq was interrupted by Max charging us.

"Domino!" Max pulled me into a full-body hug.

Max's hair was peppered with dust and sand and

the odd leaf, and his face was streaked with dirt and sweat, but was I glad to see *him*!

"I'm really sorry about nearly mowing you down and squashing you into a roadside pancake," I said, getting teary-eyed as I broke free from his grip. "How'd you—"

Max did a little dodge-and-duck move. "I've got the moves. I'm quick on my feet," he said. "I saw the tire blow and hit the pavement facedown. Thank goodness you steered away from me. The car flew right over me."

"I think Torq did that," I said, flashing Torq a smile. "Where's everybody else?"

As if on cue, our fellow CTs emerged one by one from behind cacti and trees, large rocks, whatever cover they'd found.

"Well, I'll be damned," Torq said to Max and me. "They've actually learned something." Then he addressed the group. "Excellent work, CTs. Looks like everyone dies another day." Then he grinned.

There was a general buzz as CTs gathered around us. Emma pushed to the front of the group.

"Now that's grandstanding if I've ever seen it." She pulled me into a hug. "How do you get all the luck?" When I didn't answer, she said, "Is this camp fantastic or what? Two car explosions in less than a week."

Oh, that.

Torq and the two NASCAR guys stepped away from the group and consulted among themselves while speculation ran high among the CTs and the car continued to burn off in the distance. Surrounded by sand, it wasn't going to damage anything else.

"No way that car could've exploded on its own. No way, man," Ethan said. "With that roll bar installed, it was designed to roll and protect the vehicle, not get beat up. No way the fuel system could've gotten damaged. Not from what we seen. It friggin' had to be rigged as part of the camp."

Heads nodded all around.

"But wouldn't it be dangerous to carry explosives on board?" I said.

"Hell, no," Wade said, like he was some sort of expert. "Explosives are inert until detonated."

Heads nodded. The group consensus seemed to be that the explosion was a planned part of the camp experience gone a little awry by the untimely tire blowout that almost took out Max. The eyewitness accounts all corroborated the same thing—the car exploded only once we were safely away. In my mind I couldn't figure out how else Torq knew the car was going to explode. But if the explosion was staged, how did that explain his apparently genuine urgency in getting us out?

"But why would they blow up an expensive, modified training vehicle?" I protested. The banker in me didn't see the sense in blowing up a capital asset.

"Why do they do anything here?" Bishop answered. "For the thrill."

The answer satisfied everyone but me. "The tire thing still bothers me," I said. "Torq checked them just before we went out. How would one suddenly blow? It makes no sense."

"Oh, hell," Ethan said. "Like you've never seen dead tires alongside the road. You think those were planned? Tires blow out all the time. Maybe you ran over something. Like a nail."

"On the track?"

Ethan shrugged. "You could've picked it up anywhere. Or a cactus needle. Hell, who knows?" He glanced over at the smoldering car, a look of childish awe in his eyes. "Looks like we're never gonna know now."

Rockford roared up in a Hummer and jumped out to talk with Torq and the two driving instructors. They spoke in low voices so we couldn't hear, but there was a whole lot of gesturing going on and Rockford looked none too pleased about something. I was guessing the torched car. Everyone else chalked it up to the blowout.

After a few minutes Rockford stalked over to me. "Get in the Hummer. I'm taking you back to the compound for a medical evaluation. I've called a doctor friend of mine. He's on his way now."

I waited for Rockford's doctor friend in the sick bay, leafing through the only reading material available— old copies of the *Wall Street Journal*. Geez, that Rockford was a real cheapskate. I mean, I love the *Journal*, but I read it for my job and I was on vacation, for Pete's sake. Like he couldn't afford a subscription to something fun, like *InStyle* or *Cosmo*. Even *Paramilitary Quarterly* would add a little variety.

Bored, I leafed through the most recent copy of the *Journal*, skimming headlines as I went.

IBM EARNINGS BEAT EXPECTATIONS

San Francisco—International Business Machines Corp. (IBM), the world's largest computer company, Monday posted a rise in quarterly net profit. Results topped Wall Street expectations . . .

BOEING ANNOUNCES RECORD ORDER JUST PRIOR TO FARNBOROUGH AIR SHOW

Chicago—The Boeing Company announces . . .

Movie reviews—Another James Bond collector's set is on the market—all EON Productions plus a bonus disc for each. MGM gives Bond fans a view to a thrill with this impressive collection of remastered films, with frame-by-frame restoration for ultimate picture and sound quality. Hear Goldfinger utter his most famous line, "Forgive me, Mr. Bond, but I must arrange to separate my gold from Mr. Solo," who has just been pulverized inside a Cadillac in a car crusher, as if Goldfinger were uttering the line today, not in 1964 . . .

I shuddered. The car-crushing bit was just a little too close to home right now.

. . . *see million-dollar hit man Scaramanga's third nipple* . . .

Eeuww, third nipple! *Thanks for reminding me,* I thought. This was a set I had to have.

To my dismay, the doc knocked and walked in, interrupting my reading before I could finish the article. Ever notice how doctors have a sixth sense about that? Their reading-enjoyment ESP kicks in and suddenly they're flying into your room like you're an emergency case. Like they just can't stand the thought of their patients reading something juicy. Keep them bored and waiting forever, they ought to add that to the Hippocratic oath. I reluctantly tossed the paper back onto the stack and submitted to an examination.

The doc bandaged my ouchies, prescribed a few hours of rest, and gave me a clean bill of health. "Call me if you experience any new symptoms or discomfort," he called over his shoulder as he left.

Like I couldn't have given myself the same prognosis and treatment. Without the wait.

Due to the few-required-hours-of-rest business, I missed the afternoon sessions on hostage negotiations and a war-game simulation. Instead, I took what should have been a relaxing shower but was really just an opportunity for too much thinking and my vivid imagination to run amok.

Had that double entendre talk in the car before it blew up patched things up with Torq? Is that how spies apologized, in code? I think I preferred the straightforward approach. Candy and flowers didn't hurt any, either. No matter how much I puzzled over it or wanted it to be true that Torq was trying to tell me the scene at the bar hadn't been faked, my internal jury remained hung on the matter. I turned my thoughts to other, equally serious matters.

By the time I'd removed sand from every possible

crevice and orifice in my body, I'd decided that my half-flip bootlegger was not part of the thrill-a-minute camp experience the lotto winners had paid extra for. And nothing explained the sudden blowout satisfactorily. So maybe that wasn't an accident, either. Which led directly into ... .

Two accidents in two days. Nearly being plowed down and nearly being blown up. Too much coincidence? My camera being taken took on a new, sinister context as I recalled Torq examining the first blown-up car. Had I caught something incriminating? Had someone been intentionally shooting at us? I cursed, wishing I had that camera.

It might have been only my crazy, overactive imagination acting up, but if someone *was* trying to kill Torq, Max, or me, I had a right—no, an obligation—to know and to stop them.

At dinner that night, Rockford gave a speech about safety. "All CTs will stay well away from the driving track when not in a vehicle on the course. As evidenced today, CTs should always expect the unexpected ... blah, blah, blah.

"FSC would never knowingly endanger its participants, but the very nature of the camp carries inherent risks. . . .

"The tire blowout was an unfortunate and totally unforeseen occurrence that is still under investigation. . . .

"If any CT wishes to go home we'll make the necessary arrangements—"

Which was met with a resounding chorus of boos by everyone but me. Why would they want to go home when camp was such a kick? I could have booed, too, but not for the same reasons. I was watching Rockford closely. I decided he was worried and trying to cover his ass. Which verified my assumption that the "accident" wasn't planned, even without the blowout thrown in. I didn't mention my theory to anyone, not even Emma. I didn't want to be branded a nutcase. But having been the only CT in the exploded vehicle, I still had the strong sense that more had gone wrong there than a blown-out tire. What about that pop I'd heard? I was still trying to remember if I'd heard it *before* the tire blew or concurrently with the blowout. It all had happened so fast. . . .

Add that to my missing camera and pictures, Torq's suspicious behavior around the first blown-up car, which seemed to me like more than worry that someone had used the car for target practice earlier, Pussy's gun-under-the-mattress trick—speaking of which, where the hell was Pussy?—and you came up with something sinisterly strange definitely happening at camp. And I meant to get to the bottom of it if it killed me. Of course the "if it killed me" was just a figure of speech. Which, come to think of it, suddenly seemed more sinister than it had in the past. I made a note to scratch it from my vocabulary.

Two things that made me a good bank officer were my nosy, suspicious nature and my ability to sniff out fishiness. I didn't authorize a loan until I decided everything was on the up-and-up. Right now my fishiness meter was pegged on high. Which meant one thing—more snooping!

* * *

Torq was suspiciously absent from dinner, but Fry was there in full charm mode. After Rockford's speech, he slid in next to me, joining Emma, John, and Max at our end of the table. To her credit, Emma didn't bear him any obvious grudge and flashed him a flirtatious smile, which he returned.

"Heard y'all had a little excitement this afternoon out on the track," he said, addressing me. "And, damn my luck, I chose this afternoon to run some errands in town and missed all the fun! You weren't hurt, I hope?" He put a whole lot of sympathy and concern into his softly drawled words.

If only a girl could believe it.

"No, I'm fine. Thanks for asking." I was hoping Fry didn't notice how closely I was watching him for any micro expressions that would give him away as a liar. Frankly, since the bar scene "test" bit, he'd lost a lot of his appeal to me. He was looking more and more like the traitorous 006. Especially in light of my suspicions that he'd taken Pussy to town. "Town must have been hopping today. We heard Pussy was there, too. Did she snag a ride with you? I hope she's all right. We haven't seen her today."

"You're a sharp one," Fry said, still grinning. "Poor little thing had a powerful migraine. Forgot her meds and her prescriptions back at home. I took her in to the doctor and dropped her by the pharmacy. She's still recouping. Rockford had a dinner tray delivered to her room."

I made the appropriate murmurs of sympathy as I put his response through my crap filter. I couldn't see any evidence that he was lying, but then, he was a professional spy. How easy would it be to tell? He could probably put on any micro expression he wanted, just like Torq. What had he and Pussy really been up to?

Before I could grill him further, Max broke in and started recounting his daring escape.

"He earned his secret, lucky decoder ring today, that's for sure," Emma broke in dryly as Max reiterated for the third time how he'd sprung to safety.

"I hear Torq's in some trouble over the incident," Fry said, dropping a bombshell.

"Really?" John asked.

"That accident wasn't his fault." I was a little too forceful with my assertion. Fry gave me a speculative look. "It was a weak tire." I could play the game and reiterate the official spiel, too. Not that I believed it.

Fry smiled and shook his head. "He was the officer in charge of an operation that nearly took out several trainees. The cause is insignificant. Torq screwed up. A commanding officer always takes the fall. He failed to foresee possible operation failures."

"What's going to happen to him? Will FSC fire him?" If Torq's job was on the line, I'd be obligated to share my suspicions and observations with the Chief. Though I'd prefer to have some concrete evidence first. . . .

"Don't worry about old Torq. Rockford'd never fire him. There'll be an investigation. He might get a reprimand. Not much more. How about we change the subject?" Fry looked around the group. "Anyone up for an evening paintball battle?" He pointed his fingers like guns and did a pow-pow motion.

John, Max, Emma, even Ethan, Bishop, Wade, Q, and Tanner from the far end of the table, all exuberantly volunteered.

Fry turned to me. "Domino? How about you? Wanna be on my team?" He winked.

Enticing as the offer was, I had some heavy-duty spying to do.

"That's a mighty tempting offer," I said, trying to sound Texan, or at least Old West–like, "but I'm beat. I think I'll take it easy tonight, like the doctor recommended."

"Sure we can't convince y'all?" He reached over and gave my thigh a squeeze as he leaned over and whispered in my ear. "I hear Ethan was giving you grief this morning. This is your chance to whump him one. I don't mind giving you a few pointers on how to shoot."

I shook my head no. "Pelt him once or twice for me, though, will you?"

Emma walked back to the room with me. On the way, I stopped by the pop machine and got a bottle of Sprite . . . for Pussy. My ticket into her room. No one could be uncheered by a delicious lemon-lime beverage, especially if they'd been experiencing the ravages of migraine nausea.

"I'd like to stop by Pussy's room and check on her," I said to Emma as we neared Pussy's door.

"What on earth for?" Emma's tone indicated we

should leave the bitch well enough alone and count ourselves lucky she was out of commission for as long as she had been.

"Oh, come on," I said. "She's sick." Though, of course, my kindness had an ulterior motive.

"What are you, Florence-friggin'-Nightingale now?" Emma scowled her displeasure.

I shrugged. "I'd do the same for you."

"I should hope!"

I knew a thing or two about migraines. Logan was a major sufferer. It wasn't inconceivable that Pussy had a migraine that had sent her flying to the doctor. The way Logan described them, they were like having a whole-body headache. Everything felt crappy. Even medicated, I'd seen Logan knocked out for days, spending her time in darkened rooms with cold packs over her eyes and heavily dosed with antinausea drugs. "Heed the package warning on the antinausea pills," she'd warned me. "When they say 'do not operate heavy machinery,' they mean it. Take one, and half an hour later it's boom-boom, out go the lights . . . for hours."

"Go on ahead if you like," I said to Emma. "You have a paintball match to prepare for."

"All right. I'll see you back at the ranch." Emma sounded relieved.

I knocked on Pussy's door.

"The door's open," Pussy called to me.

I let myself in. She lay on her bed with an empty dinner tray on the nightstand beside her and a pair of headphones in her ears. Her nightstand light was on. I thought it odd. Usually walking in on a migraine sufferer is like walking into a tunnel of darkness and silence, or seeing someone who has a powerful hangover. Light is bad, very bad. Sound is not so good, either. All the noise, noise, noise!

But Pussy didn't seem to mind either at all.

"How are you feeling?" I held up the can of pop. "I brought you something for your stomach." My gaze flicked to her empty food tray. Hardly a crumb left big enough for a Who's mouse, let alone a human's mouse.

She adjusted the volume on her MP3 player, pulled her headphones out of her ears, and stared at me a moment in confusion before holding her hand out for it. As I handed it to her, her earphones slid off her lap onto the floor. I bent to retrieve them. As I picked them up, I heard a voice coming through them. A faint voice, but a voice I knew—Max!

I kept a straight face, trying not to give myself away. Pussy was eavesdropping on Max. Why? She hardly paid Max any attention at all. I handed the headphones back to her. I wanted a better look at that MP3 player of hers. I had the feeling it wasn't an MP3 player at all, but an electronic ear. Yeah, I knew about electronic ears. I'd had one on my Christmas list for years. But no one ever seemed to buy me one. Guess they thought I was nosy enough as it was.

"Thanks." Pussy set the headphones on her tray.

"Tough day?" I said, straining to hear more from the headphones. But they were too far away now. "I sympathize. Migraines can be killers."

I used the word "killer" intentionally. Pussy was on my list of suspects. She had opportunity to take pot-shots at us at both the opening car blowup and this morning at the driving range. She had a gun. And now she was listening in on Max, whose room was directly next door to hers. Okay, she had opportunity, but no motive. That I could see, I told myself. Didn't mean she didn't have one. "We were all worried about you."

That was a bit of a lie, or a stretch anyway. I was getting pretty good at mastering my micro expressions. I think I fooled her.

"I'll be fine. I'm feeling better."

"You missed all the excitement this morning."

"Yeah, I heard." She sounded bored.

I dropped that line of conversation and tried a few more, which she met with one- or two-word answers. Pussy wasn't going to feed me any information. The more I tried to strike up a friendly conversation, the more the already tepid mood in the room notched toward frosty. I may be dense, but I can take a hint.

"I've got to be going," I said finally.

She gave me a weak smile that I thought was more relief than anything. "Before I go, can I get you anything?"

She assured me she'd be fine and I left. As I closed the door behind me, I turned back over my shoulder to see her sticking her earbuds back in. Listening in on Max had to be an exercise in extreme boredom. Whatever her motives, I almost felt sorry for Pussy. Almost. The bitch.

Poor Max! On a whim, I knocked on his door.

"Dom!" He smiled when he answered.

I beckoned him closer with a crook of my finger. He looked confused and I thought his eyes bulged out slightly, but he complied. When he came nearer, I stepped into him and on tiptoe whispered in his ear, "The walls have ears." I nodded toward Pussy's room and held a finger to my mouth. Then I left, leaving poor Max looking like he had expected something else entirely.

A few minutes later, I was back in my room. Emma was in the bathroom putting blackout makeup under her eyes.

"Well," she said when she saw me, "how's our little invalid?"

"She'll live." I plunked down on the bed, still pondering why Pussy would be listening in on Max. Idle curiosity seemed out of character. Given the situation, everything I couldn't explain seemed sinister. I made a mental note to keep an eye on Pussy.

"What's wrong? You sound uncertain." Emma leaned on the door frame between the bathroom and my room. She had good powers of perception herself.

"I don't think she had a migraine," I blurted out.

"What did she have, then?" Emma asked. "Your regular garden-variety tension headache?"

"I don't think she had anything at all." I took a breath. "When I went in, she was dressed. The lights were on full. She'd eaten her tray of food. I scoped the room—no meds that I could see. And she didn't have that pale, sickly migraine afterglow. Or that 'I can't think' confusion. And believe me, I recognize the signs of a bad headache, particularly a migraine, all too well. My best friend is a chronic headache sufferer."

"So she was faking?" Emma asked, frowning.

"Yeah."

"Then what was she doing in town with Fry?"

I arched a brow, deliberately leading Emma to a conclusion I didn't share. What was she doing in town with Fry? Or had they gone at all?

I was so frustrated. Since Pussy had arrived late to camp, she could have taken a shot at Max, or Torq, or anyone, on arrival during the blowup. She could have faked going to town, bought Fry off to give her a cover story, and taken a shot at our car this afternoon. But she definitely wasn't driving the car that hit Max at Hal's. I was so confused.

"Probably another flirt test," Emma said in the tone of a woman in deep denial. "She's the only woman they didn't hit on in the bar."

"Could be," I said, then smiled wickedly as an idea occurred to me. "The good news is, tonight's your chance to shoot him a good one. How often do you get an opportunity like that?"

I waited until around seven, an hour or so before sunset, and after the others had left to play paintball, before I headed out on Mission Scope the Crash Scene.

I'd changed into jogging shorts and an Underarmor jog bra guaranteed to wick moisture away from my body, pulled my hair extensions up into a ponytail, reapplied my antiperspirant, and strapped my BlackBerry on a belt around my waist along with my MP3 player. It was probably stupid since there was no cell coverage out here, but I felt safer having some means of communication on me. If worse came to worst, I could chuck it at an attacker. Or something.

Hey, I'd read a lot of Nancy Drew mysteries as a kid. I wasn't going out on a mission totally unarmed.

I touched up my lips with a brush of Lip Venom for that plumped look and stuck my earbuds in. I didn't turn my music on. The MP3 player was for decoy purposes only, to look the part of the unassuming jogger.

I headed out, bopping by the computer lab. Locked up tighter than a medieval maid's chastity belt. Maybe I'd lucked into it the first night, or maybe they had reason to lock it now. My suspicious little mind turned on all the possibilities.

Same with Rockford's office—locked, not that I blamed him. As I jogged past the garage where FSC stored the training cars, I noticed that the windows were recently soaped. When I tried it, the door was locked. Suddenly these guys were turning into security freaks.

Outside, the shadows were long and low. Crickets sang. Mourning doves and quail cooed their goodnight calls. A few clouds sat on the horizon off to the west. The temperature hovered around 95 degrees, but without the direct sun beating down, the heat was bearable.

The paintballers had agreed to meet at the orange shack, so I headed out through the orchard in the opposite direction and down the long driveway toward the gates, sneaking carefully past the trainers' cottages toward the driving range.

Once past the edges of camp civilization, I picked up my pace. I jogged out of the orchard and into the open. The landscape was peppered with saguaros, mesquite trees, and the occasional paloverde as the sun sank deeper behind me, lighting the clouds with an array of oranges and reds.

It took longer than I expected to reach the driving range and find the charred crash site. But immensely pleased with myself, and, okay, feeling a little winded and lungs burning, I examined the site, wishing I still had my camera. The car hulk had been hauled away. All that remained were bits of debris and skid marks on the asphalt. So I had braked, I thought as I examined them. Good for me.

I walked the path of the skid marks, trying to recall the accident in as much detail as I could remember. I was still uncertain about the sequence of the pop and the tire blowing, but several things were clear. The left front tire had gone. That was the side of the car facing the group of CTs.

Something was bothering me. As I thought about it, I remembered. Why had Torq warned me to stay low as we exited the car? What was he afraid of? Being shot, maybe? Did he suspect a sniper? If the tire had been shot out, that certainly explained the sudden blowout. . . .

I scanned the area to the left side of where the car had been. Orange groves, trees of all kinds. Plenty of places for a sniper to hide.

But who would shoot out the tire? And why? Pussy and Fry were ostensibly in town. But were they? What about Pussy's fake migraine? Had she fooled Fry, or was it part of their story? They had opportunity, but what was the motive? Rockford could have done the alleged shooting, but again, why? Davie, was he really out on a family emergency?

Max, Torq, and I all could have been intended victims. I ruled myself out. No one would want to kill me. My life was simply too boring to inspire that kind of hatred or passion. Even Daniel, had he seen me flirting with Torq, was more likely to dump me and run than plot any kind of revenge.

I supposed that Torq had enemies. A spy would, wouldn't he?

Max with his millions—enough said. Greed was a powerful motivator. If someone stood to inherit his lotto fortune . . .

I laughed at myself, feeling like I'd stepped out of an Agatha Christie novel. "Follow the money, Hastings," I could almost hear Poirot say.

The clouds were changing from brilliant oranges and reds to muted mauves and pinks. It wouldn't be long before darkness fell completely. I wasn't eager to be alone out in the desert wilderness, but I wanted to check out the trees and orchard. I don't know what I hoped to find—shell casings, telltale footprints, maybe? Off in the distance I heard a coyote howl.

As I scoured the nearby brush, a bush rattled. I jumped, hand to heart. What was I really trying to prove? Like I'd find *CSI*-type evidence that would solve the mystery on the spot. And if I did find a shell casing, what would that prove? And what the hell did I expect to find in the freaking dark? Brilliant, Watson. Next time pack a flashlight!

I looked around and picked up a stick for protection. Wasn't it Teddy Roosevelt who said, "Speak softly and carry a big stick"? I'd have to settle for walking softly with a small stick.

I pored over the orchard and brush probably another fifteen minutes. Overhead, the stars were coming out one by one, putting on an awesome array, making me feel small and insignificant in the big universal scheme of things.

Just then something rattled in the bushes again. The birds had all roosted, their songs gone silent. The crickets still sang, but I wasn't worried about them. In fact, creeped as I was, I kind of liked their company. Some brave spy I made.

The bushes moved. I screamed and poised my stick over my head, ready to bash someone a good one. A jackrabbit bounded from the brush and looked at me with beady eyes reflecting the moonlight.

I put a hand to my heart to steady it. "Silly me. It's nothing. Just a jackrabbit." Somehow talking out loud was calming. I decided I'd better get back to camp before talking to myself became a habit.

I dropped my stick and stretched, getting ready to jog back at what I hoped was a coyote-outrunning pace. I'd just made it back to the driveway when I heard rustling from a nearby paloverde. A stupid rabbit wasn't going to get me again.

"Fool me once, shame on you, bunny. Fool me twice, shame on me. Shoo! Go away!"

I took a deep breath and turned toward camp just as the shadowy silhouette of a man stepped from behind a lone paloverde tree into my path.

I screamed.

Chapter Twelve

"What the hell are you doing out here all by yourself?" Torq stood in front of me looking decidedly hacked off. "You're supposed to be resting."

"Torq!" I put a hand to my chest to still my racing heart. "You scared me!"

"Good." Torq's mood shifted as quickly as the light had departed. He grinned. "Was that 'honey' you just called me? And did you just try to shoo me away?"

I put my hands on my hips. "Very funny." I tried not to smile, but his grin was infectious. "I thought you were a rabbit."

"I'm not sure how to take that," he said.

"One jumped out at me earlier."

"Yeah, we have a lot of vicious wererabbits around here."

"Oh, stop. It was a jackrabbit."

He stared me down. "You going to tell me what you're doing out here?"

"Getting some fresh air." I inhaled deeply to emphasize my point.

"We have plenty of fresh air closer to camp," he said, not buying my explanation in the slightest and looking like he was ready for another showdown at the OK Corral.

I ignored him. "You?"

"Looking for you." And obviously waiting for a straight answer from me.

But I wasn't budging.

Finally, he gave up. "The Jeep's just down the road. We'd better get out of here before any more rabbits jump us." He took my arm and began leading the way just as a loud pop cracked the silence.

Torq threw me to the ground. "Stay down!" He lay flat next to me as we listened to crickets humming and a deafening lack of any more gunshot-type sounds.

"Who's jumping at rabbits now?" I said, trying to sound braver than I felt.

"You stay here and stay down. Wait for me to come back. I'm going to check things out." He popped up and was gone before I could protest.

I cursed him under my breath and stayed down for what seemed like forever. I'd just chucked caution to the wind and stood up when a flashlight beam cut past me and an armed man stepped into view, wearing a baseball cap that cast his eyes in shadow. Moonlight reflected off a barrel aimed at my chest, which did nothing to calm my already frayed nerves. He shone the flashlight in my eyes, blinding me.

Not wanting to be the latest spy casualty, I froze. And even though the capped avenger didn't ask me, I put my hands up, praying that my survival instinct would kick in soon and figure out some kind of escape plan.

My heart pounded away, crashing toward that worrisome 160 beats per minute and panic mode as I tried to remember my self-defense moves against an armed attacker and wished I hadn't tossed my puny stick aside so casually. How did Rockford do that knocking-a-pistol-out-of-the-hand move again? I glanced at the gun, bit my lip, and took a deep breath as I looked for my opportunity to attack.

"Don't even think about it."

Evidently Capped Man was also a mind reader. Damn.

He took a step back, putting himself out of my striking range. "I've taught those self-defense classes myself. I know all the moves and don't y'all forget it."

"Fry! Thank goodness it's you!" My heart rate took its sweet time slowing back into normal range.

"Domino? What are y'all doing out here? I thought you were one of the paintballers. Either Emma or Pussy. You're lucky I didn't pelt you one."

I took a deep breath of relief. "I felt better and got restless and went out for a jog." I grabbed the edge of my shorts and did a little tug.

The roar of a Jeep approaching from behind us at breakneck speed interrupted our little reunion. Its headlights appeared out of nowhere to light up the road in front of me, casting Fry and me in long, eerie shadows.

"Shit!" Fry turned around to look at it.

In the last few days I'd learned a thing or two about avoiding speeding vehicles and hightailed it off the road and into the desert, making for the cover of a tall saguaro. I stumbled as I ran over the uneven terrain, glancing back over my shoulder just in time to see the Jeep accelerate and speed toward Fry. Fry stayed rooted in place, playing a life-or-death game of chicken.

What in the world is he doing? I muttered to myself. *Damn it, he's going to get himself killed.* I cupped my hands around my mouth and, sounding like a kindergarten primer, screamed at him. "Run, Fry, run!"

Just in the nick of time he called the driver's bluff and dove off the road. The Jeep screeched to a halt and Torq, of all people, jumped out with a high-powered rifle trained on Fry.

"Slide your weapons onto the road and come out with your hands up!" Torq yelled at Fry. In the calm night air his words reached me clearly, punctuated by his vicious tone.

"Sheesh, Torq!" Fry tossed something onto the road and came out with his hands up as directed. "Put that thing down, would y'all? It's me. Fry. My weapon's nothing more than a two hundred–dollar paintball pistol. Shit."

Torq holstered his weapon and picked up the paintball gun again. "Come on out, Domino. The cavalry has arrived."

I came out from behind my cactus and walked shakily to join the two men on the road.

"Do you believe this guy?" Fry said to me. "First he

tries to run me over and then he draws a real weapon on me. I'm just trying to play me a game of paintball."

"Sorry." Torq clapped Fry on the back and explained the situation. "I came back to find you with a gun on Dom and assumed the worst. My mistake."

Fry gave him a big-old-boy slap on the back in return. "No hard feelings."

Men could make up with each other so easily.

Torq handed back Fry's paintball weapon.

"So y'all heard that noise, too," Fry mused as he grabbed it. "I thought it must have been a car backfiring."

"Must have been." Torq tossed his gun onto the Jeep seat.

Watching him, I got the distinct feeling he didn't really believe the backfire explanation. But I wasn't going to dispute him now.

"Get in, you two," Torq said. "I'll give you a ride back."

Fry jumped into the backseat. I climbed into the passenger side. Torq got into the driver's seat and we were off.

Fry leaned over the front seat, energetically giving Torq the play-by-play of the paintball war in his drawling Texas accent.

"Those CTs are wily. I'm telling y'all, Torq, they've learned a thing or two, that's for sure. They're making us proud." Then Fry went on to relate how Wade and Ethan had almost succeeded in ambushing him.

He touched me on the shoulder. "Sorry about scaring y'all out there, Domino. Just keep in mind that this is spy camp. Trust no one in this business. Do and end up dead." He flashed that grin of his and offered me his hand. "No hard feelings?"

I shook and accepted his apology.

"Hey, drop me off at the orange shack, Torq, so I can rendezvous with my troops," Fry said as we neared the paintball base.

Torq slowed to a stop. Fry jumped out of the vehicle in a single bound with his paintball gun at the ready, pausing to give Torq a slap on the shoulder and shoot me another wink before he disappeared into the orange grove.

Torq and I rode in silence. I sensed he wasn't completely happy with me. And I wasn't really sure how I felt about him at this point, either. Charging Fry with the Jeep like that and then pointing a high-powered rifle at him seemed needlessly reckless. Torq pulled to an abrupt stop in front of the lobby door.

"Thanks for the ride." I turned to jump out, eager to avoid any discussion about the evening's course of events.

He grabbed my arm. "What the hell were you doing out there by yourself, anyway?"

I gave him my best blank stare, trying hard to suppress any micro expressions that would give away my wild range of conflicting emotions or my motive for going out in the first place. "Jogging."

He arched a brow. "Really? Right by the crash site. That's a strange coincidence, isn't it?"

"Is it?" Two could play this spy game. "Rumors abound that you're in hot water with Rockford over the crash." I bit my lip as I thought up a quick half truth. "I feel responsible. I didn't mean to get you in any trouble. I should have maintained control when the tire blew. I went back to the site to see if I could figure out what went wrong." I stopped short of voicing my real concerns.

He studied me closely. I got the distinct impression he knew I wasn't telling the whole truth and nothing but the truth. Sins of omission, I'm good at those.

He squeezed my arm tighter. "I appreciate the loyalty. But I don't need your help." He wasn't looking into my eyes anymore, but staring at my shiny, plumped lips like there was a kiss in my future.

I blushed in the dark, unsure how to react. Was this another game of his? Another blasted test? If so . . . well, I was in no mood. I shook my arm loose and slid out of the Jeep.

"Dom, don't go sticking your nose where it doesn't belong." His tone was neutral.

I turned once more to face him. "Is that a warning . . . or another test?"

"Yeah," he said and put the Jeep in Drive. "Now get in the building."

I huffed off while he played gentleman hero and waited until I was safely inside before pulling away.

Emma was in the shower with the water running full force when I came in basically dazed and confused. Not to mention peeved at both Fry and Torq. What were the dynamic duo really trying to prove out there tonight? Game? Cover-up? Subtle spy dance? Had I been too close to the truth about something, say, about the crash not being accidental? Why didn't they want me out there? What didn't they want me to see so badly that they felt the need to scare me within an inch of my life?

I hugged myself, trying to fend off a shudder. If my theory was correct, I'd almost been killed today. And in reality, narrowly escaping death isn't nearly as fun as they make it look in the movies. There's no stunt double to take the blows and no new story line to resurrect your character.

Frustrated with my inability to solve the puzzle, I collapsed on my bed.

The shower shut off. I heard Emma humming and the rustle of toweling off before she knocked on the door my room shared with the bathroom.

"Come on in. It's unlocked," I said.

She poked her toweled head in.

"There you are! I was getting worried and about to send a posse out after you. Where were you?"

The clean, reassuring smell of mountain-fresh soap and herbal shampoo wafted into the room as she opened the door full out and stepped into the room. She wore a short robe and that fresh-scrubbed glowing pinkness of a nice, hot shower. Frankly, the normalness of the scene was comforting and I felt the *Twilight Zone* eeriness of the past hour begin to melt away.

"After you all left, I was feeling better and got bored, so I went for a jog. Torq found me and gave me a ride back. How was the game?"

She shrugged, but I could tell she was dying to tell me about it. "We gave those boys on the other team the what-for, that's for sure." She launched into a detailed description of the teams and the strategy, finishing up by saying, "I can hold my own. Just wait until the desert ambush tomorrow. I'd like to see those ambushers mess with me."

She lifted her robe sleeve to reveal a welt on her left arm. "The other guys only got the one good shot at me."

"Brutes!" I'd been listening, but only with half an ear. The rest of me had been working on trying to unravel the mysteries of camp.

What was really going on? What was real and what was Memorex, a reasonable facsimile of real? What was subterfuge, playacting, and outright deceit?

I made a mental list of things I wanted to know, things that would help me get to the truth—Max's true identity would be a start. And everyone else's. A good look at the accident report wouldn't hurt. I'd bet the bank's last dollar that Rockford had a copy in his office. . . .

"Hey!" Emma said. "You're a million miles away. What are you daydreaming about?"

I told her about Torq and Fry, omitting my suspicions and that I'd been at the crash scene when Torq found me.

"I'm tired of being tested and surprised. Bond wouldn't sit around waiting for the next test. He'd infiltrate."

"Infiltrate," Emma said slowly. "What do you mean?"

I spoke without thinking. "Break into FSC's central command center—Rockford's office."

Chapter Thirteen

"Break into Rockford's office?" Emma took less than a second to digest the idea. "Brilliant! I'll do it!"

Her immediate enthusiasm stunned me. I guess I'd expected more resistance. I paused, waiting for her cynicism to show. When it didn't, I supplied it for her. "Rockford keeps it locked tight. This is a former CIA training center chock-full of security cameras. And if he catches us, we'll be toast. Are you sure you're in?"

"Second thoughts already?" Emma rolled her eyes. "The very beauty of the plan is its audaciousness. Has anyone ever broken into his office before?"

"Not that he's mentioned, but—"

"Rockford's got all his important papers stashed in his office, including schedules and plans. If the information about who's going to be kidnapped is anywhere, it's in his office. So how do we get in?" Emma's eyes shone with anticipation. "How good are your lock-picking skills?"

"Don't get your hopes up."

We sat in thought a minute.

"How about a diversion?" Emma took the towel off her head and shook out her damp hair, finger fluffing it. "It works in the movies."

"You mean like pull the fire alarm?"

"Yes, exactly." She set the towel down and grinned widely. "And when he runs out of his office to check on it, we sneak in and reconnoiter."

"It's sophomoric, but it could work," I said, thinking it sounded more like a prank than a spy move. "But what about Rockford? He pulls his door closed whenever he leaves his office, even for just a second. And what if there are security cameras in his office?"

"We'll fix the door beforehand so that it won't latch. I doubt he has a camera in there. Why would he want to be watched as he works?"

"No one *wants* to be watched while they work; some of us just are." I was still worrying about cameras.

"We'll be wearing disguises." She sounded unconcerned.

"Okay," I said, giving up on the topic. "How are we going to fix the latch?"

"With a piece of tape over the latch plate. I saw someone do that on TV once, too."

I gave her a skeptical look. "Like they take no poetic license on TV?"

"Where are we going to get the tape?" Emma continued, unperturbed by my cynicism. "It's not like I carry it around in my handbag, though I've got practically everything else." She paused. "Hey! Maybe a bandage would work. I have a few of those." She jumped up and got a bandage.

We put it on the door.

"Kind of obvious, isn't it?" I inspected it, unimpressed.

Emma closed the door. The bandage crumpled. The door latched.

"Looks like a bandage is a no-go." I peeled it off and tossed it in the wastebasket. We both returned to my room to come up with Plan B.

"Packing tape would do it," I said. "Too bad we don't—" Inspiration struck. "Wait a minute. I saw some empty boxes by the recycling cans outside. I bet we could lift some packing tape off them. If the tape had enough stickum left . . ."

Emma volunteered to go. She changed into shorts and was off, returning in a flash with a two-foot-long strip of tape.

"No one saw you—"

"Of course not!" She grinned and tore off a four-inch strip.

We tested it out on the bathroom door.

"Whoohoo! Look at that. Stopped the door cold. And it's barely noticeable," I said, impressed. "He'll never see it, especially if we install it just prior to pulling the alarm."

We decided to scope out the building before morning and choose a fire alarm to pull. But before we went, we firmed up the rest of the plans.

"Most fire alarms will spray invisible ink that shows up under a black light on the person who does the pulling. We'll have to use gloves and maybe some sort of long stick to do the dirty work. And we'll have to dispose of the gloves where they won't be noticed."

"Have lots of experience pulling alarms, do you?" Emma was looking at me with admiration, like I was Prank Girl or something.

I hated to disillusion her. "That's what the installation guys told us when we had new alarms installed at—" I caught myself before I said "the bank."

"At the place where I work."

Emma looked disappointed with my response and shook her head with that "I'll just have to work with what I have" motion. "Whoever goes into the office needs gloves, too. I don't suppose you brought any rubber gloves with you?"

"No, but the kitchen has some."

We agreed to raid the kitchen for some of the disposable food-handling gloves. That settled, we moved on.

"We'll only have a few minutes in Rockford's office," I said. "We need a search plan."

"Did you see that spy reality show on TV last fall?" Emma asked. "The one that was kind of a last-spy-standing thing?"

I had and I knew what she was getting at. "We'll search his desk and the garbage. Any available surface. Taking only things that won't be missed."

She nodded her agreement. "Okay, back to disguises. We'll both need to wear masks and alter our appearances as much as possible. Just in case they check the security video."

"I brought panty hose," I said and we both cracked up at the mental image of our panty hose–covered heads.

"I'll do the searching," Emma said.

I tried not to panic. I had to do the searching, otherwise, what was the point of the whole exercise? "It's my idea, I'll search."

"You?! I'm the bolder one," she argued.

"Which is exactly why you should pull the alarm," I countered.

We bickered for nearly ten minutes before she gave in. "Fine, you go. But you have to promise to share *everything*."

This lack-of-trust business was the pits. I nodded my agreement. "But of course." I'd share exactly everything she thought I was looking for.

Emma sized me up. "You're about Ethan's size. Play this right and we could pin it on Ethan and Bishop. Wouldn't that be lovely fun?"

I grinned at her. "I like that plan."

We consulted the camp schedule and selected the morning break between classes as our operation time. Most of the CTs would stop by their rooms to freshen up and Rockford was usually in his office then. It was a daring plan. But my heart pumped with excitement at the thought of finding out what was really going on.

"Let's go gather our supplies and pick our fire alarm target," I said.

We took it as a good omen that as we sneaked down the corridor we found Ethan's door wide open and him out. We snatched two dirty T-shirts from a pile of clothes in the corner. They reeked of sweat and body odor. We wrinkled our noses in unison and giggled. Being on a mission with Emma was almost as much fun as hanging with Logan.

"We'll wash them in the sink and hang them to dry. Things dry in an instant down here," I whispered to Emma as she stuffed the shirts up her own shirt and into her sports bra for cover, giving herself some bonus T-shirt cleavage.

"What do you think?" she asked as she profiled for me. "Think the boys will notice?"

I eyed her two newfound chest lumps and cracked up. "Definitely. But socks generally give a smoother line."

She held her nose and grimaced. "No way am I putting his socks next to my skin. Yick."

"Hey, what's that?" I grabbed a prescription bottle from Ethan's nightstand.

"Viagra?" Emma giggled.

"No, but look at this." I turned the bottle label toward her. "Ethan is really Evan Jones."

"Good work!" Emma took the bottle from me and read the label for herself.

"Yeah. And you owe me how much now?" I rubbed my fingers together, indicating my money-grubbing intentions. "Ethan blew his cover before Wade."

"Nothing doing." She set the bottle down.

"Uh-huh. Leaving a prescription bottle out in the open pretty much constitutes a cover blow."

"It was in his room. That can't count."

"Wanna bet?" I said as we sneaked out with our ill-gotten goods.

"Yeah, as a matter of fact." Emma gently pulled the door closed behind us. "Let it ride."

"Still betting on Wade?" I asked.

"Why not?" She wrinkled her nose. "Now let's get back to the room before Evan/Ethan's shirt contaminates me for life and I have to take another shower."

Breakfast, oh-seven hundred hours. Desert ambush day. Tension and excitement ran high. Emma and I filled our trays and slid into a table next to Ethan and Bishop.

Ethan was bragging. What else was new?

"If I like it, I'm going to get me one of these fast attack vehicles when I get home," Ethan said, thinking ahead to the afternoon's activities. "How many Joes you know got an FAV? Ten to one I could stand out in one."

Emma flashed him a look and laid her Aussie accent on thick. "One hundred to one you couldn't stand out floating naked on your back down the river." Before Ethan could think of a comeback that involved something other than four-letter words, she picked up her fork and began eating.

My stomach was fluttery, and not from thoughts of desert assaults. With our ten o'clock mission looming, I could barely eat. "An FAV would be a poor investment. No odds needed," I said to Ethan, who shrugged like he didn't care.

"How much did you win in the lottery again?" I asked him.

"A cool two mil." He grinned like he'd just impressed

my socks and my most intimate undergarments right off me and he was liking the thought of that sight.

But frankly, that sum didn't impress me much.

"Lump sum or annual distribution?"

"Annual, baby. I'm a millionaire."

I gave him my deadpan look, like who was he kidding? "No, you're a guy who takes home roughly eighty thousand a year for the next twenty. If you invest that money, in time you'll be a millionaire. The lump sum would've been a better deal. I hope you didn't quit your day job."

"You crazy or what?" He grinned. "I can live on eighty thou a year."

I had a bad feeling about his finances. "Yeah, and assuming you're not already borrowing against that money," which many lottery winners do, "you'll run out of capital by the time you're forty-five."

He shrugged with the impunity of youth. As if forty-five could never happen to him.

"In the meantime I got plenty of free time for fun. You and me should get together after camp's over, Domino. I got a thing for brunettes."

"Good idea. I'll whip you into financial shape."

He gave me a lecherous grin. "You whipping me. I like that mental image."

Yeah, well, let him dream. He wouldn't like my financial whipping. I guarantee it.

The morning class began promptly at eight. Rockford led, passing out a thick sheaf of papers and lecturing through them with a PowerPoint presentation.

Today's topics: how to communicate secretly in an enemy environment; how to recognize booby traps and bombs and navigate minefields; how to survive a hostage situation; how to survive, and escape, when bound; how to jump from a moving car, with its corollary, how to escape from a trunk; and how to navigate without a compass.

Rockford was probably a dynamic enough speaker, if you preferred those military, commanding personas, but my mind wandered even as I wondered about the topics. Obviously, he was preparing us for the afternoon ambush and the eventual kidnapping. I should have been paying close attention. But instead I was going over Operation Break into Rockford's Office.

At the stroke of ten, Rockford dismissed class. Emma dashed off to make her quick change while I tailed Rockford to his office. Max kept hanging with me, making conversation with a monosyllabic me while I tried to shake him.

"That was some lecture. What do you think it means, Dom? Are they going to tie us up? Blow us up? Make us walk a minefield?" He matched me stride for stride.

"I dunno. Maybe." I wasn't really listening to him. I took a quick glance at my watch. I had six minutes before Emma pulled the alarm and not a second to waste.

I made my way to the main lobby with Max still at my elbow and watched as Rockford ducked into his office.

"Thirsty? Want to get a soda from the cafeteria?"

Max pulled some loose change from his pocket and flipped a coin in the air for me to see. "It's on me."

"Another time." I had my gaze fixed on Rockford's office.

"Yeah. Fine."

Max's tone made me turn and look at him. Dang! I'd hurt his feelings.

"Hey. Sorry. I'm not blowing you off. Really." I hadn't wanted to announce my visit to anyone, but I had to spare Max's feelings or feel like a heel. "I need to talk to Rockford."

Max's face creased into a frown.

"Just a few questions about my liability in yesterday's accident," I said, seeing his look of concern. "I'll catch you later."

Somewhat appeased, he nodded and walked off, glancing back over his shoulder at me several times before disappearing into the cafeteria. The CTs were slow in emptying the hall. I took a deep breath and headed for Rockford's office. I'd stuck a piece of tape to the inside hem of my tank top. As surreptitiously as possible, I palmed it.

Rockford's office door was open. As planned, I stuck my head in, leaning on the doorjamb and sticking the tape across the latch plate as I addressed Rockford.

"Sir?"

He glanced up at me from a pile of paperwork. I noted that he used one of those old-fashioned paper desk blotters. Excellent. That would be my first target.

"CT Domino." He didn't look particularly pleased to see me.

"I just wanted to let you know that I don't hold the camp or Torq responsible for that little mishap yesterday at the driving range." I tried not to sound rehearsed.

He arched a brow and I continued, stammering over my words like I was nervous. Only I was way past nervous. I was fevered, totally high on adrenaline and epinephrine like a junkie who'd just injected. And surprisingly, I loved the rush.

"I have no plans to sue, sir. Just wanted to put your mind at ease on that point." I gave the tape a little rub with my finger to make sure it was good and stuck.

"I've heard rumors that Torq is under investigation in the incident and I wanted to say that's really not necessary and we should all simply put this behind us and move on."

"You're telling me how to run my camp now, CT." He had a mean glare when he wanted to use it.

"No, sir. Just stating my opinion. I mean, no one was hurt. And the car was supposed to blow up anyway. . . ." I watched him closely for a reaction to my statement that would either deny or confirm that suspicion. I should have known better than to expect anything other than stoicism.

"I'll keep your suggestions in mind." Rockford was dismissing me. In counterpoint to his words, his tone said I could go to hell.

The old, timid Jenna would have probably crumpled under the weight of that look. But Domino the spy flashed him a smile, gave the doorjamb a good-bye thump, and pushed off.

We'd rehearsed my little Rockford encounter and allotted an estimated one minute for its completion. I glanced at my watch again as I headed for the ladies' room. Inside stall two, where we'd planted it the night before, I found a bag with my disguise.

I changed out of my tank top and bra, bound my breasts with a piece of athletic wrap that Emma kept for her bad knee, donned Ethan's newly washed, stiff-from-being-line-dried T-shirt with the picture of a large pot leaf on it, and dropped my clothes back in the bag. I twisted my hair up into a ponytail, donned my food-handling gloves and my panty hose–leg hat, and held on to my bag.

Then I peered cautiously out the ladies' room door. The main lobby was empty, as predicted. Lady Luck must've been on our side because today she was smiling. I looked at the security camera. Emma had accomplished step one of her part of the plan—she'd thrown a towel over the camera.

I waited for the alarm to sound, watching for my cue to dash—Rockford running by. And praying that Emma hadn't experienced any problems on her end. I kept an eye on my watch. At precisely six after ten, the fire alarm sounded and I breathed a sigh of both relief and anticipation. Rockford ran by just a few seconds later. The minute his back was to me, I slipped out on little spy feet and headed for his office.

He'd pulled the office door closed, as we'd anticipated. We were so darn clever. I gave it a gentle push and it fell open, no problem. I grinned like

Bond after he'd just seduced Largo's mistress. Then I slipped inside and closed the door.

We figured I had maybe a minute and a half to two minutes to complete my mission. I headed right for his desk. It was annoyingly clean. So were his in and out baskets—empty. No accident report in sight. No list of campers' registrations. Nothing! Did the man have to be so damn efficient?

Frustrated, I scanned the desk blotter. He'd written all over the top sheet. I crossed my fingers, hoping he'd doodled something useful on it as I lifted the top sheet from the two leather corners holding it down and removed the sheet just below it, stuffing the blank sheet in my bag before replacing the top sheet as it had been. I removed the second sheet from a scratch pad by his phone.

The wastepaper can was up next on my list. I peered in. It had been emptied recently and held nothing but a few used tissues and a candy bar wrapper.

I did a quick visual scan of the room, hoping maybe my camera would turn up. Nothing. Not that I expected it. If he'd taken it, it was probably in the safe. Which I tried. Locked tight.

I glanced at my watch again. I'd been in the office less than a minute, but I was already getting panicky flight-and-flee feelings. I pulled on every drawer in his file cabinet. Locked tight. His desk drawer held nothing but office supplies.

I heard the pitter-patter of grown-up feet dashing by the office door. I turned to go and caught sight of a slip of paper peeking out from beneath Rockford's file cabinet. What was a Bond girl wannabe to do? I grabbed it.

"What . . ." It was a torn printout of a travel itinerary. Someone had been in Vegas last month. Unfortunately, the passenger's name was ripped off, leaving me with only the flight times, dates, and destination.

Vegas? Don't tell me Rockford was a gambling man. Must have been a vacation.

I stuffed the paper back where I found it and fled.

Less than five minutes later, having stashed Ethan's T-shirt back in his pile of dirty clothes and ditched the papers in my room, I joined the group of CTs gathered outside under what shade they could find. To my relief, Emma had already joined them and stood with arms folded, shaking her head at the situation.

I called out to her, "Emma!"

She turned and waved to me.

"What happened here? Give me the scoop," I said as I approached her. I tried hard to sound casual. Not easy when I was elated and high from our break-in caper.

"Some idiot probably pulled the alarm as a prank." Disgust infused her voice. "It's another stinker out here today and I'm wilting in this heat. Where've you been? I was getting worried. You all right?" Emma put a hand on my arm and looked for confirmation I hadn't hit any snags.

"Great."

Emma nodded and relaxed, dropping her hand.

We'd thought of everything we could. I only hoped Max didn't put two and two together.

The alarm stopped blaring. As several of us stood around speculating about who the dirty rotten culprit was, Rockford stormed out the front entrance and began barking commands. Torq followed on his heels.

"Line up, CTs." Rockford carried the towel Emma had thrown over the lobby security camera. He held it out for us to see. "Someone here thinks they're mighty clever. I'll show you clever. Before we begin interrogating, anyone want to confess?"

Chapter Fourteen

No one was going to confess. Emma and I were ironclad, rock-solid, in lockstep, and no amount of torture was going to pry the truth out of us . . . I hoped. Everyone else thought it was all part of the camp scenario, just another spy game. For all they knew, Rockford had pulled the alarm all by his little lonesome just to rile us up. I'd give my fellow CTs credit, they were really into the spy game mind-set.

Rockford lined us up and marched us into the lobby. "The interrogation begins." He flashed us his Mr. Evil grin, complete with a menacing sparkle in his eye. "Ladies first. Ms. Peel, follow me. The rest of you wait here for your turn."

"Shit. What do you think he's gonna do to her?" Ethan's gaze followed Emma and Rockford out of the room.

"Prod her with electric shocks, probably." Ethan was easy to goad. Imagining Ethan's reaction if Rockford had indeed caught me-dressed-as-Ethan on tape and fingered him as the alarm puller gave me no end of amusement and kept my small mind from worrying too hard about Emma's interrogation. I crossed my fingers she'd been careful with that alarm and real good at dodging ink.

I sat on the sofa, sandwiched between John and Max, observing the group dynamics, trying to pick up clues to unravel the mysteries of camp. Ethan sat in a chair opposite me. Pussy sat in a chair to the right of him with Q buzzing around her like an attentive, attention-seeking fly. I wondered if he'd gotten into her tummy-control panties yet. Whether he had or not, she was definitely ready for him to buzz off. I think if she'd had a flyswatter, she would've whopped him a good one with it. I couldn't say as though I blamed her. Just watching him gave me a longing for my deluxe electric bug zapper back home at Bond Girl Wannabe HQ. The rest of the CTs clustered around us.

"Rockford must suspect Emma." Pussy smiled, full of knowing innuendo. Her eyes danced with malice, mirroring the glint of her mega-carat cubic zirconia necklace, but her voice was full of saccharine. "Why else would he call her in first?" Her gaze slid to me.

"'Cause Rockford has no clue who could've done the deed. He just picked Emma at random. Emma has no motive to pull a stunt like that. None." I let my tone and attitude imply that maybe Pussy did, though.

Pussy gave a condescending laugh. "Who does have motive? Who do you think did it?"

"Maybe you did, Pussy." I kept my tone casual.

"You seem to love the spotlight." I watched her reaction closely to see how she responded to a false accusation, thinking there could come a time when I'd be confronting her with what I believed to be the truth and the comparison could come in handy.

Pussy just shook her head and smiled. "Good imagining, Domino. Very creative, but sadly lacking in fact."

Next to me, I felt John stiffen. "Rockford seemed certain he'd find the perp. Why don't we let him handle this?" Poor John. He made a lame peace-keeper.

On the periphery of the group, Torq watched and grinned to himself before coming to the rescue. "To answer Ethan's original question—Rock will shine a black light on you. If he sees ink . . ." He made a throat-slitting motion with his finger, looking at me as he spoke.

I experienced a momentary shock of anxiety, tempered by being peeved that he'd pointed the fickle finger of suspicion at me. Did Torq know something or was he just funning? Remembering his mind-reading abilities, I quickly glanced down and laughed to cover my fear.

"Fry's going over the security tapes right now. We'll get to the bottom of this," Torq said. "Who-ever threw the towel over the camera should have left us a nice mug shot."

Just then, Emma emerged from Rockford's office, interrupting Torq's mind games with a great big grin. She gave us the thumbs-up. We were in the clear. I had to fight to conceal my exhilaration.

"Domino, you're up." Torq pointed toward Rockford's office.

"Do I have to? Why can't Pussy go next?" I put on a pout. "I'm sure she has more to hide than I do." I was only half-joking.

Everyone came up clean on the ink test. Disgusted, Rockford sent us to the firing range for our ten-thirty session. To tell the truth, I was a little disappointed in his interrogation skills . . . or lack of. I expected better from a former Special Forces guy. I mean, if he couldn't make *me* crack . . .

It was all Emma and I could do to play it cool. I could see she was dying to know what I'd found in Rockford's office. But information dissemination would have to wait. Fry and Torq presided as the ten of us took turns shooting at targets, five at a time, posed, arms locked in Rambo style, great big plastic earmuffs on to protect our hearing and make our ears sweat. Plus they rubbed uncomfortably on my Domino dangly earrings.

The firing range was outside in the open in the unrelenting heat. High temps generally made me irritable, and the sun was hell on my prized lily-white Seattle complexion. I was going through lotion and sunscreen by the gallon.

My turn came up. From the far end of the line of shooters, Torq was none too subtly eyeing my form—my shooting form. Whether he intended it to, his perusal cast a fluttery, warm-all-over spell on me, which threw my aim off. Okay, maybe my aim was never exactly on. Seeing my distress and lack of shooting ability, Torq came over to help me out. I took off my ear protection so I could hear him.

"A good marksman learns to control his breathing and pull the trigger between heartbeats to get the most accurate shot."

Yeah, well, I didn't say so, but I didn't think that was going to work. With Torq standing within a ten-foot radius of me there was no space between beats. Much to my chagrin, my heart was in hyperdrive.

He took a long look at my stance and form from the top of my head, past my breasts, my extended, gun-toting arms, down my waist, over my hips, down my legs, and past my ankles to the tips of my curling toes. He was definitely trying to get under my skin. And damn him, despite my best efforts to the contrary, he was succeeding extraordinarily well.

"Lock your elbows. You have to hold her steady." He held out his hand. "Let me show you the proper stance and grip. Here. Give me the gun."

I handed it over and he demonstrated, firing shots off in rapid succession, hitting the target dead center every time.

"Wow, lethal." I gave him the perusal right back. "You obviously have more self-control than I do."

"I don't have as much as you'd think." He grinned and handed me the gun. "You try."

I assumed the position as he assessed my stance.

"Let me just get you in the right position." He stepped in behind me and wrapped his arms around mine, his hands covering mine over the gun. "There. See how good proper form feels?"

If he meant that proper form was him pressed against my backside, then yeah, it felt great. But it was a guilty pleasure and one I should definitely be wary about, 'cause this could be another damn test.

"Okay, now pull the trigger. I'll help you absorb the shock from the kick. Ready?"

Unfortunately, from my perspective, he was the shock and the kick. I nodded anyway and squeezed the trigger. We hit the target dead center. I couldn't help smiling.

"See how easy that was?" His hot whisper teased my neck and ear and gave me an unexpected rush. He didn't help matters any, either, when he whispered again, using an extra-breathy voice, "Want to try it on your own?"

"I don't think I quite have the hang of it yet. Show me again?" I wasn't being coy. Well, okay, I was *trying* to be a little coy. Payback, mind you.

On the pretense of adjusting my grip, he leaned down and whispered into my ear again. "We need to talk. Why don't you stop by my cottage after dinner for a drink?"

My mouth went dry and I felt the telltale signs of worry—sweaty palms, adrenaline rush to the heart. Talk about what? That stupid, treacherous flirt test at the bar? A private apology would be in order there. About how I'd broken into Rockford's office? About the weather? It made a colossal difference to my anticipation and enjoyment of the evening. Not to mention my strategy.

I was definitely going to go. No doubt about that. Might as well admit I was addicted to intrigue. I'd been craving a look around his living quarters. Or maybe more accurately, a snoop around his cottage to see what I could turn up. Not to mention my feelings toward Torq mirrored Jane Austen's Mr. Darcy's toward Elizabeth—I liked Torq against my will, against my reason, and yes, even against my character.

But at least he waited patiently for my answer.

"As long as we don't talk about me being a dead woman, I'm game." I tried to sound nonchalant.

"Great." He squeezed my hand. "Ready?"

We pulled the trigger together—bull's-eye!

Fry dismissed class for lunch a few minutes late. Emma and I dashed back toward our rooms to "wash up."

"You had it going on with Torq in class." Emma gave a low whistle as we hurried down the hall.

"You think so?"

"I know so!" She looked genuinely astonished that I thought otherwise. "Looked to me like he wanted to take you right there on the firing range. Ethan and Bishop were taking bets on what was up with you two."

"He asked me over for drinks at his place later." I left out the "to talk" part.

She grinned. "You're going, of course."

"Natch." I opened the door to my room and we both tumbled in.

Emma closed the door, unable to contain herself any longer. "Can you believe we fooled Rockford?

We got away with espionage! We're brilliant, that's what we are!"

"To brilliance!" I gave her a high five.

"Okay, what did we find?" Emma said, all expectance. "What did you get? I'm dying of curiosity. It was all I could do in class not to ask."

I pulled the two papers from the drawer where I'd stashed them. "From his notepad and his desk blotter," I said by way of explanation.

Emma grabbed a pencil and did a rubbing of the notepad first. It had a few phone numbers listed, but nothing else.

"His girlfriends, you think?" She arched her brow comically.

We both cracked up.

The desk blotter was covered mostly with doodles and notes that were hard to read, partly because there were so many imprints, and partly because they were evidently in Rockford's personal shorthand and almost illegibly sloppy handwriting.

"Hey, look at this," Emma said, pointing to a drawing she'd rubbed out. "That's a diagram of the training room. And look at these arrows."

I leaned in to inspect it. "It looks like an attack plan to me."

She nodded. "I think we've discovered how the kidnapping is going to go down. They're going to burst in on us in the last training session Thursday night and take one of us."

"Yes, but who?"

Neither of us had the answer, so we simply stared at each other.

"What do we do now?" I asked.

Emma glanced at her watch and scooped up the evidence. "Don't know. We'll figure it out later. Right now, we'd better scoot to the cafeteria and eat. I have the feeling we're going to need our strength."

After lunch we met in front of the main compound building. We'd been instructed to wear sunscreen and dress for combat in clothes we didn't mind getting dirty. Two FAVs done up in desert camouflage waited for us.

Rockford greeted us. "All right, CTs, listen up. This afternoon we'll be participating in a desert ambush, just like you might experience if you were in the U.S. military.

"These are our vehicles." He patted one of the FAVs. "Let me introduce you to them. These little honeys are the cream of the crop, built by Mercedes-Benz. The German Bunderswehr, that's the German army for you civilians, uses these. The U.S. Marine Corps has used them as their interim FAV of choice.

"Each FAV has a ninety-horsepower engine that can drive up to eighty miles per hour. Each vehicle seats six—one driver and five passengers. . . ."

He rattled off some more statistics. I've never figured out why men are so impressed by these numbers. Me, I didn't even know what they meant, but I fully expected that at any moment Rockford would open the hood and everyone would take a look and be expected to "ooooh" and "aaaah" over

it. Sure enough, Rockford popped the hood. Emma
and I exchanged an "oh, brother" look, shaking our
heads in unison. Let's face it, in my book, you've
seen one engine, you've seen too many. Emma and
I stood back and let the boys, with Pussy at their
center, enjoy the show.

The FAVs looked like Jeeps or pickup trucks with
backseats. Each had a covered cab. In the bed of the
truck, two two-person seats faced each other. A roll
bar at the back of the truck bed topped off the en-
semble.

I turned to Emma. "I want to ride up front. I'm in
no mood to be wind-struck. Let the boys eat dust."

"I'm with you all the way," Emma said. "Ladies
should get to ride up front. It's only polite."

As the guys ogled the engine, Jim and Greg, the
NASCAR stunt-driving guys, came out of the building. They wore helmets and fatigues and looked
ready for battle.

Rockford looked up from his dissertation on
engine specs. "Our drivers have arrived." The guys
backed off and Rockford slammed the hood shut.

He gave us a quick lecture on battle strategy, how
to scan for ambushers, how to communicate on the
battlefield without giving away information to the
enemy, and reminded us about safety. Then he divided us into two groups. Emma, Max, Hawaiian-
shirted Wade, Pussy, and I were in one. Ethan,
Bishop, Tanner, Q, and John in the other.

I turned to Emma. "Think he's stacking the deck
here?"

"You mean by putting all three of us ladies in the

same squad?" She gave me a gentle elbow in the side. "Sure he is. We're going to kick those men's butts but good."

"No, I meant putting Wade on our team. That Hawaiian shirt could glow in the dark. Double or nothing our current wager that he's the first one out."

"Those are shitty odds," Emma said, considering. "But what the heck, I'm a risk taker. You're on."

I didn't think it mattered much because I had a feeling Emma wasn't ever going to pay up. And I'd pretty much lost track of how much she owed me anyway.

Rockford selected squad leaders for each team. We got stuck with Wade as our fearless leader.

I rolled my eyes at Emma as Rockford issued us laser-tag weapons that looked like machine guns, helmets with lights on top, and two-way radios.

I stared at the helmet. Another good hair-extension day shot to hell, hopefully not literally.

"We'll be playing laser tag today." Rockford showed off a laser machine gun. "It's less painful and more accurate than paintball." He looked directly at me.

Okay, so I'd complained once or twice to Torq about how the paintballs smarted. So now I was branded a baby?

"These guns use a safe, reliable, high-tech infrared system that includes a red dot scope with a five hundred-plus-foot range and anti-cheating technology. When you're hit," Rockford continued, "your gun makes a sound and the sensors on your helmet light up to indicate your status. Your gun is then automatically disabled for the remainder of the game." He gave a quick demonstration on how to use the weapon, showing us what a "hit" looked and sounded like. "Any questions?"

"How do we disable a vehicle?" Tanner asked.

Rockford smiled at him like he was Mr. Brilliant himself. "Excellent question. You take out the vehicle by hitting the driver. For this exercise, only camp staff are allowed to drive the FAVs. So protect your driver at all costs or you'll be defending yourself on foot. Anything else?"

He looked around the group, but no one had any more questions.

"Good. Let's load up. Squad leaders ride up front with the drivers," Rockford said. "I'll see you CTs later. Good luck with your mission."

Emma and I grumbled and climbed into a seat to sit side by side. Max and Pussy sat across from us. No one spoke as we put on our helmets and buckled up. The air was rife with anticipation, tension, and nerves.

I was actually feeling relieved. Lunch had passed with no revelations from the security videotapes. Sitting next to me, Emma was happily tapping her foot and humming. Across from me, a bored Pussy was putting the moves on Max, damn her conniving soul.

We were in FAV2. Greg drove. On a signal from Rockford, Greg fired up the engine and did zero to 80 in seconds flat, throwing me into Emma's shoulder. We flew down the road through the orange groves, past the handling shack, past the trainers' cottages, and out into the open with the 100-degree air whizzing past us. Jim drove the lead FAV. Just past the groves, he turned off the road and into the desert sand.

Cacti and brush zoomed past. All of us sat with idiot grins plastered to our faces, whooping and hollering like teenagers as Greg turned and spun in the sand. Riding in FAV2 was like riding a desert roller coaster—all unexpected spins, turns, and drops through gullies.

I sat my gun in my lap and held both hands above my head, just like I did on roller coasters. "Look! No hands."

Emma nudged me. "Better keep your gun at ready, Domino. We could come under attack at any moment."

Wade turned around and shouted over the rush of the wind and the roar of the engine. "All of you, keep your eyes peeled for signs of enemy vehicles." He turned back around and leaned his gun out the window as he searched the horizon with binoculars for signs of enemy troops.

I turned to Emma. "Who do you think the attackers will be?"

"Fry, Torq, and Rockford, most likely."

I nodded my agreement.

Greg surged ahead, swerving to avoid a giant saguaro. We headed toward the empty Hassayampa River. Greg drove full-bore down one side of the riverbank into the wash below and back up the far bank, zigzagging his way across the river in a pattern that made us lose our stomachs at regular intervals.

I smelled a setup. The riverbed was the perfect

place to attack us. We couldn't see into the distance any farther than the riverbank. Any old ambusher could surprise us by rushing from over the bank. Greg read my thoughts.

"They can't see us, either," he said, smiling at us in the rearview mirror. "Keep your eyes peeled. We're more vulnerable, but we're also stealthier down here."

Just as he finished speaking, an FAV came barreling over the far bank on our right rear flank, closing fast. Two gunners rode in the back. One attacker drove.

"Look! There they are." Max pointed them out to the rest of us, though we'd all spotted them already, and judging from their expressions, everyone felt the same rush of adrenaline and fear. Everyone but Pussy. She just looked bored.

"One vehicle." I gave the others a smug smile. "Without Davie, that's all the manpower they can muster. We're going to kick their ass." Okay, I spouted more bravado than I felt, but someone needed to build up the troops.

Greg floored it. I sneaked a peek at the speedometer. We were topped out at 80 mph.

Trying to show off, Wade yelled something about evasive action. Jim drove FAV1 up the bank and out of our sight. I hoped Wade and the FAV1 gang had a plan. I would've sent them off to either double back and cover our flank or lie in wait up ahead. Max, Emma, and I readied our weapons.

The enemy let FAV1 go and barreled in on us.

Greg kept the pedal to the floor as the enemy closed the gap and Wade yelled commands.

I was so high on thrill that the 007 theme played in my mind. I hummed it out loud.

"Would you stop?" Emma said.

"Oh, come on, you all hear it, too." I kept humming. "You know, this reminds me of that scene where Bond is racing down the mountain toward Monte Carlo and a Ferrari overtakes him," I said to Emma. "Or the chase through Hong Kong on the motorcycle handcuffed to China's top agent, Wai Lin." I could picture myself as a Wai Lin–type character—beautiful top agent and lethal shot on the run. "Only an FAV is way better than a motorcycle."

"Yeah, but we aren't handcuffed to Bond. That's a handicap I could get used to." Emma didn't look at me but kept her sights on the approaching enemy FAV.

"I don't like this," Max said. "They let FAV1 go too easily."

I aimed my gun at the approaching vehicle, waiting for a clear shot. "What else could they do? We outnumber them twelve to three."

He gave me a "yeah, but . . ." look.

Okay, so they were well trained and experienced. We still outnumbered them. I wasn't *that* worried.

I turned to Emma, whose eyes were afire with adrenaline. She had her sights trained on the driver and windshield. "When they get within range, that driver is mine."

Greg picked a path through the center of the

riverbed, dodging outcrops of rock and dips and bumps in the terrain, trying to lose our ambusher.

Unfortunately, whoever drove for the enemy matched Greg's skill. We were several lengths ahead of our pursuers, but each time Greg swerved, our pursuers made up ground.

Wade shouted into his two-way, communicating with FAV1.

"I hope he's directing them to come around and cover our flank or launch a sneak attack as we lure the enemy past them," I said to the group at large.

Wade spun around in his seat to face us. "Hold your fire. Wait for my signal."

"One. Two—"

"Over there." Max pointed to the riverbank on our left where an FAV appeared from nowhere over the edge of the bank and headed directly into our path to cut us off.

"Shit! Hold your fire." Wade got back on his two-way, screaming for backup as the first enemy FAV gained on us.

"Everyone hold on!" Greg said. "Let the fun begin."

He slowed our FAV and executed a perfect bootlegger, then gunned it and zoomed back past the first enemy vehicle.

Once we recovered our equilibrium, those of us in the back whooped and yelled.

"Whoohoo, fooled you!" Emma yelled just as a volley of fire erupted.

Our euphoria was short-lived. The enemy let fly a serious round of fire. Their aim was deadly accurate.

"What are they using, automatic lasers?" I ducked just in time to avoid being hit.

Across from me, Pussy's gun sounded off and her helmet lit up. "They got me," she said with a complete lack of enthusiasm.

Emma leaned into me. "Pussy's first out, not Wade. You owe me what now? Eighty bucks maybe?"

"I owe you nothing. Pussy wasn't even trying." I shot Pussy a look full of daggers. "We have a *Pussy* down," I yelled up to Wade. I wanted to say "wussy," but I was being nice.

The enemy FAVs executed their own perfect bootleggers and roared back in hot pursuit.

"Damn, those guys can drive, too," Emma said, stating the obvious. "It must be a stunt driver's holiday out here. Where'd they recruit all these boys from?"

Just as she spoke, Wade got off the radio. "FAV1's under heavy fire. They're calling for backup."

"*They're* calling for backup?" Emma and I said in unison.

"How many of these guys are there?" I looked at Emma, who shrugged.

"I don't know, but I'm not going down without firing a shot." Emma took aim and fired behind us at the two FAVs, which were just in range of our guns. Both shots hit.

"I hadn't noticed before that you're such a good shot," I said to her as I got off my own round.

"Just lucky."

My shots went high.

Greg gunned it through the laser fire and sped us

around a bend in the river, temporarily taking us out of sight of our pursuer.

Emma's gun whooped and her helmet light came on. "Damn, damn, damn! I'm out." She tossed her gun on the floor in disgust.

"We need a plan," I said, turning to Wade. "What do we do now?"

"I don't know," he said through clenched teeth. "Dead men don't make plans."

That's when I noticed his helmet.

"You, too?"

"And me," Greg said. "I'm going to have to pull over."

I glanced around wildly, feeling panic settling in.

"I'm still standing," Max said, giving me a thumbs-up.

I gave him a halfhearted return thumbs-up, trying to hide my disappointment. Going up against Fry and Torq with only Max at my side wasn't a thrilling prospect. Given a choice between him and Pussy, I'd be tempted to choose Pussy. At least she'd show them some cleavage and make a valiant effort to charm and seduce them, giving me a chance to escape and go for reinforcements. A man is a man is a man in her book. And they're all good.

Greg took us down the riverbed and pulled behind a large cactus before cutting the engine. "This is the best I can do for you guys. You're on your own now."

I took control. "We'll have to go on foot. If they catch us here, we're dead."

"Right, chief. The old go-on-foot trick. That gets them every time." Max nodded his agreement.

I rolled my eyes.

We unbelted and jumped from the truck, running toward the next bend in the river, with the roar of an FAV close on our tails. Powered by adrenaline and sheer survival instinct, I was pumping, really running for it. Max was six inches taller than me, with long strides and the build of a distance runner, but I managed to keep pace with him. Luck must have been on our side. We rounded the corner before the enemy FAV came into sight behind us.

"Take cover there," Max said, pointing to a large rock. We both collapsed against it, panting from the exertion and heat.

"What now?" I was really sucking wind. Probably spies should get more exercise than sitting behind a desk, looking at numbers ten hours a day. I made a mental note to renew my 24 Hour Fitness membership when I got back.

"I don't think they spotted us. They'll stop to inspect the vehicle and then come looking for us once they notice we're missing." He wiped the sweat from his brow with the back of his hand. "Our only hope is to lie in wait and ambush them when they head this way."

Okay, Max was smart. That was good. I nodded my agreement.

He wiped his brow again and frowned before pulling his water bottle from his belt. "We should be sweating more. We'd better rehydrate before moving on. If we get heatstroke, we're toast out here."

I heeded his advice. The temperature was easily

over one hundred, the sun, blistering. I took my water bottle from my belt and took a swig. Max did the same.

"Here's as good a place as any to wait for them." I tapped the large rock we leaned against.

He shook his head no. "We'd be better off splitting up. The old divide-and-conquer trick."

"Yeah, but we're supposed to be dividing *them,* not us." I took another swig of water and put the bottle back on my belt.

Max grinned and pointed downstream, if you can call any place in a dry riverbed downstream. "We don't have much time. You stay here. You're the better shot. I'll head that way and catch whatever you miss."

We tuned our radios to the same frequency and Max headed off, running downriver toward the next bend. We seemed to have ended up on the twisty-turny part of the river that snaked its way along in tight curves. Max planned to ambush them from the next bend.

He was maybe a hundred yards from me when an armed man stepped from behind an outcropping on the far side of the river and took aim at him.

Max saw him before I could let loose a scream to alert him and began running with the attacker in pursuit. I took aim, but they were both out of range of my weapon. All I could do was say a little prayer for Max.

Max was quick, but the attacker was quicker, athletically built, and moving stealthily and confidently like a predatory soldier. He was closing the gap quickly.

Max panicked. Rather than turning to face his attacker and fire, he kept running toward the bend, looking back over his shoulder like a coward.

"Turn and face him," I muttered, willing him some intestinal fortitude. "Stand and fight like a real CT."

I considered running after them, but not being a world-class sprinter, there was no way I'd catch them. Since I was the team's last hope, I was better off waiting to ambush whoever else happened by. Nevertheless, I was riveted to the scene before me.

"Go, Max, go!" I muttered, willing him to run faster.

Max tripped and stumbled, nearly falling. He caught himself and continued on. The attacker had slowed and was taking deliberate aim just as Max, still looking back over his shoulder, put on a burst of speed, lengthening his stride.

Then Max stumbled forward and screamed, falling out of sight as if off a ledge.

"Maaaxxx!!"

Chapter Fifteen

The attacker ran toward the spot where Max had fallen off the face of the earth and peered over the edge, making what I assumed was a gesture of victory. I couldn't see his face. His back was toward me.

I was stoked with worry. How dare Max scare me like this and leave me all alone to fight the bad guys. How dare he take that theatrical fall! AND HOW DARE EVIL ATTACK MAN SHOOT MY FRIEND!

I was going to get retribution on the bad man. And then I was going to kill Max for frightening the spit out of me.

With Evil Attack Man's attention diverted, I sneaked up on him, intent on taking him out, payback for Max. I sighted my weapon, aimed carefully, and prayed. I figured I had only one shot to do the job. After that, he'd be alerted to my presence. I concentrated on everything Torq had taught me at the firing range, felt Torq's hand guiding mine and steadying my aim. I took a deep breath and held it. Then I squeezed the trigger.

Attack Man's gun sounded and his helmet light went off.

"Got you, sucker." I punched the air with my own gesture of victory.

Evil Attack Man started and spun to face me.

"Fry?"

"Domino?"

Was that relief or irritation in his voice?

"I need y'all's help. Max's taken a spill." Hard to tell over his stoic, tough-guy exterior exactly what he felt as he pointed to the spot where I'd seen Max fall off into oblivion. He looked a little pale. "We need nine-one-one."

I hesitated, confused. Max wasn't just hamming it up?

"Domino? Y'all okay?" Fry frowned and took a step toward me. "Buck up and pull it together, CT. This is no time to panic. We need to radio for help . . . now!"

I took a step back from him, not exactly cowering, but not a tower of heroism, either.

"I yelled at him to stop, but the fool ran right over the ledge," Fry said softly. "I can't get anyone on my radio. We'll have to try yours. I hope to hell he didn't break his neck. Toss me your radio, Domino." He prepared to make a catch.

"No. I'll call." No way was I giving up my one line of communication to Fry.

Fry seemed to hesitate. "Tell them we need the cops."

"The cops?"

Without thinking, I dashed to the ledge. Fry lunged for me, trying to stop me, but I dodged him. My fear for Max temporarily overrode my fear of falling from heights.

"Ohmygosh." Looking down at Max, I felt as if I'd lost all my breath.

He lay at the bottom of a twenty-foot drop, his body sprawled at an unnatural angle.

And beneath him, cushioning his fall, was a very dead Davie.

Fry put his arm around me and pulled me away from the edge. "Y'all shouldn't have seen that."

I couldn't get the image of a dead, bloodless Davie from my mind. Someone had taken a knife to him. I shivered in the Arizona sun.

Torq pulled up, jumped from an FAV, and sprinted to the ledge next to us. I watched his back as he stared over the edge. Finally, he turned toward us, seemingly unfazed by the death below him. "It'll take the cops from Surprise half an hour to get here. Let's go get Max."

By the time we reached Max with the FAV, he was slowly coming to, and I was weak with relief. As weak with relief as a person who's just seen her first dead body outside of a funeral can be. Torq snapped a quick shot of the scene with his cell phone before he and Fry loaded Max into the waiting FAV.

Fry stayed with the body while Torq drove us back to camp and waiting medical help.

Mercifully, Max didn't gain full consciousness until we'd pulled out of sight of Davie's body.

"Don't tell me I fell off a cliff," he said, blissfully

unaware of what had broken his fall and probably saved his life.

If he could joke, he must have been feeling better.

I'd calmed down enough to give him an encouraging return grin. "You fell off a cliff, Max."

Emotion stole my voice as I sat beside him. Two days. Three close calls. Davie dead, and not by accident. I shuddered in the heat.

"I asked you not to tell me that!" He tried to laugh. "Ouch! That hurts." He quieted into a smile. "I missed certain death by that much!" Max held up his finger and thumb to show us just how narrow his escape had been.

Torq and I exchanged a look. We let Max chatter on happily. He'd find out about Davie soon enough.

The mission was a total and utter failure for those of us on the CT side. The enemy ambushed FAV1 and took everybody out in less than a minute. And Max, facing every kind of danger imaginable on this mission, and loving it, was going to make a full and complete recovery with only a sand burn or two as souvenirs. Davie, however, was not.

I was the only CT left standing in either FAV, probably because no one had thought to shoot me after Max's accident and word got out about Davie. A hollow victory for me.

The cops were waiting for us when we arrived at camp. They interrogated Torq and me separately.

There was nothing I could tell them. I'd seen Davie lying dead. That was it.

They were scouring Davie's room and the common areas of the FSC main building when I met Torq in the lobby after talking to the cops.

"You going to be okay?" he asked, regarding me closely, probably for signs of stress and trauma.

I felt tapped out and in shock, but I nodded anyway. I don't think I convinced him. "Will they send us home now? Davie was obviously . . ." I couldn't say the word.

"We have one more day of camp," he said circumspectly. "The cops will probably want everyone around for at least that long. We may as well finish out your vacation."

"But Davie—"

"Rockford has already talked to the police about tightening security measures. I don't think anyone else is in danger. For the rest of camp, FSC is the safest place to be."

I nodded again. I wanted to ask him who he thought did it. But now didn't seem to be the appropriate time.

He put a gentle hand on my arm. "I have to get back to work." Then he leaned in and whispered, "Eight. My place."

He winked and was off, leaving me suppressing a heavy sigh of high anxiety and anticipation in his wake for so many reasons. His tone could've been taken several ways—"I'm looking forward to some Bond-type fun" (and the billions of us who've ever watched a Bond movie know what that means) or

"Let's put our heads together about this Davie thing," or "I'm looking forward to interrogating you about the fire alarm affair until you reach the hardboil-and-crack stage."

Call me bad for going giddy and excited about Torq, especially in light of Davie's traumatic death and Max's only hours-old preempted date with death in the desert. Where was my sympathy? My compassion? My sense of timing? My fear, for heaven's sake?

Lost somewhere to my lust drive, I suspected, along with my good sense. 'Cause my Torq fantasies were strictly X-rated. But for now, I needed to get back to business.

I needed to talk to Max. What, exactly, did he remember?

An hour later, they brought Max back to his room and I popped by to check on him.

Max looked tired, but his color had returned. A bruise I hadn't noticed before discolored his right cheek and he had a cold compress pressed against the side of his head, concealing a nasty bump.

"You're looking much improved." I tried to hide my worry by going overly perky. "How are you feeling?"

"I have one hell of a headache, but I'll live. You didn't think the old fall-off-a-cliff trick would do me in, did you?" He gave a weak grin and propped himself up on his pillows. "Sit down. I could use the company."

I pulled a chair next to his bed, but before sitting,

I played Florence Nightingale and fluffed his pillows for him. "What did Rockford's doc say?"

"I'll be stiff and sore, but I'll live. He gave me some extra-strength painkillers to get me through the night and told me to rest."

"Maybe I should go, then . . . ." I was just being polite but hoping he'd ask me to stay.

"Sit. Talking isn't going to wear me out. Maybe it'll take my mind off . . ." Max paused. We both knew he was thinking of Davie. "Just promise that if I fall asleep on you, you won't take it personally. As soon as these painkillers kick in, I won't be able to keep my eyes open."

"I'm surprised the reading material in the sick-room didn't anesthetize you already. I don't suppose Rockford's picked up any new magazines since yesterday?"

"I couldn't tell. Double vision."

"Damn that double vision." I held up one finger. "I've always wondered how that worked. How many fingers am I holding up?"

He forced a weak grin. "One. You can quit with the doctor games. I'm better now."

"Max, something's been bothering me. . . ."

"Yeah?"

Figuring his memory of events was never going to be better, I bludgeoned away with my rude question. "Why did you fall over that ledge? What distracted you so much that you didn't notice it? From where I was, your fear looked real."

"A rattler, that's what they tell me." He winced and reached for a glass of water on the nightstand as he readjusted himself and set down the compress he'd been holding against his head.

I leaned over and handed the glass to him. "A snake?" They were certainly sticking to the party line. "Are you sure? Who told you? How did they know?"

"Hold up with the rapid-fire questions. My head hurts enough as it is and my mind isn't up to full speed." Max paused, clearly trying to concentrate and gather his thoughts. "Fry told me. Said he saw the markings in the sand above the ledge. And, no, I'm not sure. I can't remember a thing after getting out of the FAV until I woke up with you all crowding around me. Perfectly natural with a minor head injury and concussion. And to quote Indiana Jones, 'I hate snakes.' Would I rather jump off a ledge than face a rattler poised to strike? Probably. But I think I just tripped."

I frowned.

"What? What did you see?" Max looked interested, not worried.

I told him what I remembered, how he'd been looking back at Fry. Privately, I wondered if Fry could have been threatening him with a real gun, something that would definitely scare Max over the edge. In my estimation, Max had nearly been run down twice and now he'd been scared off a cliff onto a dead body. Fry could have been driving the car at Hal's. He could have shot my tire out on the driving range, and he'd certainly scared Max over the edge. Anyone could have killed Davie, but I still hadn't figured out why. Who'd want to kill a driving instructor?

Back to Fry—what if he was a hired assassin? Didn't old spies go bad for money every day? They did in Bond flicks.

"Could Fry have been testing you?" I asked.

Max shook his head. "I don't remember. Maybe. But why would Fry lie?"

"To avoid a lawsuit," I said, but that's not what I was thinking. "Max, how much money did you win in the lottery?"

He laughed and then winced, putting the compress back to his head. "Thinking about becoming a gold-digger and going after me for my money now?"

"In your dreams," I said. "No, Max, I'm just trying to piece things together and I'm curious."

"A hundred and fifty million."

I whistled under my breath. "Wow!" One hundred and fifty million reasons for murder. Max had to be the richest guy at camp by a mere hundred million or so.

"What are you thinking?" Max asked, watching me closely, probably trying to use his mind-reading training to see where my little gray cells were leading.

"Three accidents in two days. Three near misses . . ."

"You think someone's trying to kill me for my money?" He sounded more amused by the idea than upset.

"Why not? It's happened to other lottery winners."

"Not to me," he said emphatically. "I don't have

any enemies." He grinned. "And I made damn sure that everyone listed in my will has plenty of their own money . . . just to guard against this kind of thing."

"But how can you be sure one of those people hasn't already blown through their wad and wants more?" I argued.

"No one's trying to kill me. You'd be better off figuring out who'd want Davie dead," he stated in a tone that said case closed, discussion over. He yawned and I took that as my cue to leave. But that didn't mean I agreed with him. Davie may be dead, but I was still convinced that Max had been a target. I just couldn't figure out how Davie fit in. Yet.

In our collective opinion, Emma's and mine, Bond girls wore only a few selections of outfits: black leather—definitely too hot for an Arizona summer; evening gown—sorry, didn't bring one; short shorts; or bathing suits. Probably there was at least one bathing suit–clad babe per movie. So we settled on my prop bikini and a sarong for my evening visit with Torq. Obvious? Maybe.

But, as Emma said, "Why did FSC send you that bikini if they didn't want you to wear it? If now's not the time to be in character, I don't know when is. Plus, he has to see you in a bikini at least once. How else are you going to work up to a hot spy-sex evening?"

"I'm not sure that's what he has in mind," I said, thinking the evening could be more like heavy interrogation than heavy petting.

Emma rolled her eyes. "Oh, please."

I wasn't sure that was what I had in mind, either, but there was that recurring "satin sheet, rolling around in a fancy hotel bed with a tousled Bond" fantasy of mine. Camp had fulfilled many of my Bond fantasies, so why not go at least a few bases toward that one?

Nervous as I was about showing off my bikini-clad body, Emma made a good point. And thanks to Logan and her insistence on buying me silicone bra inserts, I now filled my glamorous, gorgeous, hot-pink FSC number. Plus the inserts made for maximum jiggle value. The bottoms were pure string bikini. Tie the matching sarong low around the waist, add my pair of heeled, jeweled sandals, and I may as well have been wearing an evening gown. Two Bond girl outfits killed with one. Double the value!

And wearing a swimsuit both allowed for an evening swim and eliminated the need for matching underwear, something I'd always been self-conscious about. Until this latest birthday shopping spree, I don't think I'd even owned a matching lingerie set. I mean, I tried to do my best to wear white panties with white bras, but that was as far as I ever took things. Because, come down to it, in the underwear department, I voted for serviceability and function over style almost every time.

Emma had straightened my hair so that it hung long and shiny around my shoulders like a model's in a shampoo commercial.

"Like the mates like it," she said.

My lips were plumped, my makeup primed so that it wouldn't melt off in the still insufferable heat, and a light, natural coat of foundation, blush, eyeliner, mascara, and shadow applied.

I squirted a dab of the fuck-me perfume on my wrists and rubbed it on my neck, behind my ears, and between my cleavage. Just in case I had to resort to using my sex appeal to gain information. Emma grabbed the bottle to douse me again. I pulled it out of her grasp before she could make her move.

"Careful with that! It's potent stuff." I grinned.

She returned my grin and stepped back to admire her handiwork. "Damn, I'm good. I should've been a makeup artist." She handed me my purse. "Now off with you. Have fun and don't do anything I wouldn't do."

I shook my head and shot her a look. "I don't think you have to worry about that."

She grinned back. "I wouldn't be so sure. If you'd just let the inner Bond girl out . . ."

Chapter Sixteen

Torq answered the door before I had a chance to knock. In direct opposition to my Bond fantasy, he wasn't wearing a tuxedo, or even a white linen suit, but cargo shorts and a T-shirt, Arizona casual. Arizona dressy, for that matter. On him, the look was simply scorching hotness. Still damp and curling over his forehead and ears, his hair had obviously been freshly washed. His face had that just-shaved smooth softness that I so love in a man; that makes me fantasize about kissing him all over . . . with a lot of tongue and sucking and licking involved. Even nervous and possibly about to be interrogated, I had to clench my fists, which tingled with the urge to run my fingers over his firm jawline and stroke his cheeks.

Torq invited me in with a sweep of his arm and a long, slow perusal of my outfit, followed by an appreciative smile that sent my heart fluttering and gave me hope that his thoughts had drifted toward my version of shower fantasies. "You look gorgeous tonight. That pink"—he paused—"outfit is *very* flattering." His tone said "sexy."

"Thank you." I suck at retorts—seductive, snappy, or otherwise. Nothing short of a miracle was going to change that. At least I'd learned the two-word art of graciously receiving a compliment and not denigrating myself or explaining the compliment away as I was prone to do. "Have you heard anything more about Davie, the poor man? Any suspects?"

Torq shook his head no. "Let's forget about Davie tonight and just enjoy ourselves."

Torq and Davie had been coworkers, maybe even friends. I decided to respect his wishes. He didn't need me throwing salt on his wounds.

Torq ushered me in and offered me a seat on the sofa. His cottage was decorated in muted Southwest colors, obviously done by a decorator, and had more of a hotel than homey feel. The only inklings of his personality were the wide array of electronic toys splashed around the place—the large plasma TV, an Xbox gaming system, a Bose stereo system . . . the list went on.

The cottage was open and spacious but couldn't have been over seven or eight hundred square feet. His great room linked to a small dining area and kitchen. He walked to the kitchen and returned with a bowl of tortilla chips, a dish of guacamole, and another of salsa. He set them on the coffee table in front of me, along with a handful of napkins and several small plates.

"Help yourself. I made the guacamole myself."

"A man who can cook?" I was wondering about

his hospitality. When did the grilling begin? And I didn't mean on the barbecue.

"A man who can squash avocados." He grinned again and walked back to the kitchen counter, where he had a row of mixers and bottles of alcohol displayed in a makeshift bar. "I promised you a drink. What can I get you? I have Hal's Flirtini recipe."

Remembering my mission, and my last drinking binge with him, I reluctantly decided to play it safe, though I really could have used a drink to loosen me up. "No thanks. I don't think I'm up for another encounter with the KGB."

He laughed. "Too bad. Once I finally found it, I realized I have plenty of it. That KGB is elusive, but damn effective."

"Yes . . . it is." I smiled and wondered when the real interrogation would begin. "Can you make a Shirley Temple version of the Flirtini? That, I could go for."

"You mean the Surely Temptini?" He winked and reached for a drink shaker from an assorted collection on the shelf next to him. I always imagined James collected martini shakers, so I wasn't at all disappointed that Torq did.

I raised a brow and crossed my legs, letting my sarong fall back to reveal my legs from my toes to midthigh as I watched him work. Two could play at temptini. "As long as it's surely nonalcoholic. I'm the designated walker tonight. Shaken, not stirred, of course."

"Of course. Coming right up." He poured pineapple and cranberry juice over ice in a silver penguin-shaped shaker, added a squeeze of fresh lime, and shook it up. Then he muddled a few raspberries in the bottom of a cocktail glass, poured the juice blend over them, topped it with 7-Up, and garnished it with a sprig of mint.

He finished making his own drink, brought mine over, and settled dangerously near me on the couch. I say dangerously, because I felt my heart pulsing toward that darn dog mode again. Only this time it had a distinct sexual edge to it, so maybe you could say it headed toward bitch-in-heat mode.

"Cheers." He raised his glass toward mine and we clinked.

I took a sip of my drink. "Almost better than Hal's alcoholic version," I said and licked my lips. A bad, nervous habit, I know, but Torq seemed to like it.

"Thanks. I graduated from mixology school."

When I gave him a surprised, questioning look, he laughed. "Did an undercover stint as a bartender once." He reached for a chip, then settled back, examining me and my freshly licked lips.

"Devious." I took a chip myself. "That confirms the stories I've heard about secret-stealing agents hanging out in bars. I just always assumed the spies were on the other side of the counter. Glad to know our government is twisting the stereotype on its ear. Did you enjoy it?" I asked. "Or was it not a real-you thing?" I didn't try to keep the barb out of my voice. He deserved a dig for setting me up with that "wanting to be the real me" line.

He grinned sheepishly like he knew I'd just zinged him. "The tips were good. Loved the hours. The sob stories sucked."

"It's easy to become jaded, I suppose," I sympathized. "You didn't answer my second question."

"That's classified information." He was cute when he smiled enigmatically.

"Is that like taking the Fifth? Anything you don't want to say is classified?" I spoke lightly, but with enough of an edge to let him know I wasn't your ordinary cream puff.

"Something like that."

We reached for a chip in unison. Our fingers grazed, lingering flirtatiously. My Domino bikini gave me surprising confidence.

When I called his bluff and didn't withdraw mine from his or the bowl, he reached for his drink instead, saying, "Why talk about me when we can discuss something interesting?"

"Why do I have the feeling you have a specific something interesting in mind?" I finished off my chip and took another sip of my zero-proof beverage, hoping it had miraculously morphed into something strong enough to cure my case of nerves.

He laughed in a totally flattering, charming way, like I was the most entertaining and delightful woman he knew. Witty. Vibrant. Totally engrossing. "Dom, you are one intriguing and perceptive woman."

He set his drink down and leaned back against the sofa, sprawling his arm along the back so close to my bare shoulders that I could feel his body heat and smell the spicy scent of that pheromone-packed cologne of his. "How about that fire alarm caper you pulled this morning? I find that interesting and very clever. Feel free to brag openly. I'm all ears." He watched me with an amused look in his eyes. "I'm dying to know what you got from Rockford's office."

My bravado faltered. The man knew how to flirt and charm. Damn him. He also knew how to feign every expression and emotion known to mankind. I could probably trust him just about as far as I could toss his heavily muscled six-foot-plus frame. We already knew that was zero. Just how did he know it was me? And, more important, did Rockford know? I opened my mouth to avow my innocence, but Torq cut me off.

"Don't even try protesting." Torq's eyes danced with a combination of amusement, appreciation, and the thrill of interrogation—predatory, searching, alert. "Your involuntary micro expressions give you away, babe."

I set my drink down and shrugged slightly, like I thought he was all washed up. "You're just guessing. And bluffing."

He shook his head no. "Give it up. I *know* you and Emma did the job. I planted the idea in your head at Hal's by telling you Rockford kept the plans there, didn't I? I'm just doing you the honor of confronting you directly with the truth."

He paused, studying me like he enjoyed it. "Looks like I've taught you something. Your poker face is improving." He grabbed my wrist unexpectedly and felt for my pulse. "But your pulse is racing, you pretty little liar." He stroked the back of my wrist with his thumb. "Much faster and you won't be able to think straight . . ."

He had that right. I slowly removed my wrist from his grip. "You don't know anything for sure."

"I know for sure, Dom. I wasn't in the CIA for nothing."

Unfortunately, I believed him. He knew. There wasn't any reason to keep protesting, but I wasn't ready to come totally clean. "What does Rockford know?"

"He knows nothing." Torq laughed at my attempt at subterfuge and then calmly sipped his drink. "Rockford's an ace warrior, terrific on the battle-field. As a spy, he has limitations. Rockford has no idea anyone was even *in* his office."

I tread carefully with my response. "Are you saying someone did a good job?"

"Passable." He grinned. "Fooled Rockford. He thinks the fire alarm was just a prank. Nice trick with the packing tape, by the way."

I paused, trying to figure Torq out. What did he want? Just toying with me? Having a little fun? "I guess the question is, *will* Rockford find out?"

"Depends"—Torq laughed—"on if I get what I want."

"And that would be?" I cocked my head as my heart fluttered out of control.

"Mutual gratification." His arm slid around my shoulders.

I felt myself flush. *I* was supposed to be the one using sex appeal to get my way, not the other way around. My mouth went dry.

"Why don't we help each other out?" He tucked a lock of hair behind my ear and whispered breathily, like he meant his words as a seduction, "Technically, you're guilty of breaking and entering. Rockford's office is monitored by a security camera. I saw the footage, but Rockford hasn't. That's not to say he wouldn't take a look if tipped off. . . ."

Stunned, I dropped my guard. "But Fry went over the surveillance footage—"

"Yeah—of the hallway by the alarm. I'm the only one who thought to check the tape of Rock's office. Clever, aren't I?" Torq traced a circle on my shoulder.

Goose bumps pilled on my arms. I shivered, thinking over the chain of events, torn between recoiling and curling into him. "I don't know. . . ."

"You want proof?" He pulled me close and tipped my face to look him directly in the eye. "You wore Ethan's pot leaf shirt and panty hose over your head. Disposable kitchen gloves on your hands. But you made the mistake of wearing your own jeans." He stroked my cheek. "Which show off your cute little ass and gave your identity away." His hand slid to my hip, where it rested warm and heavy.

"Ethan has a pretty nice butt himself," I said.

"That may be." Torq grinned. "But I've never noticed." He slid his hand up to my waist and squeezed. "But he sure as hell doesn't have hips like these."

I swallowed hard and leaned in to Torq. "Keep talking. What else did I supposedly do?"

Torq grinned and leaned in, too, meeting me halfway. Mere inches separated our lips.

"You went directly to Rockford's desk and looked in both his inbox and outbox. You removed the second sheet from his desk blotter and notepad. You looked in his wastebasket. Tried the safe.

"Then you tried the file cabinet drawers and looked in his desk drawer. And then, just as you were ready to leave, you spotted a piece of paper tucked under the file cabinet. You read it, and put it back where you'd found it."

We were so close I felt the whisper of his breath against my lips as he spoke. And his fingers at my waist performed the most gentle, sensual, mesmerizing massage.

"Sound about right?" he asked.

"About." To the minute detail. Like I was going to admit that. "So you wanted to know?"

He whispered in my ear. "What that paper said."

"In exchange for?" I brushed against him with my cleavage, hoping it was doing as much for him as it was doing for me.

"You get my silence." He nuzzled my neck, kissing it gently. "This perfume gives me ideas."

"Mmmmmm." I took a ragged breath and whispered into his thick, deep-brown hair, "Not good enough. I want more." Yeah, I wanted a lot more of everything at that point, especially him.

I steeled myself, trying to gain control over my raging hormones and my involuntary Kegel contractions and think semi-straight for a minute.

How much to divulge? I didn't see the harm in telling him what was on that slip of paper. And truthfully, with his lips on my neck, I probably would have told him anything he wanted to hear as long as he promised not to stop. So he knew that someone had been to Vegas, so what? Maybe he knew already anyway. But I wasn't showing my hand until I got something significant in return.

He nibbled my neck. "Yes?"

"I don't want you to think I'm paranoid or a conspiracy nut."

"Too late." He was sucking now.

I gave him a playful shove. "You have to promise to hear me out without judgment."

Wrong thing to say. He removed his lips from my neck, and stared into my eyes. I told him about Max and my theory that someone was trying to kill him as Torq stole an occasional glance at my silicone-enhanced cleavage. "Max says not. That no one would be trying to kill him. But he's currently in possession of one hundred and fifty million reasons."

Torq listened in silence. "No one's trying to kill Max."

"How can you be so sure?" Like a stupid dropout from seduction school, I was killing the moment. "What about him 'falling'"—I made a quote-mark gesture—"off that ledge?"

"We've been over that. He was into the adrenaline rush of the game and not looking where he was going. He saw a snake and panicked." Torq shrugged. "Didn't pay attention and went over. It's a good thing, too. Otherwise, we might never have found Davie."

The mention of Davie shut us both up.

Remembering the scene, I shuddered, feeling glad to be alive. "Poor Davie." I paused again. "I can't help wondering if the attempts on Max and Davie's death are connected." To be honest, the thought had just occurred to me. But it made a warped kind of sense.

Torq gave me a skeptical look. I ignored it. "Did Davie have any enemies?"

"Not that I know of," Torq said. "He was a likeable guy."

I nodded my agreement, remembering my driving lesson with him. "Max doesn't seem to have any special connection to him. Do you think someone mistook him for Max and killed him by mistake?"

"You have a one-track mind." His tone wasn't complimentary. "Just forget about someone trying to kill Max." He paused, frowning. "The two look nothing alike. They'd be hard to mistake for each other. They're not even close to the same height or build."

I sighed. He was right. Actually, Torq and Davie had similar builds. "Will you keep an eye on Max? That's all I'm asking."

Torq put his hand around the back of my head and pulled me toward him. "Anything for you, babe. Now let's forget about this nasty business for tonight. Can we talk about something more interesting?"

Be still my heart!

I gave into temptation and ran my fingers through Torq's hair. "Gladly."

"What was on that slip of paper?" he whispered before nuzzling my neck again.

I wondered vaguely if this was another camp test. If I told him would I pass or fail? At this point, I didn't care about anything other than his hot mouth on my neck. "Now who has a one-track mind?"

"Well?"

"A printout of an itinerary." I stroked his hair. "Of someone's trip to Vegas last month. There was no name. It was torn off." I pulled back and watched his face for any show of emotion. I thought I saw the tiniest tick in his cheek, like he wasn't happy. Without all that mind-reading training I wouldn't have seen it at all.

"And?" he said in a leading tone that left no wiggle room for me to deny knowing more.

Damn, he was good. "That's it." I made a cross-my-heart motion. "Honest."

"Did you tell anyone else about the itinerary and note?"

I rolled my eyes. "No."

"Not even Emma?" He stroked my cheek with the back of his fingers. I'd give him exactly forever to cut that out.

"Not on your life."

He grinned again and the tick disappeared, replaced by a healthy dose of lust. "You're one hell of a spy, babe. It's a pleasure doing business with you. If we don't stop now, it could definitely be more of a pleasure . . ."

He leaned forward, closing the tiny gap between us, and touched his lips to mine. Gently at first, then more insistently. "A nightlong pleasure," he whispered between kisses.

"Nightlong?" I murmured, so totally entranced by the thing his tongue was doing in my ear that I could barely think.

"Absolutely. For your own safety."

"My safety?"

"You've had too much Temptini." He was nuzzling and kissing my neck.

"What about your safety? You don't even know my real name." I threw my head back so he could kiss my neck with all the reckless abandon he could muster. "Dangerous business sleeping with an unknown."

"I thrive on danger." He sucked on my neck.

I was going to have a big old hickey in the morning, but I couldn't have cared less 'cause right now my body was thriving on its response to him.

"Do you know that Bond's slept with a total of forty-four women in his movies . . ."

"Is that right?"

"And three-fourths of them later tried to kill him."

"Once a woman has slept with me," Torq whispered with a tease and a smile in his voice, "the last thing she wants to do is kill me."

Chapter Seventeen

Torq kissed me slowly and fully as he eased me back on the couch exactly the way a Bond-type lover should, bringing out my secret longings, intriguing me with his overwhelming passion, all the while tasting deliciously of martini.

His kisses chased away my insecurities and reserve. I became Domino, uninhibited and free. A seductress. At least for the moment. My reserve and insecurities were too ingrained in my personality to be permanently banished so easily. But wrapped around him on the couch, who cared?

We kissed. And caressed. Kissed some more. Nibbled. Rubbed against each other. Stroked. Petted. Teased. All fully clothed. Building excitement. Building tension so taut I thought I'd snap.

When we finally came up for air, I stole a glance at the clock. We'd been kissing for nearly an hour, yet it felt like only minutes.

"Are you thirsty? Can I get you something?" He

leaned down and nibbled my ear, whispering with hot breath, "Another Temptini, perhaps?"

My first inclination was to take the offer at face value and decline the drink. Then I recognized the flirt in his voice and realized what he was *really* asking. Heart thumping wildly away, I hesitated. "Maybe."

"Maybe?"

Clearly he hadn't been expecting that answer. He pulled back and looked at me.

I smiled uncertainly back up at him, suddenly tentative and cautious. I just didn't have the Bond girl, no-commitment-at-all mentality. "This isn't another test, is it? Like at the bar? Tomorrow I won't hear Rockford—"

He put a finger to my lips. "That was the other thing I wanted to talk about. That was never a test." How could a man sound so sincere? "That was only about you and me."

I couldn't help blushing and grinning.

"We'll skip the drinks, then?" He flashed a wicked grin and glanced toward the bedroom.

"Do you have a gun on the nightstand and satin sheets and champagne cooling by the bed?" I said, following his line of sight.

"You mean like Bond?"

"Yeah." I nodded. "I've always had a Bond fantasy, and you *are* a spy."

"Nope. Four hundred thread–count percale cotton. But they're clean. Maybe a half-drunk, flat Coke on the nightstand. No gun. But I promise to share the Coke."

I sealed the deal with a smile. He scooped me into his arms and carried me to the bedroom.

I don't know how Torq managed it with me in his arms, but somehow along the way to the bedroom the ties to my teeny-weenie pink bikini top came loose and the top fell open. But then, he's a spy; he's capable of a lot of things I can't comprehend.

I felt a momentary lapse of confidence as the real me was exposed and nearly clamped my arms over my small, real breasts. But Torq's eyes shone with appreciation as he looked at them, smiling.

"Um, I sort of enhanced them," I said, blushing and pulling at my bikini top. "This part is fake."

He was still staring at my real breasts as if they were the eighth wonder of the world. I can't say I wasn't totally flattered by that.

"I know." Yeah, and I believed he did. What didn't he know? That was the problem with spies. "But this part is real . . . and beautiful." His words were a sigh of appreciation as he laid me down on the bed and kissed them until my whole body shuddered with delight.

Our clothes fell away and he made love to me in such a loving, erotic, Bond way, I can't begin to describe it more than to say he took me around the world . . . more than once. Oh, and one more confession—I'd never been a screamer . . . until then.

I woke several hours later tangled in Torq's percale sheets. Alone. The clock on the nightstand read five thirty a.m. Daylight was beginning to creep in. I heard the shower running and assumed the Spy Who Shagged Me was getting cleaned up and ready for the big day ahead. My smile reached ear-to-ear as I thought of the night we'd spent together and of him now naked in the shower. Joining him there was such a juicy temptation. But along with the daylight, my reserved, insecure nature reared up and voiced its opposition to my fun. If he'd wanted me to join him, he would've asked.

Maybe he just hadn't wanted to wake me, the confident Domino half of my nature argued back. Which half to believe? I was so confused.

The sight of Torq's laptop powered up and humming away on the small desk in the corner provided an allure all its own—camp secrets! Like maybe a list of everyone's real identity? Or better yet, the accident report? *What a girl won't sacrifice to get top-secret inside info,* I thought as I slid out of bed, heart racing with adrenaline.

Once dressed, I stood and crossed the room to the desk, catching a glimpse of my wild-haired reflection in the mirror. All visions of Bond girl femme-fatale perfection vanished. I looked more like the Bride of Frankenstein, only her hair was tidier. Hair extensions on end, eyes puffy, and, okay, you couldn't really tell this in the mirror, but my teeth weren't brushed— a casualty of not planning for a sleepover. So maybe it was better I didn't join him in the shower. Maybe.

I ran my fingers through my hair in an unsuccessful bid to tame my wild, unnaturally extended mane and sat down at the laptop. Torq had been totally careless in leaving his laptop out in plain view. I smelled a setup or another test. Not that it stopped me, just slowed me down a sec while I mulled over the ethics of snooping through his computer and the consequences of getting caught. What would Torq do? I grinned. Ethics lost.

I touched a key and the screen lit up. Unfortunately, the dang thing was password protected. Giving it the old college try, I took a few game stabs at his password.

What? Domino wasn't his first choice of password? I'd have to see about changing that in the future. I grinned to myself. I was just having a bit of fun. Of course, password guessing was an exercise in futility and time-wasting. I had better ways to spend my time.

I was just about to walk away and slip into something more comfortable, say Torq's shower, when I noticed a stack of magazines and newspapers next to the laptop. An old copy of the *Wall Street Journal* was open to the same review of the remastered Bond collection I'd been reading in the sick bay. Evidently, fresh reading material was scarce at FSC.

Torq was a fellow Bond fanatic! A man truly after my own heart. I smiled to myself.

I leaned over and glanced at the article again. Odd. He'd circled the word "hit man" three times in black ink. I frowned. Scaramanga wasn't my favorite villain. He only scored a seven out of ten on the menace rating. We had our first disconnect.

I noticed one of Torq's desk drawers was ajar. My first instinct, the nice, tidy, good-girl instinct, was to shut it. Then my spy gear kicked in. Hey, it wasn't locked. It was practically shouting, "Looky, looky, see what I have."

I slid the drawer open and there sat . . . a camera

just like mine. Curious, I pulled it out and turned it on. Well, look at that. Torq had taken pictures of the blown-up car just like I had. From the same angles. I frowned. Oh, and here were pictures of my birthday party.

"Damn him!" I whispered.

As I sat with the camera trembling in my hands, wondering what to do, the shower shut off and I panicked. I heard the shower door slide open. My heart was pounding wildly as I tried to think what to do. I heard him toweling off.

I grabbed my camera, replaced the drawer to its nearly closed state, and stole a couple of the magazines to read later. Hey, they were more recent than Rockford's and they might hold a few clues. Worst case, I'd know better how Torq's reading tastes ran.

Thinking fast, I slipped on my shoes, grabbed a pen and sheet of paper, and wrote a note, hoping to leave the illusion that everything was still just peachy and not arouse his suspicions. I pressed hard with the pen, hoping to hide the fearful tremble of my hands. Who knew but that Torq was a handwriting expert to boot.

Torq—
I had a *fabulous* time last night. I can't even tell you. But I need to fly back to my room before the rumors do.

XXX and *hot* OOOs,
Dom

I'd just slipped out the door as I heard him repeat the first syllable of my name. "Dom—"

My high-heeled shoes slowed me down. I pulled them off and ran like a jackalope with a coyote on its tail for the barracks, somehow making it back to my room without being spotted.

I was panting as I reached my room and came to a complete stop, ready to pull out my key and let myself in. Only there was no need. My door was decidedly ajar. I stared at it with a growing horror. So much for the safety and security of home.

"Oh. My. Gosh," I whispered, simply stunned and totally frightened. I'm anal retentive about locking doors. I had no doubt it had been latched and locked when I'd left.

Against my better judgment and my 100 percent chicken-meat nature, I pushed the door open with one arm and, heart thundering away, surveyed the room.

My closet doors were thrown wide open. And my Louis Vuitton canvas keepall, the pride and joy of my luggage collection, sat on the bed with my Domino wardrobe haphazardly stuffed into it by someone who obviously needed a lesson in how to pack without wrinkling the goods. Sleeves, pant legs, and bits of lingerie all popped out the top in a torrent of pink.

Written across it in big, black block letters were the words SMIERT SPIONAM. I'd seen *The Living Daylights* enough times to recognize the words as the same as those on the note left on a very dead 004's body. I knew exactly what they meant—"death to spies."

Chapter Eighteen

Receiving a death threat, no matter how clever or in what language, is not on my top-ten list of things I want out of life and wish someone would bestow on me. To tell the truth, it doesn't even make my top billion. And this evil, villainous jerk lost major style points for *defacing* the luggage!

Emma was still sleeping the slumber of the unthreatened and blissfully unaware, which meant the joint bathroom was empty. I rushed in for water and washcloth, intent on performing a little emergency first aid on my luggage, using cleaning as a defense mechanism against confronting the real danger—I'd rattled someone's cage with enough vigor they'd decided to lash back. But whose? And why? Who knew what I was up to? And what did I know? Damn! Everything was so frustratingly vague.

I quickly dismissed the idea that this incident was yet another camp test. No way was FSC going to intentionally ruin personal property. Not if they wanted to keep their insurance rates under control—not to mention their legal bills.

Head full of the mist of whirly, twirly, swirly ideas and vague notions, I returned to my room and scrubbed at the horrid black letters with all my pent-up frustrations and fears. But even after I scrubbed and cursed and uttered "out, out, damn ink" three times beneath my breath, the words remained, looking as fresh as the minute they were penned. Indelible ink. I tossed the washcloth onto the floor with disgust.

Now what? What did I do? Whom did I trust?

The cops wanted us to hang around for a few days. I could run, but then I'd look guilty. I could call the Surprise police and report the vandalism. But what could they do, really? I could tell Torq and hope he'd track down the marker-wielding fiend using every spy trick up his proverbial sleeve. But, sad to say, I didn't trust anyone, not even Torq. I could unpack and act as if this little event never happened while mercilessly uncovering and hunting down the perp myself.

No one has ever accused me of being heroic, not even semiheroic or passably uncowardly. I'm the one who covers her eyes during the scary parts of movies and begs others who've seen it to tell me that things turn out okay.

But I'd never forgive myself if someone, say Max, turned up desiccated and "floating" facedown in the dry Hassayampa River in the next few days. I opened my bag and began unpacking.

Ten minutes later, I tossed Louis into the back

of the closet and shut the doors, dusting my hands together like I was ridding myself of a bad experience. Then I sat down on the bed with my camera and took a good, long look at my pictures, using my newly trained spy's eye. When I blew up the photo of the charred chassis, sure enough, I found bullet holes, two of them, verifying the vague impression I'd had of seeing bullet holes in the car way back on Sunday before Torq apparently copped the camera.

The atmosphere of spy camp may have tuned my mind too far toward sinister, so I took pains to think logically. Anyone could have used that old car for shooting practice. Torq had suggested that someone had been trespassing and shooting for fun. But why only two holes? Could someone have been taking potshots at someone or something during the grand welcome explosion? Is that what made Torq curious enough to examine the burned-up car? But why did he steal my camera?

I took a sec to play "what I know."

First, there was the opening explosion. Enough said. Second, the car that mowed down Max, and almost clipped Torq and me. Was that just another drunk peeling out?

What about my accident on the driving range? Another accident, or another attempt? Max falling over the cliff? Davie stabbed? Connected? If so, how? Had he gotten in someone's way? And now my defaced suitcase—deadly warning or sick prank?

Unfortunately, there was a logical explanation for everything, except Davie's death. And the cops were already looking into that. Which only meant that I'd sound like a complete nutcase when I tried to warn people of another impending danger.

Were the threats real? I'd come to believe they were. There were just too many for mere coincidence and bad luck. And if they were real, I was certain of one thing—whoever had threatened me was getting desperate. Time grew short for our murderous villain. Just an educated guess, but I was willing to wager they'd planned to bump someone off and make it look like an accident. And it looked like that someone was Max, given that he was the common denominator in all the "accidents." Only the would-be assassin had bungled several prime opportunities and now had less than a day and a half to get it right.

I grabbed my camp schedule and took a look at what I was up against. Firing practice after breakfast, probably too risky and obvious to take someone out here. Even if our perp "accidentally" shot someone, there'd be an inquest and if a motive turned up . . .

Rappelling later this morning—an excellent opportunity for someone to take a fatal fall.

Classroom activities this afternoon—boring. Hard to imagine death by paper cut.

And then this evening, the big camp finale and kidnapping adventure followed by the rescue exercise— all perfect opportunities for a final, and fatal, accident.

Tomorrow, recap and evaluation of the kidnap rescue, followed by a good-bye assembly and a eulogy if our bad guy had his way.

Okay. Piece of cake—all I had to do was discover the identity of the intended killer, and how and why they planned on committing the crime. No problem. Right.

My head hurt with the responsibility and confusion of it all. Hercule Poirot or Sherlock Holmes I was not. I fell back on my bed, camera still in hand, wishing I had even a few little gray cells. First things first. If I could figure out who'd written the warning on my keepall . . .

The standard architecture-student block handwriting was no help. Who knew I'd been out? Torq, of course. He seemed to know everything, including my every move. And Emma. Oh, heck, anyone who was watching could have known. The hairs stood up on the back of my neck. Or listening . . .

What if my room was bugged? That would explain a lot. Bugging another CT's room had been easy enough the first day of camp. I thought I'd been pretty foxy by discovering the "bug," but what if my room really had a bug problem even now? What if that's how Torq knew what I was up to every minute?

I heard stirrings in Emma's room, followed by Emma entering the bathroom and turning the shower on. I didn't have much time. I lifted my head from the bed and looked around. The room was sparse but still had ample bug-hiding locations.

I slid from the bed, hid the camera, and began searching, muttering about losing an earring in case anyone was listening in on my searching noises, and wishing I had one of those handheld bug-detecting devices. Then I remembered something

I'd seen on a British spy documentary. I knew my Bond mania would come in useful someday!

Most bugs operate and transmit on FM wavelengths. The amateur way of finding them is to use a small, portable FM radio. All I had to do was go around the different wavelengths on the radio dial, and if there was a bug in this room, when the dial hit the bug's operating wavelength, bammo, I'd get feedback. To find the bug's lair, I'd go where the feedback was noisiest. I could do that. Really.

I grabbed my clock radio, glad that Rockford in his cheapness hadn't sprung for digital tuning, and began slowly working the dial and the room.

When I hit the desk, the feedback nearly broke my eardrum. I jumped and turned the volume down before someone else heard and got suspicious. I couldn't believe the FM-radio trick had actually worked!

There was a bug, an actual bug in my room. No way! My heart pulsed in my ears and my hands shook as I moved the only things on the desk—a notepad and an FSC pen—off and scanned the desk. It came up clean.

Okay. Pen or pad?

The pad produced nothing but radio silence. The pen, on the other hand, unleashed violent feedback. So the pen was my little snug as a bug nest. I would have congratulated myself on my own brainiac behavior, but I was simply too scared.

I turned the radio off and picked the pen up to examine it, holding it under the light. Ingenious! This was a genuine black FSC pen, not the fake navy one we'd had to substitute in the room-bugging game.

Once again, I got that hair-raising scared feeling. I thought of Torq and how he knew my every move down to what magazine I'd been reading . . . and I shuddered.

I grabbed the pen, ready to dump that puppy. With pen in hand, I opened the door to my room and surveyed the hall. Wade's door was open. I saw him disappear down the hall toward the lobby. He wouldn't be gone long, but all I needed were seconds.

Seizing the opportunity, I zipped into his room and exchanged pens. Let our listener pick up Wade's personal habits for a while.

As I dashed back out I noticed Wade's room was surprisingly tidy. Bed made. Closet doors open. A few Hawaiian shirts and a lot of conservative golf polos grouped by color hung in his closet. His shoes were neatly lined up in rows. Something about the details of the room niggled at me. It wasn't what I'd expected out of Wade. Emma had said his room was a mess when she'd searched it.

I hurried back to my room, arriving just as Emma shut the shower off. I'd just plugged my clock back in and was adjusting the time when Emma stuck her toweled head in my room. "You're up."

I looked over my shoulder at her in time to catch her frown as she watched me from behind. "What's up?"

I made a show of looking for something. "Lost an earring. Thought I left it on the nightstand. Maybe I knocked it off."

She nodded. "Hang on. Let me get dressed and I'll help you look for it."

"Don't worry about it. It's not important. It wasn't expensive."

That's when she noticed I was still in my pink bikini from the night before, and smiling knowingly, arched a brow. "Maybe you should ask Torq if he's seen it. He could try looking in his bed. How was he? I want all the details."

I felt myself blushing. "Great," I stammered. "We'll talk later."

"All right, then. I'll hold you to it." She shook her head. "I take it you haven't showered yet. Looks like you'd better step on it or you're going to be late and miss breakfast again."

"About breakfast . . ." I said.

Knowing what was coming, Emma rolled her eyes. "Want me to snag you a muffin?"

"Blueberry if they've got it." I flashed her a grateful smile and pulled her into our joint bathroom, where I turned on the water for white-noise coverage and made a pretense of wetting a washcloth and scrubbing off my makeup. "Keep an eye on Max and Torq for me, will you?"

Emma frowned. "Why? What's going on?" Then she grinned. "Jealous already? Torn between two lovers?"

I rolled my eyes. "I can't explain now, Emma. Just trust me. Don't let Max and Torq out of your sight during breakfast."

* * *

Thinking in the shower has always been a strong suit of mine. So while the hot steam swirled around me along with the subtle scent of soap, I realized I needed a gun. A real gun. No way was I playing Nancy Drew without a weapon. And I knew where to find one. Pussy had one stuffed between her mattress and box spring. If I just happened to steal it, I was killing two problems with one break-in—I'd be armed and Pussy wouldn't. It went without saying that today I was paying close attention to shooting practice. No mind wandering. No daydreaming. 'Cause the thought of me armed and on my own was really kind of frightening in itself.

That's about as productive as my thinking got. Even lingering in the lather, I couldn't put the pieces of the mystery together. I had the feeling I was a few vital clues short of a full picture.

I slid out of the shower and toweled off. Then I decked myself out as total Domino—fake silicone breasts pushed up and out, showing off in a form-fitting, low-cut V-neck tank top, signature Domino headband, crop pants, and cute little pink tennis shoes. Dressed for spy success, I was off to save the world. But not before I checked three times to make sure my keepall was still kept all to itself in the closet and the door to my room was latched tight.

Rockford intercepted me in the lobby as I headed to the firing range. "CT Domino, I need a word."

I gave him a look that said, "not you too!" I didn't

want a word. I didn't even want a syllable. "Later. I'm late to shooting practice."

"Your dedication to the craft is admirable." He took my arm. "But shooting practice can wait." He steered me toward his office. "I have someone in my office who wants to speak with you."

Turns out the someone was just FSC's lawyer wanting me to sign a statement releasing FSC from any liability for the driving range accident earlier in the week. I put him off by saying I'd have to speak with my lawyer first. I know I'd said I wouldn't sue. But, hey, if they were worried about me developing delayed whiplash or something, maybe I should be, too.

Little did FSC know that my little crash was the least of their worries. If I was right, they were looking at being the site of a second homicide.

Interview complete, I nearly collided with Rockford as I rushed out his office door. The thought had crossed my mind that with everyone in class, now was the perfect opportunity to burgle Pussy's room and get that gun. Unfortunately, Rockford had other ideas. He escorted me directly to the range in stony silence.

I arrived in time to feel relief that Max was still among the living. I considered jumping Torq about my camera. Yeah, I was a little peeved about the whole deal, not to mention suspicious. On the innocent side, he *could* have taken it as part of camp, but considering our relationship, he might have told me. Anyway, I thought better of mentioning it—too many big ears around.

After firing a few rounds, Torq and Fry led us to a small three-story building on the campus away from the main barracks and training center for our rappelling class.

"Where have you been?" Emma hissed at me as we trailed behind our trainers.

"Unavoidably detained," I said.

We assembled in front of the building, standing in the scorching desert heat. Of all the days to forget my water bottle. Almost immediately I felt a trickle of sweat drip down my back and had to resist the urge to squirm. Torq was instructing, with Fry and Rockford assisting.

"April 30, 1980," Torq said as he stood before us, "six armed Iranian terrorists took over the Iranian embassy in London's Princes Gate, holding twenty-six hostages captive and threatening to explode the building. British SAS forces rappelled from the roof to a second-story balcony and stormed the building, killing all but one terrorist, who was later captured. During the rescue, two hostages were wounded and one killed. The operation was regarded a success and became a textbook assault studied by Special Forces the world over.

"Only one small glitch during the mission—one of the SAS soldiers became entangled in his rope. This small error forced the SAS soldiers to abandon their plan to detonate a frame charge. They had to use sledgehammers to enter the building."

Torq walked down the row of us, staring us down,

pausing in front of me and looking every bit as scary as he had the first day of camp, no sign of our intimacy on his face. "Never forget Murphy's Law. If anything can go wrong, it will. Particularly during an intense, high-pressure mission."

I looked past Torq, focusing on the window behind him, trying not to be intimidated or give away my doubts about him, trying to be every bit as unreadable as he was.

"You never know when a rescue will require you to know how to rappel, which is why I'm going to teach you how to do it today." He continued staring at me. To avoid that penetrating look of his, I stared into space and tried to think calming, happy thoughts about crazy things, like balanced accounts and cool, air-conditioned bank lobbies.

Torq pointed up to the top. Ten heads lifted to follow where he pointed, all of us shielding our eyes against the sun. Just looking up gave me vertigo. My fear of heights made rappelling my biggest nightmare, right up there with bungee jumping. I felt all the classic symptoms of panic—rapid heartbeat, dry mouth, trembling hands, the irrational desire to run like crazy from the building . . .

"We'll be rappelling from the roof just like the Brits did." Torq paused once more to look at me. "Dom? Are you all right?"

I nodded mutely.

"Sure?" He studied me closely, looking concerned.

"Fine," I croaked, wondering just how scared I looked.

"Okay, then." He didn't sound convinced. "Everyone follow me. The adventure begins up top."

When I didn't move, Max took me by the arm, chatting sociably as he propelled me along with the group behind Torq. I was full of foreboding, but Max seemed blissfully unaware of impending danger.

He looked up at the roof. "This is going to be fun. Did I ever tell you I'm a rock climber?"

Thank heaven for that, I thought. Hopefully he knew how to arrest a fall.

Max began babbling on about the joy of heights and the fun of rappelling, along with all manner of possible mishaps and how to combat against them, stuff I really needed to hear.

"I think I'm going to have to miss this session. Would you believe I have a prior appointment?" I smiled weakly and unconvincingly at Max, who still had my elbow. Damn, I'd really meant to ditch rappelling. "Why don't you join me? We'll go back to the barracks and play some paintball or something. Sound good to you?" Sounded better to me than plunging to my death.

Recognizing my attempt at a *Get Smart* line, Max laughed.

"Stop with the stories, Max. You're scaring her!" Emma, who was walking on the other side of me shot me a sympathetic look while simultaneously throwing Max a warning elbow.

Max gave her a startled look. "What? What did I say? Did I say something?"

Fry came alongside us. "Rappelling's a piece of

cake, just a little old stroll down a building. Y'all aren't afraid of heights, are you, Domino?"

When I didn't answer, Fry gave me a teasing grin. "You'll get over it. One successful rappel and y'all will be dying to do it again."

Dying—that was exactly what I was afraid of. The only thing that kept me going was that I had to look out for Max.

Once we'd all assembled on the roof, Torq explained the rappelling process to the group and showed us the synthetic rope we'd be using, examining all equipment for defects and wear as he spoke. Fry gave them a perfunctory second check when Torq was done. I guess after the exploded-car incident they were going for redundancy in the equipment-checking department.

The heat made everything shimmery and wavy. I was parched. I really could've used a drink of water . . . or something stronger. I didn't have a lick of spit left in my body. Emma had drained her water bottle already or I would have asked her for a sip. To top that off, I felt panicky and dizzy. I told myself to get a grip, trying to remember those inoculation exercises and implement something to screw up my courage.

Torq strode over to two sturdy air-conditioning units that were whirling away at full force. "These will be our anchor points. Two of us will be going down at a time—one CT and one instructor. I'll wrap each rappelling anchor around the anchor point several times and secure it with a sturdy knot."

He made a show of carefully wrapping and knotting the anchor. He appeared expert at what he was doing.

"See these loops?" Torq pointed to the rappelling anchor. "These will be secured to the jump line with carabiners. Two or three ought to be enough to hold any CT's weight." He then attached the carabiners.

He stood and held up a figure-eight-type device with one hole bigger than the other. "This is a rappelling device." He took a length of looped jump line and pushed it through the larger hole, then wrapped the loop around the outside of the smaller circle. One length of the rope extended to the anchor line. He held up the other. "You'll use this line to rappel."

He held up another harness. "You'll all be wearing one of these climbing harnesses for safety."

To divert my small mind from the great big scary ledge at hand, I let myself admire him, indulging in rooftop fantasies of the sort *Playgirl* might be interested in.

I was startled out of my admiring reverie by Torq barking a name. "Max! Front and center. You're up first. I'll be going down with you."

"No!" I reacted instinctively. Max couldn't go down until someone else had checked the gear and made sure it was safe. Damn! I had to pick now to go heroic.

Every last CT had turned to stare at me.

"I'll go."

Pussy sneered. Emma looked stunned. Max looked like he wanted to clobber me. No doubt he was drooling with anticipation at the thought of rappelling. This was probably the highlight of his vacation and now I was horning in and begging to go first. He'd thank me when I'd saved his life. Shoot! Wrong thing to think, 'cause saving his life probably meant taking a fall meant for him myself.

"I bet those British SAS guys were gentlemanly enough to let the ladies go first. I've been dying to . . . go rappelling." I rushed my words before I lost my courage, crossed my arms, and looked around the group for a validation.

I got a sneer from Bishop and a snide grin from Ethan. Rockford had finally found the break-in evidence we'd planted in their rooms and grilled them mercilessly. Word was, neither cracked. Which won them everyone else's admiration, backfiring our quest for revenge.

Emma had scoffed at this. "They *were* innocent. How could they crack, those idiots?" She'd shaken her head in disgust. "They made a big scene at breakfast about taking revenge out on whoever'd framed them." She'd rolled her eyes. "Like those two are capable of figuring out that we did it and thinking up a decent revenge scheme."

Emma gently took my arm. "Domino, sweetie, I think Max had his heart set on being first up. Why don't you let him show us how it's done?"

"No." I shook my head and appealed to Torq. "I have a phobia, a real fear of heights. If I don't go first, I'm just gonna chicken out." I took a deep breath. "Right now, it's taking every ounce of courage I have to fight off my panic and not just turn tail and leave this roof." I was also trembling so hard my knees were practically knocking. "If I don't do this now, I'm never going to be able to face and conquer this fear."

I squared my jaw and stepped forward, trying to remember every conquering-phobia article I'd read. Trying real hard *not* to think about someone tampering with the equipment or shoving Max off the roof as I rappelled down. "Please."

Torq's expression softened and I thought I saw a micro expression of admiration cross his face as he clapped me on the shoulder and tossed a harness over my head. "You're right, CT. Facing your fears is the only way to conquer them." He began buckling me into the harness.

He roughly tightened my harness straps. I winced as he tugged the last one tight.

"These have to be tight." There was a sympathetic edge to his words.

"Um, Torq"—I leaned into him and whispered in his ear—"this rappelling isn't a good idea. Remember what I said about someone trying to kill Max?" I gave my harness a little tug. "This is it. This is how they're going to do it. What if someone's tampered with his rope? He'll fall to his death." I gave Torq a look pleading with him to believe me.

"No one is trying to kill Max."

I held his gaze. "I just switched places with him."

He shook his head in that way that said I was crazy and sighed. "I'll prove my point. We'll switch ropes. Will that make you happy?"

"No," I hissed back. "What if you fall?"

He didn't listen. Over my protests, he switched ropes and locked my harness to the rappelling device with another carabiner before climbing into his own harness. He tossed me a pair of heavy-duty gloves. "Put these on. Then rear back and pull to make sure the anchor can bear your weight." He demonstrated.

I let out a sigh of relief that his rope appeared to be fine and gave the rearing-back thing a go. The rope held and I felt a miniscule amount of calm return. The equipment *seemed* okay. Me, I was a mess—parched and out of water, and my sweat was evaporating off my body as fast as I produced it.

"Listen up, everybody," Torq said, "this is important. Rappelling down a building is a cinch. A sissy could do it." He shot me a challenging look, trying to incense me out of my fear.

"You place one hand on either side of the rappelling device like this. Facing the building, brace your feet on the surface and walk down the surface using small, backward leaps, just like Batman, pushing out and away as you loosen your grip on the downward side of the rappelling device. Keep that image in mind and you'll do fine." Torq looked me straight in the eye.

"Only make *short* hops. This is important. If you slide too far, too fast, friction will heat up the rope hot enough to burn your hands or, worse yet, melt the line, causing it to snap." He shot me an encouraging grin. "You have short legs, Dom. Short hops ought to be no problem for you." He looked around the group. "Any questions?"

I raised a shaky hand. "Yeah. How do we stop?"

Torq laughed like I was joking, but I was completely serious. "Clamp down tightly on the down side of the rappelling device." He clapped his gloved hands together. "Okay, enough chitchat. It's off to the wall."

I stood rooted in place, thinking, *uh-uh, no way, never, never.* Torq grabbed my arm and dragged me to the edge, where he attached a security line between himself and me. "You can do this, Dom."

Fry trailed after us while the rest of the group offered their own encouragement and I focused on positive thoughts. I could see way off to the White Tank Mountains and felt a hint of a breeze. A trace of clouds was beginning to form around the mountaintops.

Torq swung over the roof ledge, pulling me with my tether closer to the edge than I liked, and offered me his hand while Fry offered to help me over the edge. I hesitated.

"Come on, Domino, you can do it. You want to be a good spy, don't you?" Torq's voice was gentle and coaxing. "Face your fear, CT."

Steeling myself, I peered cautiously over the edge, feeling slightly dizzy at the thought of going over. *Don't look down,* I told myself. I gave a nervous laugh. "I'd rather be a good spy back in the air-conditioned comfort of the main office. A desk job at Langley is sounding pretty good about now."

Fry was right behind me. "Y'all don't really want to be a paper-pusher back at HQ. Besides, those guys at Langley do it all, don't they, Torq?" Fry winked. "Let me help y'all. Ready?"

Resigned to my fate, I nodded and squeezed my eyes shut, took Torq's hand, and allowed Fry to help me climb over the edge as I positioned my hands around the rappelling device and clamped my feet against the wall, ready to plunge to my death at any second.

"You're doing great," Torq said.

"Liar."

Torq ignored me and grinned. "On three, we take a little baby hop." Torq adjusted his hand position. "One, two, three."

I said my prayers, took a deep breath . . . and hopped. Fortunately, not to my death. The rope held. I was still positioned against the building like Catwoman. Life was good.

"Excellent," Torq said, smiling at me like a dad teaching his toddler to walk.

I opened my eyes and smiled shakily back, thinking Max owed Torq and me big, big time for being his official line testers.

"Good." Torq returned my grin. "Okay, again. A little bigger hop this time."

"Isn't once enough?" I had a death grip on my line again.

"I don't think so, babe. We've still got a whole building to scale."

I nodded, but I didn't like it.

"Again on three," he said encouragingly. "One, two, three!"

I cautiously loosened my grip and semi-fearlessly

took a tiny hop, sliding smoothly. I clamped to stop.
But instead of slowing, my jump line slid through
the rappelling device as if it were greased. Something was wrong. I clamped with all my might and
started to panic, grabbing at the line with my gloved
hands, feeling the heat through the fabric. As the
jump line ran through my fingers, I screamed.

Chapter Nineteen

I clamped down, but the rope continued its slide through my fingers.

Torq cursed. "Clamp down. Clamp down, damn it!"

"I am! I'm clamping, but it won't stop!" I felt myself becoming overwhelmed with fear and light-headedness. My hands stopped working right. I could no longer clench a fist and I felt weak.

Beside me, Torq scurried down his own rope, trying to keep pace with me, but losing ground fast.

The rope beneath my fingers was giving off heat like a backyard barbecue grill, complete with visible heat waves.

"Clamp! Damn it! Clamp!" Torq tried to reach out to grab my line. His voice became tinny and far away. My ears rang and I saw spots in my vision.

I watched beneath my feet as the ground raced up to meet me. My mouth felt as dry and rough as steel wool. The ringing in my ears grew louder, drowning out Torq's voice.

I heard a snap and screamed as my jump line broke and I began a free fall. How had someone managed to tamper with the line? How!

Above me, Torq braced himself and grabbed the security line connecting us, trying to arrest my fall and keep himself from dropping with me or being pulled loose from the building.

My field of vision dimmed and closed in smaller and smaller as the length of security rope reached maximum extension. It caught and I bounced bungee-jumper-like, twisting my back and neck like a whiplash victim. For just a second, I hung there as limp as an abandoned puppet as Torq rappelled toward me, lowering me gently as he came.

"Just hang on, Domino. Hang on. We're going to get you down safely."

Rockford, Fry, and a crowd of CTs had gathered at the top of the building, leaning over to see what had precipitated my scream.

"Don't worry," Max yelled to me from the top of the building. "Hang in there. You're going to make it."

I looked up at him and opened my mouth to yell at him, mother hen–like, to get back from the edge. I'd just risked my life to save his. No way did I want him giving a desperate murderer the perfect opportunity to "help" him over the ledge. But no sound came out.

That's when a sudden nasty gust of wind kicked up, spinning me around and lashing me toward the building like a helpless rag doll in the hands of a vengeful toddler. Seeing Torq above me struggling to maintain control of the security line, I uttered a quick one-line prayer.

"Oh, geez!" Torq said, seeing me swinging.

I opened my mouth to scream as my field of vision narrowed to a pinpoint, taking with it a view of the building rushing toward me. Then the world went dark.

When I awoke, I was flat on my back on the asphalt, staring up at a scary kaleidoscope of people silhouetted by the sun and gaping down at me. Several of them were panting as if they'd just gone for a brisk jog. Who were these tense-looking people? I blinked, confused. Then it hit me—camp, I was at spy camp. And I was alive!

Fry and Rockford were barking at people to stand back and give me some breathing space. Torq, looking shaken, yet somehow still calm, was on one side of me, holding my hand and murmuring words of comfort that sounded as far away as if he was whispering them down a tunnel.

Tanner was taking my vitals with Max assisting him. "Her pulse feels thready and weak." Tanner looked at Rockford. Whatever "thready" means. Must be a medical term. For my part, I felt clammy and slightly nauseous, which triggered the realization that I'd just passed out. Suddenly I remembered the minutes immediately preceding my delightful nightmare—I'd become the fall girl. Guess I should have been grateful to be alive. The thing was—I felt like death would have been an improvement over my present battered and bruised condition. Being an ingrate, I wasn't particularly pleased that my prayer to live had been answered. I looked up at Tanner and said, "Dr. Tanner, I presume?"

Tanner just stared at me.

"Or is it nurse?" I giggled. I may have been a touch delirious.

Tanner obviously didn't get my sense of humor. He looked at me like I was cuckoo for Cocoa Puffs. "She's either in shock or has a classic case of heat exhaustion, or both." Tanner released my wrist and rocked back on his heels. "We need to get her out of the sun and rehydrated."

"I'm fine," I protested, only I was lying through my sun-parched lips. "Only I think I owe Emma more money. 'Cause Wade was supposed to be next. Emma! Emma! Does it count if *I* outed Tanner as a medical professional? How much do I owe you now? Can we let it ride?"

"Shhh." Torq held a finger to my lips to silence me and shook his head at someone off in the distance. I was guessing Emma, but I was too distracted by his warm finger on my mouth to care about verifying my assumption.

"Don't exert yourself." Torq's voice may have been smooth and sympathetic, but he, too, clearly thought I was loco in the head. He opened a water bottle and, gently cradling my head, held the bottle to my lips. "Drink this. You'll feel better soon."

I was becoming more coherent by the minute. "How *did* I survive?" I asked.

"Later." He pressed the bottle against my lips.

I took a few sips, gracefully sputtering and sloshing

water all down my preposterously perky enhanced cleavage. I shifted gingerly. Most of me felt pretty whole and unshattered, but my left ankle throbbed, emitting pain waves of tsunami proportions. Maybe it had been throbbing all along and I hadn't noticed with the rest of me feeling like death warmed over. Maybe the pain was a good sign . . . or not.

"Does anything hurt?" Tanner asked.

"You mean besides the obvious everything?" I pointed to my left ankle. "That especially smarts."

He took a look. "Can you move it? Wiggle your toes?"

I nodded and performed the tricks.

"Probably just a little sprain. We'll ice it and wrap it back at camp." Then he motioned to Torq, Fry, and Rockford, and the three of them loaded me into an FAV and rushed me back to the main compound building with Tanner riding along as medic.

"What happened down there?" Rockford asked, speaking to Torq and Fry, not me.

"She passed out and lost her grip, sliding down too fast, burning through the rope," Torq said.

"Did not!" My denial didn't explode with as much force as I intended. I still felt weak and reedy. But it got the men's attention. All four turned to look at me.

"I was perfectly conscious until the wind slammed me against the building. *That's* when I lost consciousness." I took a deep breath for strength. "Someone tampered with the equipment."

I wasn't going to let that someone get away with attempted murder. "They were trying to kill Max.

He was up first, but I convinced Torq to let me go instead and foiled their plans."

"You're not making any sense, Dom," Torq said dryly. "We switched ropes, remember?"

"But not carabiners," I argued.

Fry and Torq exchanged another one of those "she's touched in the noggin and becoming a conspiracy-theory freak" looks.

"I checked all y'all's carabiners," Fry said. "They weren't faulty."

Tanner whispered to the others, "Classic heat exhaustion symptoms, including delusions and hallucinations. Probably had a nightmare when she passed out. Now she can't separate the dream from reality—"

"Can too . . . can too . . . can too!" I argued with all the erudition of a kindergartner.

Torq gave me a patronizing pat on the arm. "I've told you, babe. No one is trying to kill Max."

"But—" I tried to get a word in, but I couldn't get my thoughts together.

Rockford turned to Fry. "After we get her settled, gather all the gear. We'll send it to the crime lab in Phoenix and have them verify it wasn't tampered with," he said as if that settled the matter conclusively and for all times. He gave me a wary look, like since I wouldn't sign that stupid release of his, he suspected I was sue-happy.

Torq gave my hand a squeeze. "You passed out due to heat exhaustion and lost your grip." He may as well have added "on reality."

Fry turned his attention back to his driving. Torq sat in contemplative silence.

Back at the compound, they carried me to the sick bay.

"Not here again," I said, but no one showed me much sympathy. I was thinking they viewed me as a clumsy pain in the ass.

Rockford must have phoned his doctor friend as soon as I fell, because the doc was leafing through a back issue of the *WSJ*, waiting for me when I arrived, probably happy about the small mint he was making off all these compound calls and plotting how to invest his windfall profits. With Max and me around, Rockford should consider putting the doc on retainer.

Rockford's doctor consulted with Tanner before he examined me and my ankle, packed the ankle with an ice pack, diagnosed me with heat exhaustion, filled me with fluids, dosed me with pain meds, and gave me instructions to continue drinking plenty of fluids, keep the ankle elevated, and stay off it as much as possible. He dropped an Ace bandage on the cart beside my cot before confining me to bed for observation for the afternoon and went off to talk with Rockford, promising to return in a few to check on me and show me how to wrap the bandage.

"Now get some rest," he said as he left.

The thing about bed confinement—it gives a person plenty of time to think. So in between alternating ten minutes of ice on and ten minutes of ice off the ankle, I reviewed the situation. *Someone had tried to kill me!*

Well, okay, they'd tried to kill Max. My head wasn't quite clear yet, so I allowed that there was a slight chance I was wrong and they were trying to kill Torq. I mean, it had been Torq's rope that snapped, but the carabiner I'd used had been meant for Max.

I knew nothing about rappelling. I guessed some-one could have tampered with Torq's rope or they could have greased the carabiner, which would have slid too fast and burned through the rope, causing it to snap. And Fry wouldn't have checked for grease. I mean, why would he think to? But why split hairs now? I had to stop the killer from succeeding.

Damn this injury! Precious time was wasting while I tried to summon enough strength to act, or merely walk. First things first—get Pussy's gun. Then . . . then *what*? Then I stick to Max like his gun-toting shadow. Torq was on his own. The way I figured, should the need arise, he could defend himself better than I could.

While I iced, trying to numb my foot enough that I could put my weight on it, I tried to remember everything I'd learned at camp about spying and self-defense. Torq was definitely better on his own. Max was getting the raw deal, but at least I'd have a weapon.

I touched my sore ankle and winced. It was only sort of numb, but it would have to do. Some ortho-pedic surgeon somewhere was going to love me for this.

I sat up slowly, still feeling weak and slightly dizzy,

not to mention annoyingly wiped out and tired. My eyes felt heavy. I fought to stay awake. I touched my foot to the floor and cautiously applied some weight, only to wince with pain.

There was a knock on the door. Emma popped her head in. "How're you doing?"

I motioned for her to come in. "Am I glad to see you! Close the door. I need your help."

She quickly took in the situation. "You're not trying to escape? Tell me you're not."

"I have to."

She rolled her eyes. "Does this have anything to do with your crazy notion that someone is trying to kill Max?"

"How—"

"Tanner's a blabbermouth."

"Okay, yes, it does. Now come over here and give me a shoulder to lean on. I need your help to get out of here." I motioned her over, but she didn't budge.

"What's your plan?" She crossed her arms and frowned at me.

"I'm going to play bodyguard."

Emma shook her head but had the good grace not to laugh. "I can't believe this. What are you going to use for the guard part? Those lethal acrylics of yours?"

"Pussy has a gun under her mattress. I'm going to steal it." I spoke without thinking, damn drugs. What had the doc given me, truth serum?

Emma stared at me with a look of utter disbelief

on her face. "I'm with Tanner. You're definitely delusional."

"But you'll help me, right?" I gave her my helpless-puppy look. No one can resist the helpless-puppy look.

"I must be crazy, too." She walked over to me and took a look at the offending ankle. "That's nasty. You can't walk on that without wrapping it. Even then, you'll be lucky if you can support your weight for long."

I pointed to the Ace bandage. "The doc left that. Know anything about ankle wrapping?"

"I've had my share of sprains." She bent to retrieve the bandage. "Now sit down and put your foot up while I take care of it."

She carefully unwrapped the self-adhering bandage and positioned the end in the arch of my foot. "Hold your foot like this picture shows." She held up the packaging and I complied.

"Hurry!" I said. "We have to hurry. Max isn't safe out there all alone."

She rolled her eyes again.

"I'm serious!"

"Instead of bird-dogging Max you should be using your energy giving Torq a major, and very erotic, token of your appreciation. If he'd just saved my life I'd be making the most of it." She made figure eights with the bandage around my ankle and heel, wrapping slowly and carefully as I fought to keep my eyes open.

Something was wrong. I shouldn't be this sleepy.

"If not for him, you'd be a pavement pancake right now. Crow food. He was a hero, for sure."

"Hero?" I winced as she tightened the bandage. "I don't remember any heroics."

"No, of course you don't; you were out like a light. Too tight?"

I shook my head no.

She wrapped like an expert. "Torq pulled a major Bond move and hauled you down the building, fighting that damn wind the whole way.

"I tell you, it was right out of the movies, or one of those news stories you hear about where some mum gets a rush of adrenaline and superhuman strength and lifts a car off her baby or something." She finished wrapping and patted my ankle, making sure the bandage was secure.

She grinned. "Somehow he managed to support your dead weight as Fry and Rockford and the rest of us raced from the roof. You should've seen the knots of tension in his neck and how red in the face he was from the exertion of keeping the wind from blowing you both off the wall. He was dripping sweat, I'll tell you. Then he inched his way down the building, hanging on to you until he got low enough to lower you into Rockford's arms."

I frowned. "How did I get this bum ankle?"

"You hit the building hard with your foot once or twice just after you passed out. Just be grateful it was your foot and not your head."

Interesting as Emma's story was, I felt my eyelids growing heavier in a drugged sort of way and I had trouble concentrating.

The door swung open and the doctor strode in. "What the hell's going on here?"

"The patient here said her ankle was throbbing and the cot was uncomfortable. She wanted me to bandage it and help her to her room so she could rest on a real bed." I had to admire Emma's quick thinking.

"You should've gotten me." He glared at Emma and then came over to me and grabbed my wrist to take my vitals.

For my part, I could barely keep my eyes open. The doctor and Emma were fading in and out. I felt myself swaying.

"I don't think the cot will be a problem now. The meds are kicking in. Give her a few more seconds and she'll be dead to the world."

He must have seen my attempted wide-eyed expression, because he grinned as he took my shoulders and eased me back onto the cot. Dead to the world was exactly what I was afraid of!

"I gave her some strong pain meds. They have the side effect of knocking most people out for hours. I figured she could use the rest."

"Several hours!" I tried to sit back up, but my body felt too heavy to lift and I fell back.

"Don't worry. She'll be fine by evening," the doctor said. "Now you should go and let her sleep."

Emma leaned in and patted my shoulder. "Don't you worry. I'll look after Max for you." Emma gave me another pat. And that's the last thing I remembered. . . .

* * *

When I woke up, the air-conditioning unit was humming away and the lights in the room were on full. Someone, probably the doc, had unwrapped my ankle and thrown a thin cotton blanket over me. It was impossible to tell the time of day from the room, so I glanced at the clock and did *not* believe my eyes. Six thirty p.m.! No way! It couldn't be. Maybe there'd been a power glitch or something. But my watch said the same thing. I'd been out for over five hours. The class where the abduction was going to happen was scheduled to begin at seven. There was no time to lose.

Trying to avoid another fainting spell, I sat up slowly. The swelling in my ankle had gone down, but it was beginning to look bruised. My head was groggy but clearing as I reached for the Ace bandage and tried the figure-eight maneuver for myself. Fortunately, the package had directions. There was no way I was getting a cute pink tennie back on that left foot. I'd have to go back to my room and get a flip-flop.

Since no one else was around to do it, I discharged myself from the sick bay, standing tentatively on one foot and gently easing some weight on my injured left ankle. It hurt, but I was a Bond girl—tough, fearless, and still doped up. On I limped.

There was no one in the hallway as I hobbled my way back to the barracks. On a lark, I tried Pussy's door—locked tight. On to Plan B—breaking and entering from the exterior. I snagged a pair of food-handler's gloves and a left flip-flop from my room, committing a heinous fashion faux pas and a mismatch even of color. The real Dom would have owned a matching flip-flop and headband. So much for style.

My stomach growled. I'd had nothing to eat all day but a muffin. So I snagged some change and got a candy bar out of the machine on my way out.

Outside a cloud cover had formed. The air felt heavy and humid and smelled like rain. The wind came from a different direction than usual, from the southeast. It was the end of July and monsoon season. *Oh, great,* I thought. The scene was set for a scary movie. Undeterred by the weather, I sneaked off to Pussy's window.

I'd watched enough *It Takes a Thief* episodes to know that confidence is the key to breaking and entering. Heart pumping out of control, I boldly marched to Pussy's window and went rapping, rapping, gently tapping, then lunged for the cover of nearby bushes. No answer. Excellent.

I sidled back to the window and gave it a try. Locked. But not impenetrable.

If my disappearing dad had done one good thing for me, this was it. His absence had made me a latchkey kid. A latchkey kid who frequently forgot her key and whose mother could not leave work to come let her in. Several afternoons spent at the neighbor's house or on the front steps had led me to develop some very handy breaking-in skills. I knew how to jimmy a window without damaging it.

I donned my gloves, pressed my hands against the window glass, wiggled it, and within a minute had jiggled the lock free and slid the window open. I climbed into Pussy's bedroom and headed for the bed.

I slid my hand in between the mattress and box spring and, with all the anticipation of pulling out a snake, pulled out . . . an empty fist. I reached back in and fumbled around some more. I lifted the mattress and looked. Nothing, nothing, absolutely nothing! Which meant in all likelihood Pussy had the gun on her. Or she'd moved it.

I searched her closet, her drawers, and her bathroom, coming up empty on all accounts and growing more panicked by the second. Just fifteen minutes to showtime.

Her nightstand held a fine array of cubic zirconia jewelry and a very authentic-looking lady's Rolex, but no gun.

There was only one conclusion to draw—Pussy was armed and dangerous. Which really freaked me. I slid the window back into place and locked it. Shoot! No phones in the rooms. No cell phone coverage. I grabbed the notepad on Pussy's nightstand and scribbled a note to Emma, telling her about Pussy and the gun. Just in case.

It was just minutes until class and the kidnapping started. I peeled my note off the pad and dashed into the hall.

I'd just shut Pussy's door when Ethan and Bishop burst into the hall on their way to class. They were dressed in desert fatigues and had their eyes blackened. Already jumpy, I was startled by their sudden appearance.

"Geez," I said to them, hand to heart, hoping they

didn't wonder what I was doing outside Pussy's room. "Are you two the good guys or the bad?"

Ethan laughed. "Oh, we're good." He winked. "Be nice to us and we'll show you how good."

I rolled my eyes.

"The kidnapping is going down tonight," Bishop said. "We're expecting the bad guys, so we're prepared. No one's gonna get us like they got Davie." He reached into his pocket. "Wanna see what I got?"

"In your pocket? Not really," I said, knowing those two and their tendency toward lewdness. I really didn't want to see his banana.

But Bishop didn't listen. He pulled out a small billy club and a tiny electronic device. "We're not going down without a fight." He grinned evilly as he thwacked Ethan with the club. "Police issue," he said as Ethan swatted him away.

"And this"—he held out the electronic thingy—"is a tracking device. If they get one of us, the other one will know exactly where he is and how to find him."

"You two really came prepared." I should have been impressed. I really hadn't expected much out of those two. And I hadn't even thought of doing the same myself. But then, my trip to camp had been a surprise. "Genius."

Ethan grinned. "You got it." His gaze ran up and down me, lingering on my bum ankle for just a sec. "You feeling up to participating tonight?"

"Sure."

"Excellent," Bishop said, but I didn't like his tone or expression.

"What?" I said, gaze bouncing between them. "What?"

"We were hoping you would."

I had the feeling it wasn't because they just loved my company or had been horribly concerned about my recovery. "Why?"

"'Cause with that bum ankle, you're the perfect vic. They're going to take you for sure," Ethan said. "Which is just as well, 'cause you sure as hell aren't going to be much use on the rescue team."

"Hey!" I said, indignant.

Bishop put a hand on my shoulder. "Don't worry. We'll save you, honey."

I shook his hand off.

"Yeah." Ethan winked. "Then you can show us your appreciation afterward." He looked me up and down again and glanced at his watch. "You better run and change. You aren't dressed for captivity. Put something warm on. It gets cold in the desert at night."

"Gee, thanks for your concern, boys," I said. "Glad to see chivalry isn't dead."

The boys laughed and turned toward class. "See you in a few," they said in unison.

"Hey," I said, stopping them in their tracks as I felt worry well up and myself going all sentimental. "You two take care tonight. No wild heroics. Stay safe." I swallowed a lump in my throat and my eyes got misty.

They looked at me, puzzled, and, shaking their heads, walked off toward class.

I made a quick stop by my room. The boys were

right. I wasn't dressed for combat. I rushed, trying to get ready, feeling a certain desperation about everything, including how I was going to go into battle with a bum ankle and a foot clad in a flip-flop. I propped the note for Emma up against the mirror in our joint bathroom, hoping she'd see it and come to my rescue, should it come to that. Then I hobbled to my room to change.

Unfortunately, as I walked to the dresser, I stepped wrong on my bad ankle. I winced and leaned forward to catch myself on the dresser, coming face to cover with one of the magazines I'd snagged from Torq but hadn't even had time to look at. In my effort to straighten back up, I bumped it off the dresser and a printout of an Internet news article floated out from it. I was staring at a headline about lottery winners who'd lost it all and frequented Vegas, trying to win it back. Poor saps, I thought. If only they had come to my Unexpected Money Institute before things got out of hand. I could have helped them.

I bent to retrieve it and the captioned photo, a picture of an exuberant, striking woman—buxom with flowing brunette tresses, healthy and youthful, caught my eye.

I gasped.

If you looked past the differences in hair, weight, and bra size, the woman, identified as "Susan Saliner with her winning lottery ticket," was undeniably Emma!

Oh. My. Gosh! I was staring at a precancer Emma. Even though I was rushed, I hurriedly scanned the article, reading the highlights of how Emma/Susan had blown through her cash.

"Emma, you big liar," I said to myself, feeling sorry for her. She'd totally hate it if she knew I knew. And she'd probably *never* let me help her.

There was no time to think about that now. Later.

I folded Emma's picture in fourths and tucked it into my bra for safekeeping. I was probably lopsided, but I had no time to fix that now. I grabbed a track jacket and dashed for the classroom. Well, okay, maybe "hobbled" is a better description. But I looked fast in that jacket—honest!

When I arrived, I spotted Pussy sitting in the back of the room in the midst of her cadre of male admirers. I gave her a thorough up and down, looking for evidence of a bulging gun on her. Ethan and Bishop caught me checking her out and grinned lewdly as if they were imagining some lesbian action. I ignored them, thinking that Pussy could have tucked a gun in her fatigue pants. I debated warning Rockford right then, but my street cred wasn't real high and I couldn't be sure she had the gun on her. I decided to keep an eye on her instead.

The only place left to sit was in the front row between Max, who greeted me with a nervous smile, and Emma. Rockford gave me a scowl but passed on the opportunity to ridicule me. The others ignored me.

The room felt tense and poised for action. Everyone knew the kidnapping would happen soon. I felt nervous, but for different reasons.

Emma leaned over and whispered into my ear, "What are you doing here? Shouldn't you be resting?" She sounded genuinely peeved.

"We're supposed to be preventing the kidnapping. Wasn't that the whole reason for breaking into the Chief's office?" I whispered back. "I couldn't leave you to do it alone. What's the plan?"

With everything that happened, the plan-making had somehow slipped through the cracks.

She stared hard at me. "I suppose you have a suggestion?"

"Warn the class?"

"While you were resting, I came up with a better plan." She stood and everything happened rapid fire. She pulled a gun from her pocket, aiming it at Rockford. "Put the pointer down, Rockford. We're taking you hostage."

"No!" I screamed at Emma in the same instant the classroom door burst open and four armed, hooded men rushed in.

All pandemonium broke loose. CTs scrambled for cover and escape.

Emma swung around and took aim at one of the kidnappers, who was built suspiciously like Torq. I knocked Emma's arm just as she pulled the trigger. Her aim went high and a wad of paint hit the wall behind him and oozed down, leaving an orange splat in its wake.

"Are you crazy?" Emma screamed at me, shaking what was obviously a paintball weapon at me.

"Sorry! I panicked." Which was completely true. Geez, how could I have missed that she was packing a *paintball* gun? How could I believe that Emma was going to shoot Torq with a real gun? I was losing it.

In the second that I distracted her, the kidnappers seized the advantage and disarmed Emma before ordering us all facedown on the floor. We complied like lambs. Then they grabbed Wade, shoved a hood over his head, took him and Rockford and fled in a volley of paintball fire before I could warn Torq or Rock about Pussy's gun.

"Hey, what about her?" Bishop called after them, pointing at me. "Take her. She's no use to us."

He grinned when I scowled at him.

Ethan popped to his feet. "After them," he shouted, waving his billy club.

"Oh, sit down and shut up," Emma said. "We need a plan."

Fifteen minutes later, we had a plan to search the compound and find the hostage. We decided to divide into four search pairs and leave one person behind in the room to coordinate our efforts.

"Max should stay behind," Pussy said before I could speak.

"I agree." Hard to believe Pussy and I agreed on anything, but headquarters was the safest place for Max. I avoided looking him in the eye. I was about to seem like a big traitor of a friend. But, hey, all's fair in love and spying and saving someone's life. "Considering his recent accident, I don't think he should be left alone. I'll—"

Pussy cut me off. "I'll stay with him."

"You?" I pointed to my ankle. "I'll stay. I'm no good in the field."

Out of the corner of my eye, I saw Ethan and Bishop grin as they placed bets on who'd win the argument. Their body posture said they were hoping for a little hair-pulling, female wrestling action.

Pussy crossed her arms and rolled her eyes. "Someone else has had a little head trouble." She arched a brow and flashed me a sinister smile. "Someone here at HQ needs a clear head. I'm the best at coordinating missions." She smiled and winked at Ethan, Bishop, Tanner, and Q. "Right, boys?"

"Pussy stays," Q said.

The others murmured their agreement.

I glared at Ethan and Bishop. "Less than half an hour ago, you two yahoos offered me to the kidnappers because I was of no use to you."

They smiled and shrugged, obviously under Pussy's spell.

"Traitors."

Ethan and Bishop paired up; Tanner, Q, and John; leaving Emma stuck with me and my bum ankle, and us with only three field teams.

I leaned into Emma and whispered with as much urgency as I could muster. "We can't leave Max alone with Pussy."

Emma shrugged. "As you wish. I'll take care of it." She sidled off to say something to Max.

Pussy gave the plum assignments to the guys and instructed Emma and me to search the orchards and the orange-packing shack.

* * *

"I hate the orange shack," I said as we approached it, my flip-flop clacking loudly every other step I took. Try hard as I could, I wasn't exactly stealth. "And I hate that Pussy. She should have given us the rappelling building. That's where they'll be."

Emma ignored my complaining as she surveyed the shack in front of us.

"Pussy obviously thinks so. Why else would she send two teams there?" I paused and leaned against an orange tree to rest my ankle, rambling about inconsequential things to keep my mind off the real danger I was certain Max was in. "Ethan and Bishop are just going to bungle things. And Tanner and Q? John's the only good one of the bunch." I looked around. "Where's Max? Shouldn't he be joining us soon?"

"Any minute," Emma said. "I told him to give us a minute or two and then tell Puss he needed to use the loo and sneak out to join us."

"What if she catches him?" I shuddered. I didn't like leaving Max alone with Pussy for even a second.

"She won't." Emma studied the building.

I should have been concentrating on the task, too, but my mind kept coming back to Emma's situation. Even though my timing was wrong and I knew she'd hate it, I had to say something to Emma about the article I'd seen. "I know about your money problems. After this is over, you have to let me help you."

Emma gave me a blank stare. "Whatever." She returned her attention to the building. "Okay, here's the plan. While we wait for Max, we'll secure the building." She looked at me. "You go in the front and I'll take the back. We'll search the premises and meet in the room in front. If you run into any trouble, scream and I'll come running."

I made a mental note to confront her again later and nodded, agreeing that it was best to have the building secured before Max came. "And I'll do the same for you."

She held a finger to her lips. "Quietly now." Then she waved me into the building as she sneaked around back.

The orange shack was creepy in broad daylight. And really creepy at night. But since Grace Under Pressure, I'd been sort of inoculated against its haunted-housely charms. I slipped in quietly, wondering how I was going to get to Torq and warn him. Maybe the whole thing was in my head. My imagination gone wild . . .

I heard something behind me, the spin of a doorknob, the breath of wind an opening door generates, the rustle of clothing, the groan of the floor under the weight of a footstep. Instinctively, I spun toward the sound.

Bam! Something, someone, struck me from behind at the base of my head. I winced, cocked my shoulder to protect the injury, and let out a rush of breath, stunned. My head exploded with shocking pain. My ears rang with an electronic whir—like earsplitting feedback through a sound system.

I stumbled forward, trying to catch myself against the wall for support. Over the ringing in my ears, I heard a whoosh, like the power swing of a baseball bat cutting through the air. Damn! Rockford hadn't taught us how to disarm a bat-wielding fiend!

Too late, I lunged forward. Something cracked against the back of my head, snapping it forward. I slumped down the wall, fighting with everything I had to stay conscious.

Bond would not pass out. Bond would not pass out. Neither would Christmas Jones or Kissy Suzuki.

But they were fictional characters assaulted with movie props. Even my hard head couldn't withstand the crushing blow of a real weapon. I was growing thin and weak and my thoughts were jumbled and random, a potpourri of the week at camp.

"You! Why?" I whispered, or maybe only thought. "So stupid . . ." Had to escape. Had to tell Torq. Had to get help.

My assailant watched me, waiting patiently and confidently for me to lose consciousness.

I fought to keep my eyes open, to focus, to stop my world from narrowing. But it constricted to a pinprick all the same. Then it went completely, densely black. . . .

Chapter Twenty

Just call me bound and confused. I woke up lying on my side in a small, dank room without windows, shivering from a cold that put normal air-conditioning to shame. The air was thin, thin, thin and icy. I definitely was not in the sick bay. My head pounded and cried for an extra-strength Excedrin. Paralyzed by pain and fear of having my head used for batting practice again, I listened for sounds of my assailant's evil presence. Maybe some maniacal laughter or heavy, sinister breathing. Too bad I couldn't remember who my assailant was.

There was a click and I started. It was followed by a hum, like a refrigerator running. As I struggled to fight off panic, I realized I was not in the Antarctic or Blofeld's frozen Swiss Alps lair, but locked in a refrigeration unit.

On the plus side, I was breathing. No telling how long I'd been out. My head hurt, but given the power of the blow it sustained I was lucky my cranium wasn't shattered into a million tiny pieces and

I was able to think at all. My ankle throbbed. And I felt stiff from being bound. As my eyes became accustomed to the dark and some semblance of clear thinking returned, I realized I was surrounded by shelves holding crates of oranges—the refrigeration room in the orange shack!

I was lying on the floor, face flat against cold concrete, with my arms bound behind my back with zip ties. My teeth chattered and I was shivering beneath my tank top and crop pants. Somehow I'd lost my track jacket. Deciding I was unlikely to be clubbed again, I gingerly tugged at my bound wrists, hoping, fruitlessly as it turned out, for a little slack. I tried moving my feet—trussed like a turkey at the ankles, too.

If I could just reposition myself into a sit—

The refrigeration motor shut off. Too bad this wasn't a Bond movie, 'cause this would be a terrific and exciting time for James to swing in and save me. In real life I settled for a little mental screaming—where in the name of 007 were all the heroes when a girl *really needed one?*

Emma! Emma would be looking for me. Emma would come back!

I paled. Emma would be coming back all right—to kill me!

I shuddered as my memory came flooding back along with a clear image of Emma standing over me, waiting for me to pass out.

I closed my eyes and tried to think. Vague images swept through my mind. Torq had circled "hit man" in the movie review next to his computer. He'd been searching for info on Emma. The Internet article had mentioned she was from a rough section of Brisbane, and knew how to shoot and take care of herself. She came to the United States to get a new start and won, and lost, the lottery.

Emma was a hit man, or woman! The thought came from nowhere but made absolute sense. The article had said that she was desperate to get rich quick again.

"No way am I living poor," she'd been quoted as saying.

She'd been hired to kill Max. Had to be. I'd just been too blinded by my friendship with her to see it. I wondered for just a second why I wasn't dead. And if I had any hope of surviving, or if she'd be back for me.

I squirmed. My cheek came into contact with something cold and sticky on the floor. It was too dark to see, but my nose told me it wasn't orange juice. It had the metallic scent of blood.

"Davie!" I whispered to the empty room as a tear slid down my face. I swallowed hard to keep the bile from rising in my throat.

I bet she'd lured him here and killed him. Probably came back for his body the night of the paint-ball game and dumped him in the desert.

Another random thought hit me—the itinerary in Rockford's office. Was it Davie's? Had he met Emma in Vegas? I thought of the car in Hal's parking lot, of the skill of the driver. I wondered if a partnership made in hell had gone bad.

I had to get out of here and save Max. If he wasn't

dead already. Damn! I'd inadvertently led him right into a trap.

I pushed the thought from my mind, told myself to buck up, and wiggled into a sitting position. First things first—get free of these ties. With a little luck, I'd be able to get my arms in front of me.

I worked my legs through my arms a little at a time, then my hips. I was breathing hard and even felt slightly warmed by the exercise by the time I had my arms in front of me and pushed up to a stand. My ankle was killing me. With my ankles bound together it was impossible to shift my weight to my good foot.

How long had I been here? Was anyone besides Emma looking for me? I guessed they were probably still too involved in the "other" kidnapping.

I clenched my teeth against the pain and cold and felt around for something to cut the zip ties. A box cutter. Anything. Struggling would only rub my wrists raw. Nothing. The room was sharp-object-free.

I switched to Plan B—escape still bound. I inched toward the door and gave it a try. It was locked tight. One thing was for sure—I wasn't kicking the door down any time soon.

I briefly considered screaming for help. But the room was insulated. I could scream my lungs out and no one would hear me.

Panicky Plan C—jump Emma and subdue her when she returned, if she returned. I felt up the shelves around me, assessing the odds of getting one to topple where I wanted it, thinking I could push one or two over on her.

I gave one a tug. It didn't budge. On closer examination, I realized it was bolted to the wall. I tried using my highly prized acrylics like a screwdriver. Turns out they weren't as tough as grade-A steel. I broke one in the effort, shaking my finger and sucking on it, fighting back tears.

That small failure almost did me in. My courage faltered. I let out an exasperated sigh, feeling on the edge of a major crying jag and totally betrayed. How could Emma want to kill me? How could she actually do it? Swing something at my head, give me a concussion, store me here either to let me rot or to come back to finish me off in some gruesome way? All for what—money? What happened to loyalty and friendship? It sucked. It really sucked.

Exactly what *would* Bond do in my situation?

Probably pull out a Swiss army knife specially designed by Q with a laser beam that cuts through steel doors. Then he'd save Max. Only I'd probably get Torq and Fry to help me first. Bond would never give up and neither would I!

With no laser and no other weapon, I'd have to use my head. Literally. Emma was a hundred-pound pixie still recovering from chemo. I could take her. One good head-butt to the gut . . .

I heard something. I cocked an ear and went stone silent at the sound of a key being inserted into a lock. The handle to the fridge door turned. I put my head down, ready to hobble to a charge.

It was a great plan, and it would've worked, too. Except that crafty Emma had a stun gun. She waved it and reached for me. I ducked out of the way, making as much of a dash for the door as a woman with a bum ankle and bound feet can. I'd just about reached freedom, too, when Emma grabbed me by my darn long hair extensions and jerked me back.

"You should have heeded my warning when I packed your bag. I really didn't want to have to do this."

"I can't believe you defaced my Louis Vuitton like that," I said, truly indignant and trying to shame her. "Look. This is all just silly. Can't we talk it out?"

Ever eloquent, Emma stuck the stun gun in my arm.

Chapter Twenty-one

"I'll take that as a no," I said, once I regained enough muscle control to speak. I also took the opportunity to look around for Torq. No hero in sight.

"You're making a big mistake. I have fuzzy, spotty memories at best. I'm sure I can completely forget this little episode." I looked at Emma for confirmation.

"Why don't we just team up and go find those fake kidnappers?" I put on the rah-rah attitude. "Just forget this all ever happened?" I gave Emma a hopeful, Pollyanna look.

Her returning look was distinctly disgusted and cynical with a twist of "as if" thrown in for good measure.

She pointed her gun, a real gun that looked suspiciously like Pussy's, at me. "Get up and march to the car."

"You have a car?" I tried not to sound too smartass.

"What do you think took me so long to get back? I had to borrow one from the garage. I've gone soft. My hotwiring skills are rusty. Then I had to go pick up our buddy Max." She arched a brow. "He's been my target all along."

There was no use denying what I knew any longer. "Yeah. I figured that out too late." I paused. "I can't walk well with my feet and wrists bound." I held my wrists out to her. "It would speed things up if you cut me loose."

"Nice try." Emma grabbed my arm and dragged me outside to a waiting FAV with the motor running.

Large, Seattle-sized drops of rain began falling, making mud spots in the desert dust as Emma buckled me into a seat and I craned around to get a look at Max.

"He's still alive. Just drugged," she said as if reading my mind.

Off in the distance, thunder crashed and lightning lit the sky at irregular intervals.

"You picked a good night for this," I said conversationally as Emma hopped into the driver's seat and I was frantically trying to come up with a plan. When conversation stalls, discuss the weather. That's what Mom always said. "Nice gothic mood and weather tonight. Very horror-flick. All we need to make it absolutely perfect is the howl of a werewolf, or an obliging coyote."

Emma smiled. "You know, I really hate that I have to kill you. You're an entertaining girl."

"Yeah, I hear ya," I said, squirming to find a comfortable position, marveling at her understatement. "It's the pits when you have to kill a friend." I paused significantly. "You could always reconsider."

She rolled her eyes.

We jounced across the countryside, obviously off-roading it to our final destination. I was plotting escape. I figured I'd be able to unbuckle myself and then, like it or not, I was going to have to try out a jumping-from-a-moving-vehicle maneuver and go for help. There was no way I could get Max out with me. Feigning nonchalance and a fascination with the distant lightning-lit horizon, I reached for the seat belt buckle. I'd barely tickled the buckle with my fingertips when I felt a gun pressed against my head.

"Bang!" Emma laughed as I jumped from the start she gave me. "Sorry. Spy humor."

"Uh-huh."

She had one hand on the wheel with her body twisted to face me and her other hand holding the gun against my head. "Try it and your brains will be splattered over five miles of desert. Now just sit back and enjoy the ride."

Okay, I saw micro expressions serious and murderous on her face. I carefully put my hands in my lap where she could see them. "Just when did you turn into a maniacal killer?"

"Just be quiet and behave," Emma said. "I'm like every mum in the world—I have eyes in the back of my head. Try another escape maneuver and I'll shoot . . . to kill."

"Oh, come on," I said, feeling surprisingly bold and sassy. After all, what did I have to lose? "Sound like you mean it. Dear old Mom scared me more and she only ever grounded me."

"Dear Dom." Emma grinned and returned her attention to driving.

The rain fell harder and harder. Emma switched her wiper blades into high gear and punched the accelerator. It was dark, but I believed we were headed in the direction of the dry Hassayampa River. Emma was doing some impressive high-speed off-road driving.

"Boy, Davie'd be proud. I think you're the star driving student," I said, trying to goad her and hoping to make myself a real person to her again, instead of a victim. I'd seen enough *Oprah* episodes to know this sometimes worked.

Emma laughed. "Davie's in driving heaven." She paused. "He didn't teach me much anyway. I have previous experience."

"Don't tell me *you* went to Bondurant, too? Didn't know they had a branch Down Under."

She didn't reply, just grinned enigmatically.

"Okay," I said, giving the Velveteen Rabbit stiff competition in the race to be real, "you might as well tell me now—who hired you to hit Max?"

She grinned, but there was a hard set to her chin and her eyes glittered with greed. "You're too smart for your own good."

"And nosy," I added. "So who?"

"Max's dear little half sister, Kendall. She hired both me and Davie. But Davie screwed up. Twice. Then he lost his nerve and tried to bail on me. What could I do? He gave me no choice." She switched the wipers into even higher gear as the rain pelted the roof and washed in sheets across the windshield.

I was from Seattle, but I still didn't like driving in the pounding rain. This was scaring me. I fought to keep the fear and edginess out of my voice and attitude. "You don't have to kill Max and me. I know you lost your fortune. But I can give you financial counseling. Help you get back on your feet. I promise I'll never mention a word about Davie. He wasn't a good man, anyway. Why not just live and let live?"

"So you can love and let spy?" Her tone gave hard-core cynicism a heavy sarcastic edge. "I refuse to be poor again. You should have kept your nose out of my business. Then we wouldn't be in this here pickle where I have to kill you." She sounded more like a lecturing big sis than a killer.

"Hey, you can't lay that on me. You got sloppy." I pointed a broken-nailed accusing finger at her.

"My bad. I got desperate."

I shivered and decided a change of topic would be nice. "Are we there yet?"

Emma grinned and pulled to an abrupt stop. "Good timing. We're here." She jumped out of the vehicle, came around to my side of the car, and opened my door with her gun drawn and pointed at me. "I'm going to free your ankles." She cut my zip ties off. "Get out of the car."

Emma grabbed me and held me in front of her with her gun pressed to my head. "One false move and you're dead. Now help me get Max."

Somehow we managed to wrangle Max out of the vehicle. She motioned in the direction of the river. "We'll drag him there."

The rain pelted down, quickly drenching us as we dragged Max into the center of the riverbed. Tiny rivulets of water cut through the river bottom. At the heart of the rapidly filling riverbed, Emma ordered me to stop our death walk. I recognized the spot from the desert ambush game the day before, a narrow canyon that the guys had mentioned was notorious for flooding.

We dropped Max.

"Lie down beside him." Emma waved her gun at me.

I felt sick. Certain Emma was going to shoot us execution style, I hesitated.

"Let's make this quick and humane," Emma said as she shoved me to the ground.

I landed in a puddle, partially breaking my fall with my bound arms as mud splashed up my legs.

"A flash flood's headed our way," Emma said. "How long can a CT tread water?" She laughed.

I expected her to leave me to be washed away, bound and helpless. Instead, she pulled a pair of wire cutters from her pants pocket and cut the zip tie from my wrists.

"Can't have my accidental drowning victim found bound. That wouldn't look natural. If you're ever found at all."

"Stop it! Stop it. Enough's enough, Susan!" I screamed, trying to shock some sense and decency in her. I was soaked. My tank top stuck to my body. My hair was matted. But my inner sense of dignity was perfectly intact.

Emma grabbed my arms and shook me. "I don't have a choice!"

I pulled loose and rolled away from her.

She hit me with the stun gun.

I expected to be jolted and go limp, but nothing happened. I didn't feel a thing. Then I realized she'd used it on my fake breast. Embracing my good luck, I played dead instead as she tagged me twice more. The silicone inserts protected me from the electric shock. But I pretended to be jolted.

She turned to leave me to drown, or so I thought. The water was definitely rising and now covered the bottom of the river in a thin sheet. Incapacitated, a person could drown in an inch or two of water. I watched Emma, waiting for the perfect opportunity to strike. She turned and grabbed a nearby boulder with two hands and held it over her head, ready to crush me with it.

Something caught her attention and distracted her. She paused and I heard it, too. The gentle shake of a rattler's tail. God bless that rattler. It distracted Emma just long enough for me to lunge at her.

She screamed and fell back, dropping the rock. We grappled like a couple of mud wrestlers as we fought for control of her gun and stun gun. I fought using every aspect of my FSC training. I scratched and pulled hair and, disgusting as it was, reached for her nose to gouge her sinuses out. She took evasive action and dodged me.

Undeterred, I parried back. Hey, she was a heck of a lot smaller and less tough and protected than a padded Torq. And I was a whole lot angrier.

Emma screamed and fought back with equal vigor. I got the gun. Emma knocked it from my hand. It went flying, lost in the rising black water.

Emma cursed and swore and reached for her stun gun.

"Try that and you'll electrocute us both," I said, swatting it away into the rushing water as I tried another wrestling move on her.

Without warning, Emma gave up the fight. She wrenched free and raced for the shore and the waiting FAV. I took two steps to follow her and slipped in my damn flip-flop, losing her.

The water was rising quickly now. The flip-flop kept wanting to float and slowed me down as I tried to get up, pulling Max with me the best I could. I kicked it free and staggered back to my feet with Max in my arms, fighting the rising water. I took a step and froze.

The rattler was back, shaking its booty-thing just inches from us. I'd always been told that snakes are more afraid of us than we are of them.

"Shoo," I said to the snake, trying not to make any sudden movements that might remind it of prey. "Shoo. Go away. You've done your job and I'm very grateful, now scat!"

To my surprise, the snake skedaddled, though I think self-preservation had more to do with its departure than my intimidation tactics. I heaved a big sigh of relief as I fought to remain standing in the rising water.

And then suddenly a light appeared on the dark water. I looked up into a pair of headlights hydroplaning across the river directly at us.

Chapter Twenty-two

So what did I do? Run like hell? Nope. I couldn't leave Max. I cowered, resigned and ready to be mowed over and join the roadkill of the world, ruing my bum ankle and Max's lack of consciousness. As I was saying my final prayers of contrition and wondering why my life wasn't passing before my eyes yet again, the FAV jolted to a stop next to us in a fanfare of murky water. Torq jumped out, taking in the situation with a glance.

"About time you showed up, Spy Guy. I was beginning to doubt your spook powers." I think maybe Torq grinned. I was faltering under the weight of holding up Max. Torq took him from me and I helped load him into the FAV.

When we finished, I reached into my bra and pulled out the now-soggy picture of Emma/Susan and held it out to him, tapping it. "Did you know that Emma, aka Susan Saliner, is trying to kill Max?"

"Yeah," he said, taking the disintegrating paper from me. "Get this from my room, did you?"

"Yeah. Well, I figured you owed me for taking my camera."

Best I could tell in the dark, he was still grinning and amused. "I'll explain that later." He took my arm. "Let's get you in the car before we drown out here." He pointed to the tires, where the water had risen so fast it was midway up the hubcap. "We have to get out of the river before we're washed away."

I was nodding my agreement when I was blinded by yet another pair of approaching headlights.

Another FAV barreled toward us.

"Oh, brother! Not again!" I said.

"Emma! Shit!" Torq shoved me toward the driver's side. "Jump in and drive!"

"No, you drive," I said. "You have more experience. You've been to the Bondurant School—"

"And you have a perfect driving record." His voice was only slightly mocking.

"Only if you discount that one blown-up car," I retorted, wondering what the world had come to when I started pointing out my driving failures.

Ignoring me, he buckled himself into the passenger seat. "I'll ride shotgun. I have a hell of a lot more firearm experience than you do. If we manage to get out of her path, she's gonna come at us with all the firepower she can muster. The woman's part of a major crime family and she can shoot to kill. Now move!"

I jumped into the driver's side, buckling up and adjusting the mirror.

"To hell with the mirrors," Torq said. "Punch it!"

Emma was flying at us on the perpendicular, ready to T-bone us right into oblivion.

I hit the gas pedal and we peeled out, wet sand and water flying in our wake.

"Veer right. Take us up the far bank. We'll never make the east bank here. It's too steep and she's cut off our downriver path." He paused. "Once up, get us a few hundred feet away from the river so she can't ram us back in," Torq directed.

I followed his directions, remembering the spot he meant from our ambush day. I got us ashore, but barely. By the time I'd pulled out of the riverbed, the water had reached our undercarriage. Another inch or two and we would've been floating.

Emma turned and pursued us with her brights on, trying to blind me in the process.

"We have to get back to the camp side of the river," Torq said as he craned around to watch Emma's progress. "If we can outrun the water, there's a spot a mile or so ahead where the county built an access road, complete with a bridge across the riverbed. Emma will try to stop us."

I nodded my agreement with his plan. "Just tell me where and when to turn."

Emma had now turned and was following us, hot on our tail, closing the gap. "She must have the souped-up FAV," I said. "You couldn't bring the fast one?"

"Maybe it's the driver, not the car. Look out!" Torq grabbed the steering wheel and took us around a large saguaro.

"Sorry!" So narrowly averting a collision and being

impaled on a cactus rattled me, though I would have thought I'd plumbed the depths of fear hours ago.

"Just keep your eyes on the road. This was the fastest beast in the garage." He kept looking in the rearview mirror, preparing to fire if necessary.

"Sure thing," I said. "But where's the road?"

He grinned.

Our trip around the cactus slowed us down. Emma gained on us, coming up alongside us on the left.

"Damn!" Torq said. "She's going to ram us. The most effective place to ram a car is the left rear bumper. Brace yourself. And if the airbag deploys, ignore it. It'll deflate in a second. It'll be hot in your lap, but it won't disable the vehicle."

"Aren't you going to shoot her or something?"

"Just—"

Wham!

My head snapped forward and backward from the impact. Max bounced around in the back. I screamed. Torq grabbed the wheel and straightened us out. "Foot back on the gas," he yelled.

Emma fell back.

"Whoohoo! We did it. We lost her." I peered into the rearview mirror. I grinned, spirits soaring. "We left Emma in the dirt."

"Don't get cocky, kid. She's not done yet." Torq looked back over his shoulder. "She's back. She's riding in your blind spot, preparing to ambush us."

"What? I knew I should have adjusted the mirrors! Then I wouldn't have any blind spots!" I craned around to get a peek at Emma. "Well, don't just sit there, shoot her!"

"I never realized you were so bloodthirsty." Torq smiled.

"That bitch has tried to kill us too many times this week. I'm losing patience with her."

"Our best bet is to outmaneuver her. She's raising her gun." Torq took aim right back at her, positioning his gun in the window behind me, trying to get a clear shot at Emma. "In a moment, she'll let loose between twenty and thirty rounds of quick semi-automatic fire. And she's accurate as hell, a prize markswoman. Once she starts firing, we have two options—slam on the brakes or perform the bootlegger. I say go for the bootlegger."

"But we'll be going in the wrong direction then."

Zing! Emma hit my side mirror with her first shot. A volley erupted, just like Torq predicted. Torq was firing back, yelling instructions for the bootlegger.

"Foot off the gas."

I removed my foot, trying to cover my head and duck as I did. "I hate this! I don't like being shot at."

"Nobody does, Dom," Torq answered calmly.

The car veered wildly.

"Spin the wheel! Pull the emergency brake." Torq kept firing.

"Where's the emergency brake? Is it one of those floor buttons? I can't find it." I was looking around wildly. "I'm not familiar with this car! Is it American or Japanese?"

"It's German," Torq said through clenched teeth and pulled a lever between the seats.

The car spun around perfectly, wet sand flying in all directions.

Something was wrong with Torq. I turned to look at him and noticed he was clutching his arm. "You're hit, aren't you? That bitch got you." My voice pitched up several octaves with worry. I felt woozy just thinking about it.

"Don't panic, Dom. We can't afford panic right now. Release the emergency brake and punch it! We need to fly. Take us out into the open desert. Then we'll loop back around and head for the bridge. Let's hope to hell we get there before Emma or the water does." He reached under the seat for a first-aid kit as he spoke, still clutching his arm.

"How bad is it?" I steered according to Torq's directions, afraid to look at his arm. "Should I pull over?"

"Hell, no! It's just a flesh wound. She barely grazed my arm. It'll bleed like hell for a few minutes until I can get it bandaged. Then I'll be fine."

I didn't believe him. "Did you hit the bitch?" Cold anger, when it erupts, is a very scary thing. In that moment, I lost sight of Emma as a person and wanted her dead as a Dickensian doornail.

"I doubt it." Somehow Torq managed to single-handedly apply a bandage, give directions, and reload his weapon as I drove.

A few minutes later, the bridge came into sight. So did a car blocking the bridge entrance.

"Good, the bridge is intact." Torq sounded calm and confident.

"And what about that car?" Okay, so I sounded shrill. I think I had a right.

"A one-car roadblock. No problem," Torq said.

I gave him a "you're so crazy" look. "We didn't cover roadblocks in class. Why don't I pull over and let you drive?" I tried to match his calm, but I was already white-knuckling the steering wheel.

"Worried about those insurance rates again?"

If he was trying to goad me into action, it wasn't working. "No, seriously, I can't ram another car. It's not in my nature. I'm basically conflict-averse—"

"This from the woman who was screaming for blood a minute ago?" He paused and sighed heavily. "Dom, I can't drive with this arm and ride shotgun at the same time. I'll talk you through it."

I did my own big shoulder-heaving sigh, which Torq took for acquiescence.

"Put on your high beams. Let's blind the bitch. Aim for the rear fender between the rear wheel and the bumper. Hit at an angle and keep the accelerator floored through the collision. No matter how badly the FAV is damaged, keep going. Get us across that bridge."

Torq braced his arm and winced, ready to take a shot at Emma as we passed by. "This time, the airbags will almost certainly deploy. Be ready."

We were closing the gap quickly.

I looked but didn't see Emma anywhere. I tuned everything else out and focused on my target area, holding the wheel in a death grip.

We were almost there. Seconds to impact. I braced myself, repeating Torq's instructions, flooring the gas pedal. Aiming . . . aiming. At the last second, I closed my eyes and plowed into the left rear quarter panel of Emma's vehicle.

Metal screeched against metal. My foot lost the gas pedal. I felt the whiplash of the impact and my airbag deployed. Unable to see, I held the wheel straight, found the gas pedal again and punched it. We were either going across that bridge or into the river with gusto.

Just as Torq had promised, the airbag deflated into my lap. Emma's car spun out of the way. We sailed onto the bridge. I was scared to the very edge of panic. The rain pelted down so hard that even with my wipers on high I was having trouble seeing through the flood on the windshield. We could have actually been underwater for all I knew. I wondered briefly if I'd been mistaken and we'd taken a wrong turn into the river.

In my rearview mirror, I saw Emma appear from behind a cactus and jump into the car. Seconds later, she was barreling across the bridge after us. I headed straight into open desert. Behind us, Emma had cleared the bridge.

Suddenly, up ahead, a pair of headlights appeared.

"It's Pussy!" Torq said. When I gave him a questioning look, he grinned. "Didn't I tell you? She's my colleague, my cohort in crime. A P.I. Max's brother hired to protect him."

"I think you left that part out," I said, feeling suddenly jealous and a bit guilty for making fun of Pussy. The world was certainly on its head when I was trying to kill Emma and glad to see Pussy. "Is she just a cohort or a co-cavort?"

Torq grinned that sexy grin of his again. "Jealous?"

Before I could think up one of my infamous boring retorts, another pair of headlights appeared. And another. Overhead, I heard the roar of a chopper as it led the charge toward us.

"Look. Pussy called in reinforcements. Good girl," Torq said.

"Who are they?"

"FBI. Local law enforcement."

Behind us, Emma swerved and headed back toward the river.

I yanked on the steering wheel and gunned after her.

Chapter Twenty-three

Torq grabbed the wheel and spun us away from the river. "Let her go. She'll never make it. The water's too deep."

Before our eyes, Emma's car shot into the raging water at full speed, as if extreme mphs would fly her to the far bank.

"Suicide," Torq whispered under his breath.

Emma charged partway into the river before the car lost its grounding and began to float. Guiltily, I was half-hoping she'd make it. Just disappear and start a fresh, new life. Use her spy camp skills to create the perfect alias and cover life.

No such luck. In just a couple of seconds, the current slurped the FAV into the heart of the raging, bubbling torrent. The FAV did several 360s in the water before a wall of water toppled it end-over-end like a scale model in a Bond movie. It sank without fanfare, disappearing from sight into the murky water.

I stared hard in the dark, looking for a figure to emerge from the car. Looking for Emma with a sick feeling in my stomach and a profound sadness for her choice.

"Do you think she made it?" I asked stupidly, hopefully, fearfully.

"Slow her down and stop," Torq said, avoiding an answer. "Let's get back to civilization." Torq picked up a two-way radio and began communicating with Pussy and the other rescue vehicles. He reached over and squeezed my hand as he barked commands to the others. In seconds we were surrounded by cops and agents of all variety and badge.

Torq jumped out of the FAV. "Stay here."

I'd had enough high-performance driving for one night. Torq could take over. I slid over to the passenger seat.

He stood in the rain, talking with the law enforcement boys for several minutes before he ran back to the FAV and jumped into the driver's seat. "Some of the boys are headed downriver to make sure Emma didn't somehow manage to escape." He gave me a look probably meant to convey hope. He wasn't as unemotional as he'd have people believe.

"The chopper's going to land in the open area up ahead. They'd like to ask you some questions and take you and Max to the hospital for observation."

"What are my options?" I wasn't in the mood to be questioned and, though the thought of a helicopter ride was tempting, I much preferred being with Torq.

"You could drive back with me."

I bit my lip and nodded toward his arm. "Maybe you need to be in the chopper."

"Nah," he said and grinned.

"Okay, I'll stay with you." I grinned back.

"Let's go let 'em know they can take Max and the chopper home." Torq revved up the engine and put her in gear.

"Are you sure you can drive?" I asked, worried about his arm.

"Can I drive?" He snorted and took off toward the chopper, showing how fast he could accelerate just to prove a point. As soon as we stopped, Torq jumped out and went to talk to the cops and the chopper crew. The crew ran over to the FAV with a stretcher, loaded Max in, and took him away.

A few minutes later, I watched as Torq returned to the FAV in the pouring rain, his shirt molded to his chest, his hair slicked to his head, curling at collar length, a big old bandage around his upper left arm. He was walking his cocky, badass walk and looking a lot like he had when I first saw him, only wetter. There was something hot and sexy about having just defeated death together. Maybe that's why Bond always gets the girl at the end.

"You going to be all right?" Torq asked as he climbed into the driver's seat next to me. He was asking about more than my physical condition. My sanity seemed to be at stake.

"Define 'all right.'" I couldn't really say I was unchanged, or at that moment, totally steady. But I'd found an inner strength I hadn't known existed. That was enough for now.

"Should I insist you go in the chopper?" His voice was soft, sultry, concerned, but somehow still begged me to refuse. His gaze slid to the tank top molded to my form.

I shook my head no. "I'll be fine. You're the guy with the gunshot wound."

He shrugged and nodded at the cadre of vehicles around us as we watched the chopper take off. "We're going to caravan back."

Torq put his good arm around me and pulled out behind the rest of the law enforcement vehicles, driving with his bum arm. The rain still poured down, but the lightning had subsided. I pushed thoughts of Emma aside, deciding to dwell on the positives and ponder the dark stuff later.

"So I guess I win," I said, cuddling into him like I belonged there.

"Win?" he said.

"I thwarted the kidnapping, didn't I? A real kidnapping. Not to mention, I saved your ass—"

"My ass? Who showed up with the FAV at the key moment?"

"Yeah, but I stayed alive until you finally made it. And just so you know, I was trying to escape and warn you."

He shook his head, but he was grinning.

"Plus I did all that fine high-performance driving. I get bonus points for that. I get to go down in the annals of FSC, right?"

"Yeah. Sure. Too bad there's no prize money, *Jenna*." He made my name sound sexy.

"Okay, so you've outed me." I paused. "What about you? Who is the real you? And after all this excitement, will you be able to stand another boring camp session, or will you return to the real spook life?"

He smiled at me, looking a bit sheepish. "Actually, I *am* still a bit of a spook. I run my own consulting firm. I'm a corporate spy. I do a session or two for FSC for fun from time to time."

"Oh." I took a minute to digest that info. He was certainly a man of mystery. I stared at him hard, willing him to say more, but he remained mute. I changed the subject. "How did you find me?"

"Pussy sent out an SOS when Max went to the can and didn't return. I knew Emma was really Susan. I'd been keeping my eye on her. But I had nothing on her. She was pretty clean in her hit attempts."

I digested that info.

"As soon as Pussy contacted us, I called and told Rock and Fry what I suspected. Pussy checked the garage and found an FAV missing. The FAVs are all equipped with tracking devices. Led me right to you."

I nodded.

He gave my shoulders a squeeze. "Are we good?"

"Well . . ." I paused, trying to phrase my question. "You still have some explaining to do. Like why you stole my camera?"

"Oh, that," he said as if breaking into and entering my room was no big deal. "I took it for your protection. I suspected someone of taking a shot at us during the opening car explosion. I was worried that someone might not like you having those photos." He gave me another playful squeeze. "I was going to give it back. Honest."

I pointed an accusatory finger at him. "You bugged my room using an FSC pen, too."

"Yep." He didn't sound the least bit sorry, either. "To keep on eye on both you and Susan. I figured Susan would check for bugs in her room, but not yours. You threw me off for a few when you stashed it in Wade's room." He smiled as if he was impressed. "Anything else?"

"Yeah. I'm guessing Torq isn't your real name?"

"Good guess."

"So?" I spoke with a leading-question intonation.

"'So,' what?"

"You're not going to tell me your name?" I fell back on Mom's flirting advice and batted my eyes.

He smiled. "Spooks don't have real names."

"Oh, come on. Your mother named you *something*." I looked him over, not having a clue what name he looked like. "Jason?" Hey, half the guys my age are named Jason. It was a safe bet guess.

"No."

"Justin?"

"Not a chance."

"Rumpelstilskin?"

He shook his head and grinned. He gave my cheek a playful stroke. "You can call me just about anything."

Then he stopped the FAV, leaned over, and kissed me.

"I wish—" I said.

"What?" He slid his warm hands up under my wet tank top, favoring his left arm only slightly.

"I wish you weren't in such a weakened condition." I traced his wounded shoulder.

He gave me a quizzical expression.

"Famous last lines. *Octopussy.*"

"Ah," he said, understanding. "To hell with the arm. The part of me we need right now isn't hurt at all." He pulled me close and kissed my neck, working his way slowly upward, one hot kiss after another.

"Oh, James." I'd always wanted to say that. I ran my fingers through his hair, reveling in the heat of his kisses and the rush they were working on me.

He ran his hands along my ribs and down the plane of my stomach. I guided them lower.

"Oh, James. Oh. *Oh!*"